DIVINE

JUSTICE

Also by J.J. Miller

Brad Madison series:
FORCE OF JUSTICE
GAME OF JUSTICE

Cadence Elliott series:
I SWEAR TO TELL

Email: jj@jjmillerbooks.com
Facebook: @jjmillerbooks
Blog|Website: jjmillerbooks.com

ISBN-13: 979-86-57274-00-4

For my dear late mother

DIVINE

JUSTICE

(Brad Madison Legal Thriller, Book 2)

J.J. MILLER

CHAPTER 1

The sounds were loud, sharp and unmistakable.

I didn't need six years in the Marines and two tours in Afghanistan to tell me they were gunshots. Two of them; half a second apart.

A dreadful high-pitched din erupted from within the adjacent theater. Screaming, hundreds of young kids screaming. Within seconds, a flood of frantic bodies came spilling out. They ran for their lives, tears streaming down terrified, baffled faces, heads swiveling desperately in search of the quickest way out.

"He's shooting at us!" one boy cried.

"There's a gunman! Run!" shouted another.

Everyone around us was doing exactly that—bolting for the exits.

I pulled my seven-year-old daughter Bella close. Then I lifted her up. Her face was pale with fear. Her arms tightened around my neck.

"What's happening, Daddy? I'm scared."

And just like that, our world changed.

Just a few minutes earlier, I'd been enjoying my first moments of ease in what had been a morning filled with drama, tears and fury ... all on account of a monumental screw-up by yours truly.

Weeks ago, I'd surprised Bella with two tickets to VidCon, something I'd never heard of until she'd breathlessly mentioned it to me months back. A three-day love-in for the world's most popular YouTubers and their fans. At the time, my social media prowess pretty much started and ended with a neglected Facebook page, so I'd have thought the local McDonald's would have been a big enough venue for such an event. But here we were at the Anaheim Convention Center—sold out and swarming with kids.

It wasn't just the prospect of going to VidCon that had rocked Bella's world. I'd managed to get us into a limited-access performance and meet and greet with Cicily Pines, a young singer Bella had been raving about. When I'd delivered this news by phone, Bella's squeal of delight almost burst my eardrum.

But come the day, I'd steered the good ship *Awesome Dad* straight onto the rocks.

I only got Bella every second weekend, and yet over the past few months I'd managed to sabotage our time together regularly. Usually, the excuse was work—a criminal defense attorney's job can't always be shoehorned into a Monday to Friday work week, and I'd had to leave Bella waiting while attending to some client's predicament that couldn't hold until Monday.

Other times, there was no one to blame but me. I'd been cutting loose a bit lately, and more than once I'd woken up late with a blank memory and a strange woman, only to realize I'd broken yet another promise to Bella. Today, I hate to admit, was one of those days. I'd spent the night with a young paralegal—getting slam drunk in some bar before winding up in my bed. Both of us slept through my alarm. Only the persistent calls from my ex-wife Claire managed to rouse us.

When I'd picked Bella up it was clear we were going to miss the start of the meet and greet. Claire said we'd be lucky to make it before it ended. And she was right. In the car, after Bella had cried and scolded me, she'd fallen into a silent funk. Then she ordered me to turn around and take her back home. I tried reassuring her, telling her we'd make the show, but she knew I didn't really believe what I was saying. And in the past few months, she'd learned better than to take me at my word.

The Cicily Pines gig was scheduled to run for thirty minutes. It had already been going for twenty by the time we got our wristbands.

A dead weight tugged at my arm as I pushed through the crowd of teenagers crossing one expo hall after another. Holding my hand was not just fifty pounds of seven-year-old daughter but about two hundred pounds of resentment.

When I finally caught sight of the venue we wanted, there was, to my immense relief, a queue forty yards long parked outside. The show had been delayed. Though I didn't deserve it, the gods had smiled upon me.

Bella bounced up onto her toes, her spirit soaring. As soon as we joined the queue it began to move. Relieved, I made some stupid dad jokes. Bella laughed and bumped against me as we shuffled forward. I almost felt like a decent father.

We'll cherish this day for the rest of our lives, I thought.

A thought that was obliterated by gunfire.

Run! That's what everyone's survival instinct was telling them.

But amid that sudden chaos and frantic evacuation, I knew I couldn't run. It had been almost ten years since I'd served, but that Marine instinct flipped on like a switch.

Like most Americans, I'd wondered many times what I'd do if I was ever caught in a public shooting. Even though my daughter was with me, that didn't give me pause—I had to neutralize the shooter.

9

I looked around and saw a nearby stall. Between us and it, though, was a stampede, a boiling river of chaos. People were sprinting, tripping over each other, pushing, screaming, crying. We had to get through. I tightened my hold on Bella and stepped steadily through the turmoil, buffeted by the frenetic torrent of bodies. When we reached the stall, I swung Bella down and knelt beside her.

Seeing her terrified face did make me stop and think twice. For a brief second, I landed in mental quicksand.

Do I get Bella out or go for the gunman?

How could I live with myself if I get us out safely while defenseless kids are slaughtered?

My mind was made up.

"Daddy, what are you doing? We need to get out of here!" Bella pleaded, her face sheet white. I didn't know how to explain my actions to her. It was part instinct—I was hard-wired to engage the enemy—and part duty. I just couldn't let another Columbine go unopposed.

"Bella. You'll be safe here."

"What do you mean? What are you doing, Daddy?"

"Sweetheart, I need to stop this man," I said breathlessly as I lowered her down and moved some large plastic storage containers out of the way. "I can't let him go on shooting innocent people. I need you to stay here. You understand? Don't move. Please. And don't make a sound."

"Don't leave me here, Daddy! What if you get shot?"

It was the obvious question for which I had no answer.

"Darling, I'm going to come back for you real soon. You hear me?"

The noise all around us was unearthly terror. Sadly, it was something I'd heard several times before when we'd stormed

10

villages in Afghanistan. But here, it felt surreal, and I struggled against the fatherly instinct to save my daughter's life above all else.

Under my guiding hands Bella obliged. She lay down, her expression still bewildered yet trusting.

"Please come back, Daddy. Please come back for me."

"I promise," I said, as I quickly piled up the containers around her to conceal her presence. "Now not a sound, under any circumstances. Is that clear?"

She nodded. It killed me to see her so afraid, but I snapped myself out of it and got to my feet. I leapt back into the tide of hysterical kids and pushed my way upstream until I reached the entrance of the theater.

I'd heard no more gunshots, but that didn't mean the killing was done.

CHAPTER 2

I slid in through the doors and crouched low in the middle aisle to scope out the scene. I fished my phone out from my pocket and flicked the airplane mode on. I was going after a shooter unarmed. I didn't want an incoming call ruining the element of surprise.

At first, I couldn't see anyone in the dimly lit room. Further up, towards the stage, I could make out rows and rows of empty seats. Past them was a dance floor area just in front of the stage. As I panned to the right, I saw him. A man standing dead still. I had no idea if he was the shooter, whether he was solo or whether there were others at large. But there was an eerie silence and no shouting, so I figured no one else was being hunted down.

I stayed low and crept up the aisle toward the stage. As I did, I noticed people hiding behind the seats. I didn't know whether they felt too petrified to move or thought it was a good place to hide, but they all noticed me. Some looked up from lit phone screens. Probably texting their parents. This triggered the realization that word of the shooting would be spreading like electricity down a wire. In a distant corner of the room, I heard a phone. It rang twice before the owner snuffed it out.

I paused next to a young man, about sixteen, who was breathing hard. Relief came over his face at the sight of me. I was a grown-up, so I must be the cavalry.

"Did you see the shooter?" I whispered.

"I think so. Up there. The black guy in the blue hoodie."

I nodded. That fit the description of the figure I'd seen standing to the right of the stage. At least the blue hoodie part.

A few seconds later, I was at the front row. I stuck my head out for a peek. It had been about ninety seconds since the shots were fired. I couldn't see his left hand, but there was no weapon in his right. I didn't know why he was standing there, but I couldn't waste any more time. I had to act. I shuffled to get around the end seat, put my hands to the ground like a sprinter and prepared to launch. It was about twenty yards between me and the shooter. If I was quiet and quick enough, I could tackle him before he heard me and swung his weapon round. I'd drop my shoulder and hit him hard in the ribs, then pin his arms to his sides as we crashed to the floor.

Just as I was about to spring, two figures rushed the shooter, doing exactly what I'd planned to do. But after tackling him to the ground, they struggled to contain him. He broke free, rolled away and got to his feet. Now it was my turn. The guy swiveled around and saw me. He was a young black man in his late teens. I launched at him. Seeing me come at him, he turned and ran. I was barely two short yards into the pursuit when a voice boomed down from the stage.

"Freeze, asshole, or I'll shoot!"

I knew better than to assume that whoever called out knew I wasn't the bad guy, so I stopped in my tracks, raised my arms, and looked up at the stage. A security guard had his arms straight out and his weapon pointed at the shooter.

"Don't you move an eyelid, you son of a bitch!"

This was another voice, coming from behind me. I turned slowly around to see another guard walking forward steadily, his weapon firmly trained on the shooter, ready to unload if the target so much as scratched an itch.

"We've got this, sir. Thank you," the second guard said, tapping my shoulder as he walked by.

I watched as they closed in on the suspect and ordered him to the ground. He was just a kid—eighteen or thereabouts—but he was physically imposing, tall and solidly built. For a moment, I thought I recognized him. There was something vaguely familiar about his appearance that I couldn't quite put my finger on.

"I didn't do it," he kept telling the guards. "It wasn't me."

Of course, he didn't do it. What else was he going to say?

Guilty or not, he was going to need a lawyer, and a damned good one at that.

The suspect lowered himself onto his knees. One of the guards stepped forward and kicked him in the back to flatten him. Then they both jumped on and cuffed him.

"I didn't do it!" the suspect cried out again. This took a great deal of effort as he now had an overweight guard sitting on his back.

My eyes fell to the dead body on the ground a couple of yards from my feet. From the clothing, it appeared to be a young man. Next to him lay a Glock 17 pistol.

"Shut your mouth!" shouted the guard before smashing the suspect's face into the ground.

I figured the kid was lucky in one respect: he'd probably avoid being lumped with a judge-assigned public defender who couldn't give a shit. A sensational crime like this involving hundreds of teenage kids? His case was sure to be a media circus, and that meant every publicity-starved defense attorney in L.A. would come sniffing. I half felt compelled to step in. But I had to go.

I turned and ran to get Bella.

"Bella!" I called as I rounded the stall where I'd left her and began pulling away the storage containers.

"Bella, darling. It's Daddy. I'm back, sweetheart. Everything's okay."

But my words fell away as I removed the last box. My blood went cold with a dreaded revelation.

Bella was gone.

CHAPTER 3

Now I was the one running through the Anaheim Convention Center in a state of panic. An internal monologue helped me keep a lid on my worry, saying Bella wouldn't have moved unless it had made absolute sense for her to do so. She wouldn't have just disobeyed me and fled. But no one would have just taken her ... surely.

I shouted out her name as I ran, stopping to check a few obvious hiding places where I thought she may have taken new refuge. I swept back through the vast, now empty expo halls, through the ticketing area and then out to the large foyer. Everywhere was empty. I called and called but got no response.

Outside, hundreds of people stood huddled together in groups. Many looked at me, having emerged late, as though I'd have some answers for them. But all I had were desperate questions.

"I'm looking for a young girl. My daughter. She's seven. Long light-brown hair. Have you seen her?"

Their blank but sympathetic faces made it clear how idiotic my quest was. As if, while running for their lives, they'd have noticed a young girl by herself and thought it odd enough to recall.

"Sorry mister, but I haven't seen her," one teenage boy said. "But a lot of people went that way."

He pointed down Convention Way, a broad promenade leading away from the venue.

I thanked him and ran on. People were milled around the fountains and statues, many embracing one another. Others were on their phones calling loved ones to let them know they were okay.

My phone!

I'd wondered why Bella hadn't called me. Then I remembered I'd switched it to airplane mode. As soon as I reconnected, the phone began ringing.

With a flash of alarm, I saw it was Claire. Unable to say where Bella was, I didn't want to answer, but I had to.

"Hello."

"Brad!" Claire was breathless. "Where have you been? I heard there's been a shooting. Are you okay? Is Bella okay?"

"Yes, we're safe. It's over. They've got the guy."

"Oh, thank God. How's Bella? Can you put her on, please?"

"I can't right now. I've got to do something."

"What do you mean? I just want to speak to her quickly."

I wasn't about to tell Claire that that wasn't possible.

"I'll call you back," I said and hung up.

I resumed searching for Bella but there were so many people it was impossible.

I was flicking through my phone to find a photo of Bella to show people when it rang again. It was Claire.

Somewhat defeated, I answered.

"Claire, I'm just—"

"I cannot believe you. You left her?!"

"What? What are you talking about?"

"I just got a call from a lady who's with Bella. She says you left her by herself and ran off!"

"Claire, that's not what happened. I hid her. She was safe."

"What do you mean she was safe?!"

"I had to do something Claire. I wasn't going to stand by and let a bunch of kids get shot while I ran to save my own life."

"Your job was to keep our daughter safe."

There was nowhere else for this conversation to go.

"Where is she?" I asked.

"How insane is it that *you* have to ask *me* where your daughter is?! My God. She's in Starbucks, waiting for you."

"Thanks. I'll bring her home right away."

I walked to the coffee shop feeling yet again like I'd let my daughter down. Now, my idea of playing the hero seemed like just an egotistical glory dash, an extravagance performed for dubious reasons.

Within a few seconds, I had Bella in sight. Our eyes met, and she ran towards me as I walked through the doorway. I lifted her up and held her tight, never so relieved and thankful to have her in my arms. The dread of not knowing where she was or whether she was safe had spun me into a place I never wanted to be again.

Her own relief came in a flood of tears. Amid her sobs, I felt her rest her head on my shoulder.

"Daddy. Why did you leave me?" she said.

I realized it was going to be a huge job to convince Bella that abandoning her at a time of mortal danger had somehow been the right thing to do. She wasn't versed in America's history of mass shootings. Both Claire and I had done a good job of shielding her from the worst of the news.

"Darling, I didn't want to leave you. But I made sure you were safe, and then I had to do something to make other people safe too."

"What did you do?"

Suddenly I was stumped. *What had I actually done?*

"I tried to make sure no one else was hurt, honey. I wanted to make sure everyone else would get back to their families again. I thought ..."

A steely female voice from behind interrupted me.

"I thought it best to get her properly out of harm's way."

I turned to see a rather stern-looking woman aged in her late-thirties. She wore a gray skirt suit and very little make-up. Her blond hair was pulled back with a black band and her sole piece of jewelry was a string of pearls. She regarded me with an expression that was at once pleasant and disapproving.

I extended my hand.

"Thank you, ..." I said, searching for something to add in place of a name. Neither "miss" nor "ma'am" seemed appropriate, because I took an immediate dislike to her. Maybe it was self-defense; after all, she clearly didn't wish to hide her judgment of me.

"I'm Francine. Francine Holmes."

We shook hands quickly and coldly.

"I'm ex-services," I tried to explain. "I had to see if I could help nullify the threat."

Francine smiled and looked down at Bella, patting her on the head.

"Quite the hero, your daddy."

"Thank you for helping Bella," I said. "I'm sure you meant well."

She sensed, rightly, that I was having a hard time conceding that I didn't have everything, my daughter's safety included, under control.

"Well, I think it turned out for the best. What a delightful young woman she is."

Bella piped up with some news.

"Francine says she can arrange for me to meet Cicily Pines," she said.

"Really?" I said. "Wouldn't that be something? How could you do that?"

Francine's bearing softened, as though she was prepared to entertain the possibility that I wasn't entirely a deadbeat dad.

"I'm part of the Halo Group," she said. "We run UpliftInc, a promotions company for YouTubers, and we put on the event for Cicily today."

"I don't understand. You're her manager?"

"Not quite. We're her primary patron. We love what she does and want to help her flourish, that's all. Her and others like her."

"So you're like the Motown Records of YouTube?"

Francine practically shuddered.

"No, we support a select number of young people who we think are the flowers among the weeds."

I figured Halo must be behind the stable of Christian stars I'd read about. I'd done my homework on Cicily Pines and watched just about every post on her channel. The clips were all similar—just her, an acoustic guitar and a voice from heaven. She was sweet without being guileless. She seemed humble and genuine. There was a hint of religion about her but nothing overt. She occasionally expressed her gratitude to God, but that was about it. A few minutes on Google revealed she was aligned with a Christian

20

network of social media "influencers." I was okay with that. Wholesome is just fine when it comes to a seven-year-old girl's role model. I didn't expect Bella to grow up a saint, but I wasn't going to complain if her influencers were people who encouraged her to like herself and not strive to please others—boys, namely—in order to feel validated in life.

But there was something about the company's name that rang a bell in a dim corner of my brain.

"The Halo Group. That sounds familiar to me."

"We have been around for ten years. We used to be the Halo Council, a non-profit group founded by Victor Lund. We ran security and development projects in war-torn countries. But these days, we are purely US-focused. Everyone in our YouTube stable is American as apple pie."

My mind was ticking. I was sure I'd heard the name Victor Lund before, and the Halo Council too. Then suddenly, the grim realization clicked. It was the name of a place I wanted to keep well behind me: Bati Kot, a dusty village in Nangarhar province, east Afghanistan. My unit had gotten into a firefight there, one that resulted in several civilian casualties, including the death of a foreign aid worker. In response, Lund had launched a vociferous public slur campaign against my men in the media. A few years later, as I recalled, the Halo Council had been expelled from Afghanistan by President Karzai, apparently under intense pressure from the US ambassador in Kabul.

"The Halo Council. You were in Afghanistan, for a while," I said flatly.

Francine's eyes narrowed.

"Yes, we were."

"So was I. Am I right in thinking Halo was kicked out for some reason?"

"It would take too much time to answer that question now. I will leave you two alone. When things calm down, we will organize another event." She rested a hand on Bella's shoulder. "And when we do, young lady, you will be the first to know. You will be welcome as our VIP guest. By then, this dreadful experience should be well behind us."

"That would be wonderful. It's very kind of you," I said. "Here, I'll give you my card."

I fetched one from my wallet and handed it to her.

"So you're a lawyer?" Francine said as she read the print. "A man of many talents." It seemed like she wanted to tack "except for fatherhood" onto the end of that statement. "Well then, Bella, I will certainly be in touch, and we will arrange for you to come and meet Cicily another day. How does that sound?"

"That sounds great. Thank you," Bella said, all smiles.

I put my arm around my daughter.

"I'd best be getting her home."

"Yes," said Francine. "What a dreadful ordeal. She will want a big mommy hug, I imagine."

We'd only just begun walking back along Convention Way when a teenage girl walked straight up to Bella with an excited smile.

"Excuse me. You're Bella Madison, aren't you?"

Bella nodded silently with a half-smile.

The girl was looking her up and down with admiration. It was clear she was taking stock of Bella's "look." Until now I'd barely given Bella's outfit a moment's thought. Normally I'd compliment her, but this morning my admiration got lost in the rush. She did have a striking talent for putting clothes together, something that was evident even before she was out of diapers.

"Oh my gosh, I follow you on Instagram," the girl said. "Can I get a photo with you?"

Bella looked flattered. As I watched her chat with the girl and join her for a selfie, I felt proud of the humble, graceful way in which Bella conducted herself. I never liked the idea of her having an Instagram account. According to the platform's terms of service, users had to be older than thirteen. I'd argued with Claire about it a couple of times, saying she was too young to be making images of herself public. But Claire insisted I was overreacting and that Bella enjoyed having a dynamic outlet for her love of fashion. She assured me she had total control of the account and that she'd had the social media version of the "birds and the bees" talk with Bella. When I raised the subject of creeps who followed kids online, Claire said she scanned Bella's account daily, blocking and reporting anything inappropriate. I remained dead against it but eventually gave up arguing.

The girl worked her phone and asked Bella to choose the filter she preferred.

"I like that one," Bella said, pointing at the screen.

"So do I," said the girl who then tapped away again. "Done. Posted. I'll tag you. You'll be sure to like it, won't you? That would be so awesome."

"Okay, no worries," said Bella. She pulled her phone out of her small handbag and tapped away on the screen. "There you are. Done."

The girl swooned at what she saw.

"You're following me! You're amazing. Thank you so much."

A minute later, as we continued to the car, my phone buzzed. I took it out to see five desperate text messages and several missed calls from Bella. All the frantic calls being made around the convention center must have jammed the networks.

"Your messages just arrived," I said.

"Well, they're no use now, are they? That's just not good enough, is it Dad?" She'd applied a remonstrative tone to her voice.

23

I knew she wasn't directing the comment at me. I did that myself. *A bit like your daddy*, I thought regretfully.

"No, it's not, sweetheart."

Bella and I barely spoke as we drove back to Claire's house at Venice Beach. I asked her a few times how she was feeling, and it was clear she was still in shock and struggling to process things.

But I had to ask why she moved from where I'd left her.

"Francine found me and told me it would be safer outside."

"She found you?"

"She said she saw us go behind the booth."

"What else did she say?"

There was a long pause before Bella answered.

"She said she couldn't believe you'd run off and left me like that."

I did not like this woman at all. I just kept my mouth shut.

"It's okay, Dad," she said before everything went quiet again. Eventually she resumed talking. There was a train of thought she wanted to share. "You know, it was weird. I was so scared. And there was all that screaming. And I knew you were there. But ..."

"But what?"

"Well, you were there. Just not for me."

That winded me. She said it like it was a lesson learned, something for her to store away as a coping mechanism for future disappointment.

"Bella, I'm always going to be there for you. That's a promise."

I said the words knowing she believed them to be, on current evidence, hollow. From my end, I meant every word—I never wanted her to feel like this ever again.

But that's just the sort of thing a father says. Right?

24

CHAPTER 4

We're proceeding in single file along a raised dirt bank between poppy fields. The crops are in bloom, just a few weeks from harvest. Beyond to our right flows a fast, shallow river. The carpet of crimson and white flowers and the lush greenery bordering the river form an oasis lodged in a dusty expanse of desert. Ahead lies a village, an accretion of mud-walled housing compounds. Men and women in robes and turbans walk the dirt streets. It's a vision straight out of an illustrated children's bible, a way of life that has barely changed for centuries.

As we approach, we file onto the inroad. Kids in dusty, flowing garments run out to greet us, shouting out hello, wanting to shake hands, and asking for money. Their parents look on from a distance, wary about their offspring fraternizing with foreign fighters but hopeful they will return with a few dollars.

We walk through the town unthreatened. Men and women appear relaxed as we pass by. We get a nodded greeting here, a lifted hand there. They look as though they are glad to see us, but there's no telling what they really think.

We round a corner into another dirt street flanked by mud walls. It's empty. There are no kids to be seen, and the only visible adult faces poke out warily from windows and corners up ahead. The hypervigilance kicks even higher. There's no telling whether those faces belong to cautious civilians or insurgents. You only know for sure when an AK-47's pointing at you.

Four of my men are up ahead—Hunter, Blanchard, Shaw and Jeffreys. All slowly pivot their torsos from one side to the other as they walk; rifles held to chests, index fingers resting on trigger guards.

Everything is quiet; the dominant sound our own breath. Our focus is cranked up by the constant expectation that all hell could break lose any second. In this state of supreme acuity, you are so attuned to your environment you actually think you can see a fraction into the future. It's this wired condition that makes readjusting to life back home—the cozy bed, the comfortable silence, the lawnmowing mundanity—so hard. This is an elevated, superhuman sense of being alive. Feel it enough and you come to like it, the same way a skier stands above a cliff-scarred double black run, the same way a BASE jumper steps onto the edge of a skyscraper in the dead of night. In these spells of lucid intensity, nothing else matters but the now—not the past, not the present. Nobody, no one matters but you and your men and the determination that you will all get each other out alive.

We look for tell-tale wires, freshly padded dirt—any sign of an IED in waiting.

We see none.

Suddenly there's a huge blast ahead. I see Hunter literally torn to pieces even as I'm lifted off my feet and thrown back by the shockwave.

In a cloud of choking dust and smoke, I crawl forward. I get to Jeffreys. He's shaken but otherwise okay. I crawl further forward on my elbows, making my way toward Shaw as fast as I can. He's bleeding from the abdomen and shoulder—probably shrapnel from a pressure cooker filled with explosives, nails, bolts and nuts.

"Medic!" I scream, but Shaw waves me off saying he's okay.

I keep crawling again, now toward Blanchard. He's a bloody mess. Half his face is gone. It's as though some ferocious beast set its jaws into the side of his face and ripped off everything to the bone. I actually see the flecks of white bone within the red mess of flesh and blood. A chunk of his skull is gone. His right eye is protruding from its socket, forced out by sudden, violent pressure. Somehow, he's alive. But all he can do is writhe and moan on the ground, his legs bending up and down, his bootheels scraping channels into the dirt in a macabre jig.

"Medic!" I scream again. "Medic!"

I kneel beside Blanchard and rest his deformed head in my lap. I talk to his good side, as if I know that that part of him can still hear me, understand me, believe me. He is just nineteen years old, this Blanchard kid. He is something else. Smart, funny, empathetic, he is one of the most popular members of our unit. And he has become a hell of a soldier. Born and raised in Ohio, he is grounded in that good-stock, rural-family way and has an old head on his young shoulders. We are two weeks from tour's end, and he has plans for when he gets back home. Now here I am, holding what is left of him as he lies dying in some shitty war in a shitty town that has not changed since Attila the Hun passed through.

"Medic!"

Where's the damn medic?!

"Mom! Mom!!" Somehow, with half his head gone and his mouth choking with blood and dirt, Blanchard can still form the word.

"Mom?!"

As I look into his clear blue eyes, they go still on me, never again to be lit by ambition, humor, desire, or good news.

I feel him draw one last heaving breath.

I look up and see a small figure walking towards me. A young girl shuffling quickly through the dust cloud. She is carrying something. She walks straight up to me and stops. I realize the thing she's carrying is her own arm. Blood is running freely down the side of her face, a face wet with tears and smudged with dirt. The blood flows faster and thicker.

She looks at me and her eyes roll to the back of her head and turn white.

"Salaam alaykum," she says. Peace be with you.

She says it again, and again. Faster and faster. First her voice is trance-like, but then it gets louder and louder until she is screaming, high-pitched right into my face.

"Salaam alaykum! Salaam alaykum!"

✳✳✳

I woke up bolt upright and cold from drying sweat.

It was four-thirty.

I hadn't expected to sleep at all. When I got home after dropping Bella off, it was hard to put my mind at ease. I sensed the VidCon shooting could be a PTSD trigger. I'd had enough whiskey and beer to get me drowsy, but sleep remained elusive. Yet I must have dozed off. And that was the kind of shit that awaited me when I did.

There was no way I was getting back to sleep now. I didn't want to. Not after that lurid regurgitation—albeit distorted—of my Afghanistan experience.

And there was no way I was going into the office. That was partly why I'd set out on my own despite several offers to join large law firms. This PTSD thing only came occasionally, but when it

29

did, I'd rather not explain why I was playing hooky to co-workers and partners who considered fourteen-hour days to be the bare minimum.

This dream was one of a few packages my mind had edited for me to remember; a kind of sick playlist that provoked me in various ways, like ripping the bed covers off, hitting the floor, reaching for weapons or ammo to kill an imaginary enemy that felt so real in my warped headspace.

I had my coping mechanisms. Hitting the bottle hard was not one of them. I knew where that path led: alcoholism, misery and a gun barrel in the mouth. I kept it at a half-bottle of scotch plus whatever beers were on hand to chase it down. But my real battle buddy in this war of unwanted remembrance was cannabis. At home, I always kept a vape pen and a stash of Blue Dream cartridges on hand. I didn't vape every day, but it sure as hell beat the useless pills—the anti-depressants, the anti-anxiety drugs—that the Veterans Association threw at you.

I got out of bed, grabbed a beer from the fridge and pulled out my vape pen. I settled down in front of the TV and took a couple of hits. For whatever reason, getting stoned was a good transition from nightmares to normality, at least for me. It enabled my mind to dislocate itself from a riptide of horror that could easily suck me into madness and dead-end despair. The worst things I'd seen during combat could be put where they belonged: in the past. It allowed me to relax, to regain a sound, rational perspective. Hell, it even made me laugh.

I scanned the news channels. I was always interested in news from Afghanistan and Iraq. Watching reports from the war was never a trigger for me—it was more a reminder that my experience was real, an affirmation that I'd been there, that what I did had some purpose. But as to what the overall game over there was, who knew.

I mean, if we wanted to beat the Taliban, Afghanistan wasn't the place to be. To win that war we'd have had to invade Pakistan—that was where their headquarters were, where their madrassas or training schools were, where they radicalized young men into fundamentalist robots. Half the time the enemy fighters I'd faced were just plain insurgents, some Joe Blow Afghan out for revenge after his brother or entire family had been killed by a mortar we accidentally lobbed into a wedding party. He could be someone who just hated the sight of foreign soldiers running around his neighborhood telling him what to do, pushing him off his roads, pointing guns at him and, yes, telling him he shouldn't grow opium, the one crop he knew he could make money off amid all the hardship and uncertainty that went with living in a war zone.

There was nothing on the news about the Afghan war. Hardly surprising, since it was again fading fast from America's conscience, even though we'd been fighting there longer than Vietnam.

I aimed the remote at the screen. But then something stopped me from touching the button. A headline scrolling across the bottom of the screen caught my eye. It was about the VidCon shooting. The text said a seventeen-year-old male had been apprehended. I stuck around to see if there was a story. Sure enough, it came within a matter of minutes.

The piece detailed how YouTube sensation Luke Jameson had been gunned down at a concert where he was about to perform and noted that a young man from Pomona was being held in custody. The reporter said the alleged shooter could not be named because he was a juvenile.

I continued flipping through the channels and stopped when I landed on the movie *Moneyball*. It had only just started. I hit pause, got up for another beer, and returned to the sofa and movie. It was going to be a chill kind of day.

From my bedroom came the sound of my phone buzzing with a message. I was in no mood to engage with anyone, but curiosity got the better of me: who would be texting me at five in the morning?

31

When I picked up the phone, I was surprised to see the name "Jasmine Torrell" as the sender.

Last time I spoke with Jasmine, it was the hardest call I'd ever had to make. I'd rung her from our base in Jalalabad with the worst news. Her husband, and my dear friend, Sherman "Tank" Torrell was dead. He'd taken four AK rounds to the chest. He'd have taken more if he hadn't shot and grenaded the five insurgents that had ambushed us from the top of an escarpment. Until that day, we had thought the giant of a man—the finest physical specimen I'd ever seen, and the most courageous, selfless fighter— was indestructible. But we'd tempted fate. I'd covered him as he scaled that escarpment and hit the enemy's flank. I thought he was unscathed because he was still standing after the insurgent guns fell silent. But by the time I joined him he'd collapsed, dead. Later, I'd listened to Jasmine's untold shock and grief as I relayed the news she'd prayed would never come.

Her text read: "Hi Brad. Sorry to bother you out of the blue, but my son Demarco has been arrested. Police say he killed someone. Please help."

I called the number right away. Jasmine answered, but the connection was so poor I couldn't hear a word she said.

"I'll come see you!" I shouted.

Jesus. The news report said the alleged shooter was from Pomona. That's where Jasmine lived. The kid I saw being arrested in the theater must have been Tank's son, Demarco. No wonder I thought I'd recognized him.

My plans for the day changed in an instant. Up until now all I had in mind was more Blue Dream hits, more beer and the movie followed by a long session of *Red Dead Redemption* on the PlayStation. The only foreseen interruption would have been the pizza delivery boy. Well, that was out the window now. The wife of my old friend needed me.

To help clear my head, I walked to the pull-up bar I'd installed in my bedroom and pumped out thirty. I followed that up with eighty Marine push-ups and a hundred crunches. Then, I hit the shower, shaved, and headed for the door.

Yeah, I was still a little stoned, but otherwise I was good to go.

CHAPTER 5

The late-January day was cool and the sky was as clear as cut glass. To be moving felt good, but to be flying down the freeway in my Mustang GT felt even better. It was a glorious way to put distance between me and the headspace I'd awoken to earlier that morning. I was grateful to Jasmine for giving me a purpose outside of myself, forcing me to abandon my planned isolation.

It had been about eight years since I'd last made this trip out to Pomona, a few weeks after we'd buried Tank. We'd spent almost eighteen months in Afghanistan together. He died just a couple of weeks before our second tour was due to end. Through Tank I'd learned Jasmine hadn't been in good health back then: diabetes had struck in her early thirties and there'd been complications. I wondered if she'd improved.

Her home, like most others on her street, was small: single level, two-bedroom, driveway up the side, single garage, cement path from the sidewalk to the front patio, no steps, and two camp chairs where you could take in the view of the street whenever the urge struck you. I knocked on the door and heard the volume of a television drop.

"Is that you, Brad?" Jasmine's voice was shaky. She sounded older than I knew she was.

After I hollered back, she told me to let myself in. Once inside, I turned left to see Jasmine sitting in an armchair in front of the television. A small table to the side held a jug of juice, an empty cup of coffee and a box of Kleenex.

The house was untidy. I could see dishes in the sink and spent fast food bags on the kitchen table.

"Sorry not to get up," said Jasmine. "It's my heart."

I was shocked at Jasmine's appearance. She was obese—no other word for it. She hadn't always been that way. Tank had shown me photos of when they were dating and just married. Back then, she'd been fit and radiant.

I bent down, kissed Jasmine on the cheek and gave her a big hug. Her arms held me tight for a few seconds.

"Lovely to see you, Brad," she said. "Please, have a seat."

As I lowered myself into the armchair opposite, Jasmine reached for a pill container, opened it, took two or three out, placed them in her mouth, and swallowed them with some water from a plastic bottle.

"My heart. It's not going so well," she said.

"I was about to ask how you're doing, Jasmine. But it seems you're having a hell of a rough time."

Her eyes filled with tears, and she reached for a Kleenex. She dabbed the corners of her eyes and her nose. I pulled my chair closer and took her hand.

"I hate to see you so upset," I said. "Please, tell me about Demarco. What happened?"

She took a deep breath, withdrew her hand from mine and began folding her Kleenex.

"They say he killed a man in Anaheim. Shot him point blank in the chest." Just saying the words led Jasmine to break down. I waited a few seconds before replying.

"Jasmine. Was this the shooting at the convention center?"

"Yes. Yesterday afternoon."

"I was there."

Jasmine looked at me, puzzled.

"I was at VidCon, a YouTube expo, with my daughter," I said. "I took her to see this singer she's obsessed with, and all of a sudden all hell broke loose."

Jasmine listened intently, hoping that whatever I said was going to bring her some relief, that I'd somehow know more than the police were telling her and could reassure her that Demarco was innocent.

"Jasmine, do you have a photo of Demarco I can take a look at?"

I already believed Jasmine's son was the alleged shooter—I just wanted to be absolutely sure.

"The most recent one is up there," she said, pointing to a shelf beside the television.

I stood and picked up the framed photo of a smiling boy aged about twelve. Unfortunately, I was sure it was this boy's older self that I'd seen the day before.

I returned the photo to the mantle and fell back into my seat.

"Let me tell you what I saw. We were waiting to get into our show when we heard gunshots. I ran towards where the shots came from, hoping I could stop a mass shooting."

"What about your daughter?"

I felt a stab of guilt but decided to speed on through the story.

"I hid her. When I reached the theater, I saw a man's body on the ground and, I'm afraid to say, Demarco was standing over him."

Jasmine rocked back and forth gently and put a hand to her mouth.

"My son is not a killer," she said with defiance.

"I'm sure he's not, Jasmine. I'm sure there's some reasonable explanation. And I'm going to find out what the hell it is. But first I need you to tell me about Demarco. Has he ever been in trouble with the law?"

It almost seemed like a dumb question. Tank had told me years ago that Demarco had been a bright but troubled kid. That was when Demarco was about eight years old. He just hadn't coped with Tank being away and Jasmine becoming more and more debilitated. He'd been increasingly disrespectful towards his mother. After Tank's death, I'd thought about offering to help try and keep the kid on the straight and narrow, but I never acted. And Demarco had strayed as Tank feared he would.

Jasmine told me that the boy had always missed his father terribly when he was on tour, and the distance between her and her son had only grown. When Tank was home things were better, but his presence never really settled Demarco. Besides, the Tank who came back from Afghanistan was not the same man who had left. He didn't spend much time at home, always finding some excuse to be out. Sometimes with his buddies, but most times just by himself—at the gym, the shooting range or out hunting. He didn't seem inclined or equipped to steer his relationship with Demarco to a better place.

Demarco had been a promising student, but in the year leading up to his dad's death, he became defiant and disinclined to apply himself to anything. After Tank died, the counseling he had failed to overcome his anger and confusion. What the kid had desperately longed for—a present father—had been cruelly yanked away.

37

With her own health problems, whatever strength Jasmine had to reach the boy steadily faded. From the age of ten, the two barely conversed. She just got grunts in reply to her questions.

At school, Demarco got into too many fights and acquired a reputation as not only a tough kid but a bully. He missed classes, and at age thirteen was expelled for smoking pot. That same year, he began running with the Sintown Crips, a black criminal street gang from the west side of Pomona. It wasn't long before he left home without so much as an angry word.

That had been two years ago, and Jasmine had neither seen nor heard from him since. Well actually, she had once. After her repeated appeals to police, they brought him home one night. He'd walked out again the same night.

It was the saddest of sights to see this good woman detail the pain and suffering that had befallen her.

There was nothing I could say to ease her worry, except that all the details about the Anaheim shooting were not yet known.

"Please, Brad. My baby sure ain't no angel, but he ain't a cold-blooded killer either. I know that, deep in my heart. There must be some mistake."

It was going to have to be some mistake. For the life of me, I couldn't begin to fathom what a street kid would be doing at a convention like that, let alone killing a man there in cold blood. I had to speak to Demarco.

"Jasmine, I'll go see him. Right now."

"You have to clear this up. Please, Brad. He doesn't belong in jail. He's just a boy. My dear boy. You've got to save him."

Her pleading eyes flooded with tears.

"I'll do my best, Jasmine. I promise. But I need to know as much about Demarco as possible. Do you have anything you can show me: you know, what he excelled at, awards, school, reports, anything and everything?"

Jasmine nodded.

"In my bedroom closet, up high on the right, there's a box I keep everything in. It all seems like distant memories now."

"Great. I'll just go get it."

Armed with the box, I made to leave. Jasmine looked a little embarrassed not to stand and see me to the door. Suddenly, she broke down again. But, after a moment, she rallied to speak to me.

"Brad. I have to tell you. I don't have long to live. The doctors say I'll be doing well to last another year. Please, don't let them take him from me. Just one more time, I want to see him walk through that door and give me a hug. Just like he did when he was little."

I crossed the room and hugged her. She was now sobbing, her body trembling. I gave her one last squeeze and made for the door.

"I'll do my best, Jasmine."

CHAPTER 6

I walked into the meeting room at Juvenile Hall to see Demarco Torrell leaning up against the corner wall in blue short-sleeved overalls. He was tall and athletic, leaner than his old man but still an imposing physical specimen. It was incredible how much he looked like his father. But while I felt I knew him, he was eyeing me coldly.

"Hello, Demarco. You may not remember me, but we've met before."

I put out my hand. He kept his in his pockets. Apart from following me with his eyes, he hadn't moved an inch since I'd entered.

"Who the hell are you?" He delivered the words like a jab, his deep voice belying his youth.

"I'm Brad Madison. I was a friend of your father. We were in Afghanistan together."

"Killing sand niggas. Or getting killed by them. But you got your ass outta there good enough."

I'd seen this a lot in younger men in jail. The "can't break me" posture was an automatic survival response. Show no weakness, no vulnerability. It was actually a sign that they'd have a chance of gaining respect. The need for a hard, protective shell applied just as much in juvenile detention as it did in prison.

"Well, yeah. I made it back. That was years ago now, but your dad and I were good friends. I saw you at his funeral, eight years ago."

"I don't remember."

There were a few seconds of silence. Demarco pushed his shoulder off the wall and turned to me square on. He then folded his arms. The skin from wrist to sleeve cuff was covered in tattoos.

"So, you're going to get me off this bullshit charge, is that right?"

"I'm going to try."

"How you gonna do that? The way I see it, my ass is fried."

"At least let me try. You've been arrested on suspicion of murder. You're going to need a good attorney."

"Maybe this is my destiny."

I was confused. I was expecting the silent treatment from Demarco or, if he talked, a vehement denial of guilt mixed with a tirade against the cops. Not philosophy; not something that sounded awfully close to surrender.

"What are you talking about?"

"I mean, maybe this is what God wants for me." He shrugged his shoulders and took a seat, leaned forward and rested his arms on the table. "These past few years I've done some bad shit. Maybe this is karma coming back to bite me in the ass."

"I'm not following you. This is something that needs to be fought. You don't just go with the flow when you've been arrested for murder. If their story's not right, you, me—we—have to get the truth out. We fight this thing with your truth."

41

"My truth? My truth is that God delivered me here. So it must be what He wants for me. This is the path He chose for me. It's the path I have to take."

I was glad Demarco was talking, but I was disturbed by the words coming out of his mouth.

"Sorry, we need to back up a little here," I said. "Tell me exactly what happened yesterday."

"Yesterday I listened to God, I followed His word and it led me here."

"God told you to kill someone?"

"Not exactly. And I didn't kill no one."

"Okay that's a start. So how did you end up standing over a dead man who had just taken two bullets to the chest?"

Demarco leaned back in his chair.

"You ain't gonna believe me. No one is."

Hell, he was afraid of sounding stupid—just like any kid.

"I will believe you, Demarco. I just want you to be honest with me. What on earth were you doing at VidCon?"

"I went to deliver a message from God."

"What does that mean? I need specifics."

He adjusted himself in his chair. "I was at the mission."

"The mission?"

"The Los Angeles Mission."

The homeless shelter in Skid Row. It was run by volunteers trying to save people from getting lost in the wasteland of drugs, crime, insanity and prostitution.

"I'd seen too much shit with the Sintown Crips and wanted out. A friend of mine, older than me, started looking out for my ass. I respected that dude, and when he started telling me I had to get out and make something of myself, I began to listen."

So he did inherit some of his old man's smarts after all.

"Anyway, after a couple of good friends got killed, I kinda took this dude's advice to heart. But I was doing it tough. Eventually, I came downtown to the mission."

"And what happened there?"

"They were good to me. I stuck around, learned a thing or two about my life and found God. And on the day I truly believed, I walked out of the mission and got a direct sign from Him."

"You got a sign from God? What kind of sign?"

"That I was chosen to serve Him."

"What was the sign?"

"A dude outside the mission asked me to deliver a message that would help a sinner repent."

"Please, go on."

"He asked if I wanted to serve God. 'Yeah,' I said. And he said, 'Well how about you deliver this message and I pay you a thousand bucks?' And I was like, 'You shittin' me.' And the guy goes, 'Five hundred now, five hundred after you've delivered the message.'"

"He offered you a thousand dollars to run an errand?"

"That's right. So I said, 'Yeah, sure thing.' It was like God giving me a kickstart for my dream."

"What dream, Demarco?"

"I was gonna get my shit together. I was gonna join the Marines. Just like dad. I'd been out of the gang for a year and I needed to get my life on track. I wanted to enlist, but first I had to go back to school, get my high school diploma."

43

That was a big ask given where he was starting from, but I admired his ambition. Actually, I could have hugged him. I could only imagine how touched Tank would have been.

"You decided you wanted to join the Marines?"

"Yeah. I had no money to get myself cleaned up. I didn't want to go live back home in Pomona because the gang's there. So I needed money, I needed a job, and I needed to finish high school. And to me this grand was a helping hand from God just reaching out to me."

"So then what happened with this guy?"

"He showed me a photo of the dude I was supposed to give the message to."

"Did he give you the photo?"

"No, I just had to remember this guy. And I didn't need a photographic memory to do that. He had punk hair and nose rings and shit. There was no doubt I'd recognize him if I saw him. And so I went with this dude, he dropped me off, gave me a pass and told me to follow the other guy into this concert and then tap him on the shoulder and give him the message."

"You didn't think this was odd?"

"Yeah, of course, but he gave me five hundred bucks just like that."

"Did he tell you anything else?"

"Yeah, he said he was going to be filming it all. He said this is what he wanted to do for a living: filming pranks where famous people get punked by strangers off the street. They get a cream pie in the face or something like that. But he said the dude would be shocked by the message."

"Why would he be shocked by this message?"

"I don't know."

"Then what happened?"

44

"We got in his car and headed over to Anaheim."

"Did this guy have a name?"

"It was Toby, or something like that."

"What did he look like?"

"White, tall, skinny dude. Had a Lakers cap on."

That didn't exactly narrow it down, but it was a start.

"Go on. What happened next?"

"He dropped me off outside the center and told me to go on in."

"What about the rest of the money?"

"That's what I said: 'What about the other five hundred?' But he told me to chill—that he'd find me as soon as the filming was done."

This was one of the weirdest stories I'd ever heard, but if Demarco was making this up, he was a damn good liar.

"So then you go find this guy. It's Luke Jameson, I assume?"

"Yeah, that's the name. So I make my way in. Security look at me like I got no business being there, but I flash my pass, they check it out and then put a wristband on me and I'm through."

"Then what do you do?"

"I try to find my way to the theater. Toby said the Luke dude would wait until everyone was in before going in himself. He was the star of the show but he liked to make an entrance from the crowd. That was his thing. Toby said I should wait at the door. He said the dude would be wearing a hoodie or something like that to hide his face. But I picked him easily enough."

"Did Toby tell you why Luke was a target?"

"He said he'd turned his back on God and that he needed to heed God's word again. That was part of the message."

"What was?"

"I had to say to him, 'You've been served by God.'"

"Right, so he was a lapsed Christian?"

"I don't know, something like that I guess."

"So then what happened?"

"I got in right behind him when he walked in."

"He didn't see you?"

"No, it was real dark."

"Was there anyone else with him?"

"No."

Maybe a posse would have blown his cover. That made sense. Kind of.

"And?"

"And so I follow him through the crowd, the music comes on and he stops. Then I tap him on the shoulder. He won't turn around. I tell him, 'You've been served by God,' like I was told. But he still won't turn around. So I say it again a couple times, louder, and then he swung around. He was pissed and I didn't really take a shine to him either. But then BAM a gun goes off right beside me and this guy goes down. Then it all went crazy."

"Tell me."

"Some light from the stage comes on and everyone turns around and sees him on the ground. They all start screaming and running for their lives."

"And what do you do?"

"I'm standing there. I couldn't move. I wanted to run too, but people were looking at me like I'd shot him. I thought other people might think I was chasing them if I ran too, so I stayed put. I bent down to check on the dude, but he was dead. I watched him die right in front of me."

I was thinking how this story would go down in front of a jury. It wouldn't fly. The prosecution would tear it to pieces.

"Are you telling me the truth, Demarco?"

"I swear to God."

"Yeah, I know, but this story is out there. What did you tell the cops?"

"Not a lot. A short version of what I told you."

I was surprised he talked to the cops at all. Most gang members know that if you're ever arrested you keep your mouth shut. Maybe that was a good sign—that Demarco wasn't afraid to tell his side of the story. It suggested he had nothing to hide.

"Okay, but from now on you keep your mouth shut. Don't open your mouth to anyone at all in here, you understand me?"

"Who you think you're talking to?"

"It's just something I have to say, Demarco. You'll be facing murder charges soon. And with your history, it's going to be a big ask for anyone to accept that you were there on some Christian mission to help a fallen angel."

"So, like I said. Maybe this is what God wants from me—this is my challenge. No one said it would be easy."

"Well, it's my challenge now too. I'm going to defend you, Demarco. So you are going to have to help me as much as you can. That means I need you to be one hundred percent honest with me, understand?"

"I have been."

"Good. Let's keep it that way."

CHAPTER 7

After leaving Juvenile Hall, I made some calls. I needed to confer with my secretary Megan Schaffer and my investigator Jack Briggs. I asked Megan to get together all of Demarco's priors and I briefed Jack on my meetings with Jasmine and Demarco. Then I dropped in on the cops to get a copy of the arrest report. It was midday by the time I got back to the office. Jack and Megan were seated in front of my desk. Jack was re-reading Demarco's rap sheet.

"You really going to waste your time on this case?" he said by way of a greeting, holding up the offending document.

"Why shouldn't I?"

"Because it looks like your boy is full of shit."

"How so?"

"All that born-again, message-from-God crap he fed you? I mean, the kid's been running with the Sintown Crips, not selling boy scout cookies."

"He admits he's done things he wasn't proud of."

Jack slapped the rap sheet with the back of his hand.

"Like vicious assault. Like auto theft. And that's just what we know about. The Sintown Crips are just another mafia—seven homicides pinned to them in the last two years alone. They deal ice, crack, coke, heroin, weapons, you name it. And this kid, who's probably just carried out their latest homicide, says he just so happens to have left the gang cold, found God, and decided to go back to school and enlist? I'm not buying it. It says here he's already done two stints in juvie. But what I want to know is what his rap sheet doesn't tell us. Was he in the car when those Crips did a drive-by? Was he standing watch while someone got knifed? What was the *real* shit he actually got away with?"

Jack had never been a straight-up gun for hire, so to speak. He had a mind of his own and enough money from his IT business and tech stock trading to retire. Add to that the looks of a matinee idol and the drive to keep himself supremely fit and you had a full-fledged alpha male for whom work was basically an optional extra. He liked investigating because it was interesting and real, and he liked working for me because we kept innocent people out of jail. But he was not at all interested in helping me let the guilty walk.

"Have you ever heard of Ramon X?" he asked me.

"Can't say I have."

"Well, these past couple of hours I've been busy putting together a picture of your boy, and from what I've gathered so far, it ain't pretty. This guy Ramon X, like your boy, comes from northwest Pomona. He's only twenty-four, but he's moved high up in the Sintown Crips, and no Dudley Do-Right gets to scale that chain of command. But he did, and fast. And in his downtime, he's a talented rapper."

"Still, I've never heard of him."

"He just founded Hemlock Records, but that ain't all—he's what you might call an entrepreneur."

"How so?"

"He's got a YouTube channel with twelve million subscribers."

49

"Twelve million? What kind of money do you make from that?"

"The plenty kind. The guy's loaded. Probably stinking rich from YouTube alone."

"How so?"

"YouTube pays a certain amount for views and then there are ads, product placement and merch."

"Merch?"

"Merchandise. With a captive market of millions of people around the world, you can sell anything, create a sideline business that'll earn you as much as the channel."

"So what's this got to do with Demarco?"

"Well, my guess is that he and Ramon X were tight."

"No," I said. "Demarco said he left the gang."

"I know. But come on. He would say that. And if they are still tight, that's of concern to you, because Ramon X and the dead guy—what's his name? Luke Jameson—they were open enemies."

"What, warring YouTubers?" I laughed.

"It's no joke. These two have been at each other's throats, waging a YouTube version of battle rap. You know, dissing each other in the videos they post. And there was also the matter of a stolen channel."

"A stolen channel?"

"A while ago, when these two were more palsy, they joined forces to trade off each other's celebrity and make some extra cash. Within a few days their new channel had a million subscribers. But then Jameson decided to take it for himself, so he changed the access password to lock Ramon X out and kept the revenue all to himself."

"Why did he do that?"

"I don't know, but it's possible it was in response to something Ramon had done."

"How serious did their hostility get? Don't tell me—a boxing match."

"Close. That's actually what many fans wanted to see, but Ramon X's idea of getting square was much darker than that. He made no secret of the fact that he wanted Jameson dead."

"Did he ever make that threat explicitly?"

"Who knows what he said to the guy face to face, but on YouTube he was careful. You know, keeping it within their guidelines so he didn't get his channel shut down. But on other social media platforms, he didn't hold back. He came right out and said he wanted to see Jameson dead."

"So you're thinking..."

"I'm thinking your boy has fed you a load of crap. I'm thinking he's decided to earn himself some coin and some gang kudos by doing Ramon X a favor. Any young Sintown Crip gangbanger would want to earn Ramon X's respect. The dude's got an entourage almost as big as Floyd Mayweather Junior."

"You have been busy. So your theory is Demarco volunteered to be a gun for hire?"

"Look at his record, Brad. What the hell was this gangster from Pomona doing at VidCon? He wasn't there collecting autographs, I know that much. He went there to kill."

"I'm not sure you're right, Jack."

"Who knows what's right? But one thing I do know—this stinks like a dead cat. It's a lost cause. Why waste your time on it? Can you imagine what the cops and prosecution are going to do with this case if he pleads not guilty? They will destroy him."

"I can't do that."

"Why not?"

"Demarco's old man is a buddy of mine. At least he was. Tank Torrell was my closest friend in the Marines. I loved and respected him, and we looked out for each other. Until the day he got killed."

"Right. I see. And let me guess: you're doing it pro bono?"

Jack had assumed right. I wouldn't be taking a cent from either Demarco or Jasmine.

"You got it, but that doesn't mean I expect you or anyone else to work this case for nothing. I owe it to Tank to do my best to look out for his boy. And my gut tells me he's telling the truth—as preposterous as that may seem to you. But think about it: if your theory is right, then it was a suicide mission. Why would Demarco commit a murder for which he was almost certainly going to be caught?"

Jack shrugged his shoulders.

"Just because it seems screwed up to you, doesn't mean it doesn't make sense to someone else's twisted way of thinking. We see it just about every day—mass shootings, terrorist attacks. A lot of people seem to want to make a name for themselves by slaughtering the innocent."

There was something that had been on my mind since meeting Demarco. If he was telling the truth about leaving the Crips, his life would be in danger if he ever went to jail.

"Jack, Demarco isn't sick in the head. He'd started making some good decisions in life. But I'll tell you something: if he goes to prison, it's game over."

"Sure, if he's found guilty there'll be no parole."

"That's not what I'm talking about."

"Then what are you talking about?"

"I'm talking about the Westside Pomona gang. They're a Latino mob controlled by the Mexican mafia. Right now they are in a serious blood feud with the Sintown Crips, two members of which were shanked in San Quentin this month."

"But if he's left the Sintown Crips, they won't target him, right?" said Megan.

"No. He's an even bigger target. To the Westside gang he's still a Crip. And they will kill him because he'll have no protection inside."

"Oh my God," said Megan.

"If I don't keep him out of jail, he's dead. That kid's life depends on me."

Jack shook his head.

"I hate to say it, but to me this looks like mission impossible."

"I hear you. But I intend to find out exactly what went down at that convention center, and I need your help. Are you in?"

Jack smiled.

"Sure. But I warn you. Someone's got to play devil's advocate on this one—and that someone's going to be me."

"Well, let's get to it."

I looked over the arrest report I'd brought with me.

"Jack, there are a few names here. Witnesses who told the cops Demarco was the shooter. We need to speak to as many as we can find."

"I'm on it. I'll also check to see if any eyewitnesses spoke to the media."

"Let me guess: Tara McClean will be your first call. She's always happy to oblige."

Jack smiled knowingly. Tara McClean was a television reporter who had a soft spot for Jack.

"She's only human," Megan scoffed light-heartedly. "Jack, are you going to keep spinning the wheels or are you at some point going to stick around long enough to have a family?"

"Kids are over-rated," Jack said. "Besides, I've got plenty of nieces and nephews."

Somehow Jack's words didn't ring true. He'd be a great dad, and I could tell Megan thought so too. She'd been trying to hook him up with a friend—a former Olympic downhill skier who was an absolute knock-out. Jack was particularly coy when it came to set-ups. They emasculated him slightly, as though they implied he didn't have the gumption to get the job done himself.

"Speaking of kids, I've got to go," I said. "Let's touch base later. See where we're at."

My next meeting was something I was both looking forward to and dreading. I was going to check in on Bella, and I knew Claire would want to "talk." I knew what was coming—she may have chewed a butt cheek off me when I'd dropped Bella home yesterday, but I figured she wasn't done. She'd want another chance to sink her teeth back into my ass.

***

I pulled into the double garage of Claire's Venice Beach home, finding just enough room next to her silver Porsche Cayenne. She'd done extremely well in the two years since her jewelry business had taken off and we'd gotten divorced. Her $2.3 million, three-level house sat between Strongs Drive and the canals. The ground floor, which opened out to a small lawn and the waterway beyond, was an open studio. I walked down the side pathway and entered via the yard gate.

Claire was busy at a large drawing table. Her assistant Caitlin—a fashion tragic who I guessed worked for practically nothing—was carrying sketches or something over for Claire's inspection. In the far corner I could see Bella, lounging on a white sofa, headphones on, immersed in her iPad. Obviously, today had been a stay-at-home day, and for that I felt guilty.

I steeled my jaw and walked in.

Bella was the first to notice me. Instead of the usual leap-off-the-sofa-and-open-armed-dash, she didn't move. Then, I assumed, she decided the right thing to do was come give her father a hug, or at least say hi. She shifted herself lazily off the sofa and ambled up to me. She went all floppy as she reached me, smiled gently and threw her arms around my waist before I lifted her up. I was relieved to at least have earned her partial forgiveness.

Her mother, on the other hand, was a different story.

Claire sat watching until I put Bella down.

"Looks like you're busy, as usual," I said, a standard compliment. Claire had been flat out for eighteen months and was delighted to be so. Every day that her jewelry business moved forward, the memory of our marriage dropped further behind and her status as an independent fashion success story grew stronger and stronger. The celebrities who'd once only known her as the name behind a brand recommended by their stylist now ranked as friends. She was happy, and I was happy for her.

"It's hectic. I've got to have the fall collection locked down and shot by the end of the week," she said.

"I'm sure it will be a huge success, as always."

I couldn't help but read the fawning press over Claire's designs. She was no longer a doe-eyed ingenue who could be flattered by a positive review or a celebrity endorsement. She was now an artist, a designer who validated her powers of vision and design with each and every collection.

"Thank you, Brad. Let's go upstairs where we can talk."

I followed her upstairs into the main kitchen. I declined her offer of coffee or a drink. We sat at her kitchen table.

"So what is it you want to say? Are you not done with telling me what an asshole father I am?"

She shook her head.

"No, that's not it. Even though for the life of me I cannot understand why you did what you did. I just can't get that out of my head—that you chose to leave her alone to endure that nightmare."

"Well, I can't explain it to you any better than I have. The short of it is, if that had been a mass shooting, I could not have looked in Bella's eyes again if I hadn't tried to prevent as many deaths as humanly possible. If you've never watched the news and wondered why nobody did anything, or felt that someone surely must have been able to do something to end the carnage, then what can I say? You and I are fundamentally different people."

"I don't want this to be an argument."

"What do you want this to be then?"

"A conversation about what's best for our daughter."

"I have a feeling you're about to tell me what's best for our daughter."

She bowed her head and smiled ruefully.

"Okay. I took her to my therapist this morning, and I want to tell you what she has advised."

"She talked with Bella?"

"Yes."

"Alone?"

"Yes."

"And?"

"And, as you might expect, this was an extremely traumatic event for Bella. She is super anxious and does not want to be left alone at all. She slept in my bed last night."

"What's the advice?" I could tell there was news coming my way that I wasn't going to like. I just wanted it out in the open.

"She doesn't feel safe with you. We hope you can agree to a change of conditions regarding your access."

I was half expecting this, but it still came as a shock. I only had Bella every second weekend, so there wasn't a lot of fat to trim off.

"Changes? Such as?"

"Now this is proposed as a temporary arrangement."

I was glaring at her. She looked at the bench between us.

"You get to see her as usual every second weekend but only during daylight hours. No sleepovers."

"So she wouldn't stay at my place?"

Claire nodded.

"Is this what Bella wants?" I said.

"This is coming straight from her."

"Via a shrink and via you."

"You can't expect her to tell you."

Despite my anger I knew any kind of hot-headed reaction from me would only damage things more.

"How long do you propose we do this for?"

"That depends."

"On what?"

"Brad, we need to be patient. *You* need to be patient, for your daughter's sake. When she's ready she'll let us know. I hope you can see that is not an unreasonable thing to ask."

It took me a long time to get accustomed to only seeing Bella every fortnight, but to Claire's credit she was not black and white about the rule. I got to take Bella skiing and hiking, and we had gone to various other events outside my allotted days. Yet, as much as I hated the prospect of an even more restrictive arrangement, I wanted to give Bella her space. If that's what she wanted, then so be it.

"Okay," I said.

"Okay what?"

"I agree. No sleepovers until Bella decides she's ready."

"That can't be something she just tells you—she has to tell the psychologist and me."

"Of course. In triplicate. As if I could put words in her mouth."

Claire smiled, relieved. There was something condescending about her and that irked me. Maybe I was being unfair, but when it came to our parenting, or leading by example, things always seemed to be a case of mom knows best and dad's a bumbling fool in need of ongoing tutoring. That made me think of how Bella had become enmeshed in Claire's fashion world. Her Instagram account was essentially a fashion magazine populated by a single model, her. I thought of the girl who had fawned over Bella in Anaheim.

"I meant to tell you something."

"What?"

"After the shooting, this girl—late teens—came up and practically drooled all over Bella."

Claire smiled fondly. "She gets that a lot. Better get used to it."

"That's the thing. I don't want to get used to it. And I don't think it's okay that you're used to it."

"It's what she loves doing."

"What, posting photos of herself? She just came up with that all by herself? Don't act like you didn't set it all up for her."

"True, I got her started. But if she wants, she can stop any time she likes."

"If she wants? She's a seven-year-old girl. How could she not be enamored with all the praise and affirmation she gets. But there are probably—no, there are certainly—all manner of creeps panting over her thinking God knows what. You know what kind of sick individuals are out there."

"Maybe. But you could say the same thing about walking down the street. How many sickos do you think we pass every day? And I don't just mean the ones who catcall, I mean the ones who keep quiet, the ones with sleazy eyes. The completely hidden ones. How many men who come across as totally harmless are up to something perverted on their computers in the comfort of their own homes? It's no different—there's no telling who the creeps are or who they aren't."

"It just seems like asking for trouble."

"That's one way to look at it."

"Or a great way to help market your jewelry designs. That's another way to look at it."

She glared at me.

"This is not about me! I've shown you the income she makes but you barely seem interested. And now all of a sudden, when you've screwed up, you come out with this."

"This is not a reaction to what you just told me about my access. It's not a response to the shooting. I'm not comfortable with it.

Never have been. And I'm her father, no matter how much you like to mess around with the time I get to do that."

"Me, mess around? Don't you ever forget—what's happening here is a result of your own actions, your own decisions. How about owning up and taking responsibility for it?"

"Look, let's just stop. I need to get going. And there's something else I wanted to tell you."

She stood there, arms folded, waiting.

"I'm defending the alleged shooter."

Her mouth dropped. "You're what?!"

"The young man who was arrested for the VidCon shooting. I'm his defense attorney."

She stayed silent as I began walking out.

"I can't believe my ears," I heard her call after me. "You just can't help yourself, can you? Just have to be the goddamn superhero. The man who shot someone in cold blood, who terrorized hundreds of people, including your own seven-year-old daughter—you're trying to get him off?!"

I stopped at the top of the stairs.

"There's a lot more to it, but yes, that's it in a nutshell. See you in a couple of weeks."

"God help us. Oh, and look who's addicted to fame," she called out as I started down the stairs. She was alluding to the amount of press I'd gotten for previous cases.

I stopped.

"That's not it, Claire. Not by a long shot. He didn't do it."

60

CHAPTER 8

The VidCon organizers gave me a number for Ramon X. The only problem was getting him to answer. For three days my calls went straight to voicemail. Finally, he called back and invited me over to talk.

I don't know what I imagined a gangster rapper's house would look like, but a cream-colored, palm-tree shielded mansion sitting high in what appeared to be the Beverly Hills of Pomona seemed kind of fitting. The driveway led up a slope and underneath one wing of the house.

Two barking Rottweilers escorted my car to a stop, positioning themselves at the driver's door, spit flying from their hostile jaws. I stayed put.

A young black guy wearing an NWA t-shirt and shorts came up to the car and shouted at the dogs. They shut their fang-filled traps and backed off a little. He waved at me, assuring me it was okay to get out.

"They're all bark, these bitches," he said. It was a friendly line, but he wasn't smiling. Underneath his cap brim, his eyes squinted at me. Nothing to do with the sun—just plain street scrutiny. "You the lawyer?"

"Yes, I am."

"I'm Trey. Follow me."

He turned for the house, and I followed with the dogs trotting beside us. Inside we passed through the lounge area where a bunch of guys were watching a massive television screen through a haze of pot smoke. They didn't even look at me.

"He's in the studio," Trey said over his shoulder. We continued across the house, through a kitchen, pool room and then a huge dining area. At the far end of the house, we followed some stairs down. The beat coming from the studio grew louder. Trey opened the door and rap music burst out, along with the scent of weed. I walked in to find Ramon X sitting behind the mixing desk nodding to the music. A guy next to him tweaked the levels. Then a rapper started in. I looked through the glass to see another guy holding cans to his ears and punching out words with commanding venom.

Ramon X motioned me to come over so I did. He extended his hand.

"Just getting this down," he said. "You mind?"

"Not at all," I said, somewhat taken aback by the courtesy.

From what I'd read, Ramon X never denied being a gangster. But since gaining success as a rapper, he'd proven to be an astute businessman. His first YouTube videos were freshly written raps recorded with the most basic of gear: a phone and a YouTube account. He recorded everything on his phone from the raps to the beats to the video footage. He even edited everything on his phone. In some videos he spoke of his passion for his craft, and the difficulties he faced trying to make it as an artist.

After I'd waded through the clips on his channel, I understood how his openness, honesty and personality had won him more and more subscribers. He was tough and edgy but always civil. He displayed an easy charm and a great sense of humor. On occasion, he'd speak out about the injustice of how cops treated young black men.

From what I'd seen, Ramon X was no black revolutionary calling for the overthrow of the white patriarchy. He was an engaging voice of protest, a man who humanized the lives of black people subjected to white hate. But he was also no pussy. He touted his gangster history as a badge of honor. He may not have been a man of the world, so to speak, but he was a man who knew how to thrive in *his* world.

After the rapper finished his lines, the mixer cut the backing track.

"Yeah-ah boi!" Ramon X yelled getting up on his feet and pumping his fist in the air to salute the rapper's effort. "That was sick. That was the freaking dope, right there."

The rapper emerged from the booth looking totally unfazed by the compliment. He then clasped palms with Ramon X and chest bumped. "True," he said before bursting into laughter, as did Ramon X.

My host then turned to me, smiling.

"Come on, we can talk out back. It's nice out."

We left the studio, climbed the stairs, then headed outside.

"You want something to drink? Soda? Beer? I can get my man Tito to make you a killer chocolate shake. What you want?"

We skirted a large pool, passing two girls enjoying the mild warmth of the winter sun.

"A Coke would be good," I said.

Ramon X shouted out: "Yo! Tito!"

"Yo!" came a reply from the kitchen sliding door.

"Can you get us a couple of Cokes out here?"

"You come get 'em!"

"If I have to come get 'em, your ass better be gone for good by the time I reach that door!"

"Coke it is."

We walked over to the pool and took a seat at a square glass table underneath a brick gazebo.

"So, how's Demarco doing?"

"Not so good. He's in a shitload of trouble."

"The cops think he was shooting for me, right?"

"You've spoken to them?"

"They came and asked some questions."

"About your beef with Luke Jameson?"

"Yeah. You know about that?"

"I know that I can't take what I read as gospel. But it's hard not to miss the fact that you hated Luke Jameson. You weren't shy about saying so."

Tito came, placed two cold bottles of soda on the table and left without a word.

"Here's what's true: We used to be okay," said Ramon X. "We did some stuff together to boost our own channels and it worked. But then it didn't. He got to the point where he decided he didn't need me anymore, and all he wanted was to promote himself and make sure he had more subs than me."

"Then he insulted the Crips."

"That's how much of a dumbass he is. He got to thinking he could say whatever the hell he wanted and there'd be no consequences. For real. But if you going to cross me like that, you either make amends or amends is going to be made for you."

"What did he say, exactly?"

64

Ramon X was slouched way back in his chair, the reflection of the pool filling the frames of his sunglasses.

"He dissed the Crips. And by that I don't mean some shitty remark that's going to upset nobody. He was trying to make a fool of me."

Ramon X reached for his phone, then flicked and tapped his screen before handing it to me.

The video showed a cocky white male (Jameson) taking the piss out of black gangs. He was dressed up in a blue bandana, the color of the Crips, did a facetious rap, grabbing his crotch and chopping his hands in front of the lens. The lyrics labelled gangster rappers as losers, and at one point Jameson likened Ramon X to a Kinder Egg. He held up the candy to show its brown chocolate outer coating and white chocolate inner layer. The message was clear: "Ramon X wishes he was me."

"That's not the smartest thing I've seen," I said, handing the phone back. "And you threatened to kill him over that?"

"That's not quite right."

"I thought it was pretty clear. You tweeted something to the effect that he'd just signed his own death warrant and that he had days left to live. And it turns out you were right."

"I was saying what every nigga was saying. It wasn't that I was going to kill him. It was that he practically dared every member of the Crips *not* to kill him. It's the stupidest, dumb-ass cracker shit you can imagine. That's what it was, that video of his—either a death wish or the work of the dumbest motherfucker on the planet. You think homies are going to take that shit? He seriously had no idea who he was fuckin' with."

"Tell me about your relationship with Demarco. You were friends?"

"We hung out together starting a few years back. We both rolled with the Sintown Crips doing the usual petty crime shit, hanging out thinking we were hard-assed gangbangers."

"But you rose in the ranks, and now what? You're out?"

"Yes and no. I'm not going to disown the boys. That nigga who got your Coke's a Crip. The nigga that laid down that rap you heard is a Crip. We're not all gun packin', crack smokin' hateful sticks of TNT, you know."

"So how come you haven't seen much of Demarco?"

"He just took off. About a year ago now. Something heavy went down and he checked out."

"You can do that? Just up and leave?"

"Depends on your intentions. But a gang's not the army. You don't get busted for desertion. It's just that it becomes a life most dudes never find an alternative to."

"And were Demarco's reasons for leaving deemed kosher?"

"Hell, the main thing is you're not leaving to go snitch. And Demarco was trusted."

"Why?"

"Because he'd seen some shit go down and the cops tried everything to get him to betray the gang, but he kept his mouth shut. That got him some time in juvie."

"The assault case, right?" I said.

Ramon X nodded.

"So he really had severed ties with the Crips?"

"Yeah."

"You think he would ever take your words and act on them, to kill Luke Jameson for the honor of the Crips?"

"Are you his lawyer or a fucking cop?"

"Got to look at it from their angle. Don't think they won't be stitching all this together as Demarco's motive."

"He didn't commit shit. You're gonna get him off, right?"

"I won't lie. It's not going to be easy. Black on white crime, gang connections, motive—it could all add up to a pretty compelling narrative for a jury."

"Who else you talking to?"

"I've only just started. Why?"

"Because I ain't Luke Jameson's only enemy."

"Like want-him-dead kind of enemy?"

"Yeah, there was no shortage of them."

"Like who?"

"Like Evan Harrington."

"Who's Evan Harrington?"

"He's a two-faced, lying son of a bitch posing as a goody-two-shoes Christian family man."

"So I take it you guys are tight."

He coughed up a laugh.

"Yeah, right. I don't have anything to do with the dude, but you say Jameson and me got history? Well this shithead tried to knock Jameson's lights out. Dude had to get a restraining order on that oily little freak."

"What happened?"

"I'll give it to you as well as I know. You see, this Harrington dude has this channel that is all about his little family. He's got the cute wife, the cute kids. And then he was caught cheating on Tinder."

"He denied it, I take it?"

"Initially, yes. But he fessed up eventually. Of course, they posted a video about it, and his wife said God had forgiven him and that she had forgiven him, and on they rolled."

"So what about Jameson?"

"They go back a ways. Became friends at some Christian summer camp before Jameson started his channel. But then Jameson got famous on Vine."

"Vine? What's Vine?"

"Used to be massive. A platform for making short videos fast. Jameson made it big on Vine before Twitter bought and buried it. That's when he switched his whole focus to YouTube. And when Jameson started to get big on YouTube, Harrington decided he wanted in on it. He had nothing—no talent, no personality, no money, so he basically just pimped his life and the life of his wife and kids on YouTube. Suited that lazy son of a bitch too—he realized he could make a living out of doing nothing. Nothing but lying, that is. He does nothing. Creates nothing."

"Why was there a rift between Jameson and Harrington?"

"Jameson called Harrington out as a faker, and Harrington didn't take too kindly to that. I mean, when you're trying to up your subs—which we're all trying to do—the last thing you want is a big-time influencer dissing you. And yeah, Jameson was also saying that Harrington was buying subs."

"You can do that?"

"Hell yeah. Man, this YouTube thing is a frickin' gold rush, and there are some bent ways to get ahead."

A bad business deal was sometimes a catalyst for murder, but I wasn't convinced this was why Jameson was dead.

"Collaborating to build up your subs seemed to work for you and Jameson."

"It did up until he stole the channel off me. But Jameson went at Harrington pretty hard. And this is while Harrington was trying to get merch out, set up his website, build his Instagram. The guy was desperate not to take a backward step."

"Did he confront Jameson?"

"Yeah. He didn't do it in his posts or anything, because he always had to be, like, the nice Christian boy—thanking God for this and that and making every day so rich and rewarding. But off camera he took any opportunity to get in Jameson's face."

"And VidCon was one of those opportunities?"

"Yeah. Like the day before Jameson was shot, I think. Yeah, it was the first day. Harrington jumped him and started laying into him. You didn't see that?"

"No."

"It was all over Twitter, man."

"Yeah, well I'm not."

"The point is, it just goes to show what kind of person Harrington is. I'd say even if he was the world's number one YouTuber, he'd still be as strung-up and insecure as he is now. You ask me, that's one fuckin' dangerous dude."

I leaned forward to get to my feet.

"Thanks for your time, Ramon."

"Will you be wanting me to testify?"

"I'm not sure I'd put you on the stand as a defense witness. Your background just gives the prosecution too much ammo to discredit you. That said, they might see a purpose in calling you so they can discuss your tweets and whether Demarco might have wanted to kill in your name."

"But that's bullshit."

"Maybe, but it's the sort of bullshit a jury might swallow whole. If I were you, I'd get your story straight and clear but with no elaborations. They could really screw you."

"Thanks for the heads up."

My pace quickened slightly as I made my way to the car. And it wasn't just the two Rottweilers sniffing at my heels. This was what I loved about the law. Things were getting exciting. We were behind the eight ball, sure, but there were plenty of shots still left in play.

CHAPTER 9

Demarco's case was automatically prime media fodder: a brazen public killing with a strong racial subtext. To get the most bang for their buck, the District Attorney's Office wanted Demarco tried as an adult as opposed to leaving him to be processed in the juvenile system. The person who had the power to make that decision was Justice Meredith Callaway. On her reputation alone I believed the result was in long before the race was run.

As I approached the entrance to Eastlake Juvenile Court, I saw the one and only Jessica Pope waiting outside. I can't say it was a surprise to see her. As the assistant district attorney prosecuting the case, she'd wasted no time filing for a transfer to the adult system.

It was always a pleasure to see Jessica. Tall, blonde and drop-dead gorgeous, it was a surprise she never followed her famous broadcaster father into the media. There her smarts, drive, pedigree and looks would have most certainly fast-tracked her to a national broadcasting gig. Maybe that's just what I'd have preferred, because it meant I wouldn't have had to go up against her in court—not that she'd ever gotten the better of me professionally. Outside court we'd always enjoyed a flirtatious relationship, one that had once moved into the bedroom. We never dated. There was always something about our relationship that meant we'd be professional adversaries first and "just good friends" second. But she didn't mind blurring the lines for fun. And that was a distraction I could do without, because whenever we met, the simple thought of having her again was never far from my mind. I'd always prided myself on my self-discipline, so she never knew, as far as I could tell, just how close I always came to pulling her into my arms and kissing those fast talking, quick drinking, sassy lips of hers.

"Brad, just the man I wanted to see," she smiled.

I didn't return the cheer. I hated having her gunning for Demarco. Judges loved her and the press loved her, but as her opponent I could only love her as much as a pit bull with its teeth bared inches from my balls.

"Hello, Jess. You wasted no time filing for a waiver."

"If it wasn't for Proposition 57, I'd have been able to do it myself. But something tells me Judge Callaway will oblige."

Until recently, when a person under the age of eighteen was accused of a serious offense such as rape or murder, they could be tried as an adult purely on the discretion of the public prosecutor. But after Proposition 57 had been voted in, that decision lay in the hands of a judge. Still, for the most part, the extra layer of protocol just delayed the inevitable.

At least Demarco got a hearing. I was well prepared, but with his priors and the police case building against him, I didn't hold much hope he'd be spared.

"You look particularly hungry today, Jess. Have they run out of raw meat down at LADA?"

"Don't worry your pretty little head about me, Brad. I get plenty of whatever I like. Speaking of which, I haven't heard from you in a while. Are you avoiding me?"

"No, just trying to keep my nose clean."

"How's that beautiful daughter of yours? Is she going to follow in daddy's footsteps, or will you let her in on the fact that there's a far more noble and rewarding path to be taken in the law?"

"I'm not pushing her to be anything. She's only seven. That said, right now all she wants to be is a fashionista."

"Yes, I know. She's quite the Instagram star. She's adorable."

"Don't tell me you follow her."

"No, but I've checked out her account. She is a stunning girl, Brad. And the way she puts clothes together? It's divine. Is that all her own doing, or Claire's?"

Jessica and Claire knew each other remotely, having met in social circles. If you wanted to find a fashion icon of the law, Jessica Pope would top the list.

"It's all Bella. It's just a gift she has."

I said this with my eyebrows raised, clear that the situation wasn't all to my liking. Jessica paused, seeming to wonder if she should say what she was thinking.

"What?" I prompted.

"No, sorry. Nothing. I was just wondering, are you totally comfortable with Bella having so many followers?"

I'd recently become aware that her follower count was nearing half a million. I let out a "don't go there" sigh.

"Look, I'd prefer she had interests that she could pursue in private, but this is Los Angeles," I said. "Doesn't everyone need an audience? If she was a wannabe pro skater her sponsors would no doubt be pushing her to build her profile and cash in on her marketing good looks. Hell, this is the home of Hollywood. How many kids out there want to be famous actors, or pop stars or whatever? It's out of control. And these days, if it's not online, it never happened."

"Whoa, I didn't mean to push the 'discouraged dad' button. Can I have my money back?"

"Bitch."

She gave me a wink.

"That's why you love me. Or at least why you want me. Am I right?" Before I could answer, she opened the door and invited me in. "Come on, let's go. It's time to kick your ass."

Rightly or wrongly, I had half a boner. And I think she knew it.

I waited at the defense table, and within minutes two bailiffs escorted Demarco into the courthouse and sat him down beside me.

"How you doing?" I asked.

"All good, except they won't give me my phone, and I missed the game."

I couldn't help but be impressed: Demarco had certainly mastered the art of nonchalance. He knew full well what this waiver hearing was about, and he was making damn sure to act like the prospect of going to men's prison didn't faze him. He knew as well as I did that, on top of every other threat a young man faced in jail, he would be a target for rival gang members. I had to wonder whether he had really severed ties with the Crips. Renewing his allegiance to his old gang would be a smart move, an insurance policy for life inside. On a first-degree murder charge, Demarco would be looking at life without parole. In that event, the best way to boost his survival chances would be to become a Crip for life.

Judge Callaway didn't waste any time getting down to business. Before Jessica could open her mouth, Callaway addressed Demarco.

"I'm sorry to see you here again, Mr. Torrell," the judge said.

A surprising look of shame came over Demarco. He bowed his head briefly.

74

"If I remember rightly," she continued, "at our last meeting you said you were going to change, that you had found faith and you were determined to lead a life that would make your parents proud. Is that right?"

"Yes, Your Honor."

"That was only six months ago. You were here on a shoplifting charge, but I let you off. You said you were on the streets and were desperately hungry. And I believed you. We talked about how you needed to change because the path you were on was leading you to one place—prison. And you assured me you had stepped away from the gang life and crime for good. Isn't that right, Mr. Torrell?"

"That's right, Your Honor."

"Well, I'm very sorry to see you here again, young man. Let's hear from Ms. Pope. Counselor?"

Jessica got to her feet and went straight for the jugular.

"Your Honor, what we have here is the ruthless, audacious killing of a young man. A murder that was carried out in public and witnessed by several people. I believe the evidence already acquired by the police indicates very strongly that the accused not only carried out this murder, but that he did so with malice aforethought."

Malice aforethought. AKA "premeditated." Jessica was gunning for first-degree murder.

"As you can see from the police report," she continued, "the accused was found standing over the victim, Luke Jameson, a young, successful social media star. While the accused was not caught holding the weapon, traces of gunpowder were found on his right hand. And three witnesses say they saw the accused tap the victim on the shoulder and say to him, 'You have been served by God.' Seconds later, two shots were fired into the victim's chest.

"Your Honor, as you have noted, this is not the first time the accused has appeared in juvenile court. Two years ago, he appeared on auto theft charges. Then there was an assault charge. Both these led to time spent in Juvenile Hall. And finally, there was his last appearance here—a minor shoplifting charge you referred to earlier. Each of these appearances come on top a list of prior offenses I have submitted to you, and which I assume you have already read. The accused has a track record of criminal activity that has only escalated in seriousness. He is a known member of the notorious Sintown Crips criminal gang, and the bulk of his run-ins with law enforcement have been in the company of other Sintown Crips members. Now, he stands accused of committing cold-blooded murder.

"I would argue that the accused has been given ample warning and ample time to change his ways, yet he has chosen not to do so. I think it is abundantly clear that there is no hope that he can be rehabilitated by the generous services offered by our juvenile justice system. No, while the accused is just months short of being legally defined as an adult, his actions are that of a hardened criminal who deserves to be dealt with as an adult. I believe the loved ones, family and friends of the late Luke Jameson would agree that it is our duty to ensure the accused faces the full weight of the law."

With that Jessica sat back down. Demarco was leaning back in his chair like it was all okay. That didn't mean he was indifferent to what was going on, but the sense of fatalism he displayed worried me. I had no issue with believers, trust me, but it is hard to help someone fight a powerful adversary when they are nourished by a belief that whatever becomes of them is pre-ordained, tailored even, by God.

In our meeting prior to this hearing, Demarco had said he would never plead guilty, that he owed it to God to maintain the truth—that he was innocent—no matter what. So from the get-go, I knew I wasn't going to be approaching Jessica for a plea deal. And I knew Jessica would be delighted to learn that Demarco was standing his ground. That way it would go to trial, and she could put him away for life with no chance of parole.

I had to admit, I felt hamstrung by what I could offer to counter Jessica's cold assessment of my client. But I was going to give it my best shot.

"Your Honor, to properly judge someone, we need to not only be aware of the facts as they are recorded by the police, but also the facts as they are recorded by others in a position of social authority. I know it has only been a matter of months since Demarco was before you, but I can assure you that in that time he had indeed embarked on a corrective path, all of his own volition.

"Based on the documents I have filed, it is a recorded fact that he entered the Los Angeles Mission of his own accord six months ago. This was when he told you, Your Honor, that he was following the path of God toward redemption. And his actions have reflected a commitment to that end. At the mission, he took part in charitable works and underwent counselling to help equip himself for the significant challenge of making deep changes in his life.

"Your Honor, I think you would agree that such a commitment to change for the better is rarely seen in people of a similar age to Demarco, whatever their background.

"As for the crime for which Demarco stands accused, I believe there is a lot of room to question the presumption of guilt that the prosecutor seems so willing to accept without weighing all the facts impartially.

"It cannot be questioned that Demarco was there at the time of the killing and that he engaged with the victim verbally moments before the shooting. Yet, it is another thing entirely to accept that Demarco pulled the trigger."

"Counselor, gunpowder traces were found on your client's hand," said Judge Callaway.

"Well that indicates his proximity to the shooting, but it does not necessarily mean he was the shooter."

Judge Callaway almost groaned.

"Your Honor, if we look at motive for this murder, Demarco Torrell possessed none. He was running an errand of sorts for which he expected to be paid a total of one thousand dollars. Money that he could not refuse. Money that he planned to use to return to school, graduate and then join the Marines and serve his country, just as his father did."

I had a few more words to say, but Judge Callaway held up her hand.

"Counselor, I'm sure you will have a very thorough and detailed defense to mount for your client, but this is not the place to present it fully. I'm not here to judge whether Mr. Torrell is guilty of the crime for which he is charged. My duty is to determine whether the circumstances dictate this case be transferred to the Superior Court."

I was about to interject, but I thought better of it and sat down.

"Now, I need to make a decision based on a few considerations," said Judge Callaway. "Does the seriousness of the crime for which Mr. Torrell is charged warrant him being tried as an adult? Yes, it clearly does. Does Mr. Torrell's background, history and actions tell me I should direct him towards adjudication and, if necessary, rehabilitation in the juvenile justice system? No, I think not. What I have before me tells me that Mr. Torrell's commitment to changing his ways is not abundantly clear. It could well be that he is impervious to any benefit on offer from such services. To that end, I am granting a waiver that will allow the case of Demarco Torrell to be tried in the Superior Court. Good luck to you, Mr. Torrell."

Jessica couldn't help herself. She gave me a smug grin as she stood, swept up her belongs and made for the door.

I turned to my client. "I'm sorry, Demarco. This was to be expected, but it's still a blow. I just need to gather the evidence to make the strongest defense possible."

"I think you'll be fighting an uphill battle," he replied. "They are going to pin my ass for this no matter what the truth is."

"Not if I can help it. But I need you to help me."

The bailiffs were at his shoulder.

"Hang in there, Demarco. I'll see you soon."

"You know where to find me," he said with a wry smile.

CHAPTER 10

"Still no word. He's disappeared. No one's seen him for over a week now," said Jack over the phone. He was talking about Toby Connors, the young man Demarco said paid him to go to VidCon. "I've spoken to his mom and his girlfriend again. Candice Levine, the girlfriend, said she hasn't heard from Connors since the day he met with Demarco."

"That doesn't sound good," I said.

"No, it doesn't. Doesn't sound good for Demarco, doesn't sound good for you, and sure as hell doesn't sound good for Toby Connors."

As we spoke, I was headed San Diego way to pay Evan Harrington a visit. I wanted to ask about his altercation with Luke Jameson the day before he was killed. I needed to see for myself if he had anything to hide. To my mind, the police should consider him a suspect.

But we desperately needed to speak with Connors so he could corroborate Demarco's story. Jack had been on the hunt for days. Turned out he was a wannabe YouTube star who lived with his mom and did little else but make prank videos.

"His mother didn't know a hell of a lot about his videos," Jack said. "She said he was obsessed. All he ever did was go out to get footage then spend hours on end editing."

"Have you checked out his channel?"

"Yeah."

"And?"

"It's just what you'd expect from a young kid who thinks a string of really dumb stunts is going to turn him into a celebrity."

"How lame are we talking?"

"Take *Jackass*, subtract the imagination and the pain and the humor, and then what you have left is the Toby Connors channel. You know that scene in *Napoleon Dynamite* where he goes over that ankle-high jump and crushes his nutsack?"

"Yeah."

"Well, that's too good for this guy's channel."

"Have to start somewhere, I guess."

"That's what his mom says. His girlfriend said he intimated to her that he'd been hired to do a job. He was excited about it."

"Like what? Was he hired to prank Luke Jameson?"

"She couldn't say. She said Connors was super hush-hush about it all. Didn't tell her anything. Normally, she'd go along for his shoots—you know, drive him around, help talk down pranked strangers who were pissed off with him, but he insisted he had to do this job solo."

"So she knows absolutely nothing about it?"

"Nope."

"Did they report him missing?"

"Yeah, a few days ago. They thought he might have run off for a couple of days with some friends, which he does sometimes, but none of his friends know where he is either and, obviously, he's not returning calls."

"He's dropped off the grid completely?"

"Yep. I know one of the cops looking into the case, and he's going to give me a heads up if anything surfaces."

The case against Demarco was building. Jack had interviewed all the witnesses listed on the police report. One young woman was adamant she saw Demarco follow Jameson into the theater with an angry expression on his face. Another two witnesses who were standing right next to Jameson when the shots were fired said they didn't doubt Demarco pulled the trigger.

"Where does this Connors kid get a grand to pay someone to help out?" I said.

"Assuming you believe Demarco's story."

"Jack, the cops found five hundred bucks exactly—five hundred-dollar bills—in his pocket. To me that backs his story. Still, it seems like a lot of money to pay someone to help you humiliate Luke Jameson."

"That's the thing—you put 'Luke Jameson shamed' into the title of your video and you'll get millions of views. That's called strategy."

"Was he hoping to use Jameson to build his profile?"

"Looks like it."

"Okay. Have you made contact with Cleo Jones?"

Cleo Jones was one of the VidCon organizers I'd spoken to to get Ramon X's number.

"No."

"Can you touch base with her. Ramon X said there were quite a few people who disliked Luke Jameson intensely, but he didn't have names besides Harrington. Can you check with her?"

"Sure thing."

"Thanks. Keep me posted."

✳✳✳

As I cruised south, I lost myself in thought. The more I learned about the social media world, the more it disturbed me. My mind returned to Bella and her Instagram account. Claire had never ceded any ground to the objections I'd raised, and now, with me even more on the outer, I had less sway than ever.

Of course, I knew that parents these days held a disproportionate amount of fear about the dangers children face. When I was a kid in Boise, Idaho, we'd leave the house on our bikes in the morning and come home for lunch before heading out again with mom calling out: "I want you home by six at the latest." We smoked cigarettes, made mischief and explored. Our boundaries were set by time and geography, not fear.

According to Claire, things today were not so different. The interactions Bella had with her "fans" were almost always positive, Claire had told me, save for a few naysayers critical of what she was doing. She'd rattled off a list of pre-teen fashionistas with larger followings than Bella's. She could actually cite the number of followers each of them had—all in the millions. I couldn't tell for sure, but I wondered whether Claire nursed an ambition for Bella to outdo them. Hell, this was LA—if you're going for something, you want to be number one, right? Otherwise, what was the point?

It all made my head spin.

The sound of my phone ringing jolted me back to the here and now. I glanced down at the screen. It was Jack.

"Hey, you got something?"

"Yeah. I just heard from my cop buddy, the one looking into Toby Connors' disappearance."

"And?"

"They just found his body in a disused lot near the Santa Ana Freeway, a few blocks from the convention center. Some homeless guy noticed the smell. Connors was in the trunk of his car. Shot twice; one to the head."

"Any idea when this happened?" I asked.

"Too early to say, but my buddy tells me it's been a few days at least, maybe even a week."

My mind shifted into a higher gear. We were never going to get to speak to Connors now, but the next best thing was to get hold of his phone. And the only way to do that was to be a very good friend of the good folk at the city morgue.

"Jack, any chance you could ..."

"I'm going to head to the mortuary after I'm done with Cleo. The kid's body won't be there yet. But all his belongings will go with him, including his phone."

I liked that about Jack: often you just didn't have to ask; he just knew.

"Good. Hopefully, you can get every call and text message Connors exchanged in the last few days of his life."

What Jack was about to do was not what you'd call legal. But I needed those phone records ASAP. Sure, the police would get them and that meant they'd eventually be made available to me via the discovery process, but I couldn't wait that long.

If Demarco was telling the truth and he had been framed, then Connors' phone might help us find the real killer.

I ended the call and sped on south.

***

A few seconds after I knocked on the door of a perfectly middle-class-looking house in Grantville, a young woman appeared carrying an infant child. The pink floral headband told me the baby was a girl.

"You must be Amy. I'm Brad Madison, defense attorney for the man charged with killing Luke Jameson. I spoke with your husband earlier today."

"Yes, of course," Amy Harrington said with a warm smile. "Evan's just ducked out—we ran out of diapers. He'll only be a few minutes. Come on in."

Amy had that beautiful girl-next-door radiance. She just seemed perfectly wholesome—a wellspring of positive vibes. As I stepped through the door, she lifted the little girl's hand to give me a wave.

"This is Rhapsody," she said.

The little button squinched her face into a gummy grin. Total heart-melter.

"Oh my, what an absolute cutie. Lovely to meet you, Rhapsody. How old is she?"

"Nine months."

I was surprised, and relieved, that Amy didn't answer the door holding a camera. I'd arrived ready to insist that my appearance and interview was not to be recorded for their channel.

Since Evan Harrington had appeared on my radar, I'd taken the obligatory dive into the internet, checking what I'd been told, reading his posts and what others had said or written about him. In their vlogs, Evan and Amy were an openly Christian couple who wanted to share the trials and tribulations of a young family pursuing life in God's name. The channel had been running for two years. When they started out, they posted every few days, but for

85

the past year they'd committed to posting daily. The degree to which they'd opened their lives to the public drew criticism. More than a few said they were commodifying the lives and privacy of their children, who had no say whatsoever in the fact that they were being watched by millions.

I couldn't help but marvel at the determination they possessed to film the whole day, every day. Everything they did, from going to the supermarket to taking one of their kids to the hospital, was done with a selfie stick in hand so it could be captured for the channel. To date, they had built a following of two million subscribers, and their commitment to daily vlogs meant they had to devote almost every minute of the day to shooting or editing footage.

Along the way they'd become a magnet for trolls. Every video they posted drew a swathe of negative, judgmental comments about their parenting, their motives, their choices, Evan's infidelity, and the rumors that they'd bought subscribers. In the end, to block the haters, they'd disabled video comments.

Yet they'd managed to do well enough to buy a new house. It was a two-story picture-perfect family home. As I walked in, I glanced around the walls of the living room, where photos of the family plus three framed YouTube awards hung.

Amy saw me looking at them.

"They're for when we reached half a million subscribers, then one million and then two million," she beamed.

"You're doing well."

"Well, we've worked hard at it."

"And what's this?"

A framed letter hung next to the YouTube awards. "The Halo Group" logo was printed across the top. I leaned in closer to read the text. It was a note of congratulations and thanks from Victor Lund himself. He expressed his pride in their work and said he looked forward to their continued growth and success. "Your family is a bright, shining beacon amid a sea of darkness. God bless you."

"The Halo Group has been very supportive of what we're trying to do," Amy said.

"Are they your primary sponsor?"

From her reaction, I could tell Amy didn't really want to say. "Well, we couldn't have gotten this far without them. What with the Tinder scandal and all. They helped us get through a really tough time, and now it's all paying dividends."

As she spoke, a young boy, about four years old, came running into the room. Amy broke into a sweet laugh.

"Isaiah, say hi to Mr. Madison."

The boy and I high fived.

"Where's Daddy?" he asked.

"He's gone to the store, honey. He'll be back soon."

"Are we going to the waterslide?"

"Yes we are, sweetheart, once Daddy's finished speaking with Mr. Madison. Why don't you run outside and make the most of this beautiful day?"

"Okay," he said and turned for the back door beyond the kitchen. A few seconds later, I heard a dog's happy bark before a big, blonde, hairy lump of enthusiasm appeared at the sliding door. Isaiah tackled the dog with loving arms.

"That's Honey," Amy laughed.

"I actually know that."

"Ah, so you've watched our videos."

"Some of them. I don't know how you do it—day after day, through the tantrums and meal times. Parenting is stressful enough without having to shoot and edit a video diary of it. Every day."

"Well, that was kind of how we looked at it too a while back, but it's just become a way of life, the way we do things as a family."

"I know you've caught some flak for making the lives of your children so public."

"Well, that's fair enough if people disagree with what we're doing, but they don't know the amazing things that have come from it. And I'm not talking about money or the house. A lot of people really connect with what we're doing. We're not movie stars, we're real people with real issues that we deal with day in, day out. And we have the Lord to thank for this precious life we lead."

"You must be thrilled with how it's going."

"Well, I think people think it's a piece of cake to do this. But we don't pretend to be the perfect family, you know? We have our ups and downs, our fights, our disappointments and our goals. But that's what people see, and that's the beauty of it all. It's genuine. You just can't do this on a daily basis and have your whole family working to create some kind of fake image you've pre-prepared. The Lord will decide where our lives travel—we just have to open our hearts to His will, and He will make the journey clear to us."

For a moment I thought of Demarco Torrell and how similar his words had been despite his horribly different circumstances.

Just then there was a sound at the front door.

"Hello?!" a man called out.

"That's Evan," Amy said. "In here, sweetheart."

The sight of Evan Harrington didn't match my expectations. I wasn't sure why, but I'd expected a shorter man. Yet he was six three and, like his wife, he exuded a terrific sense of bonhomie. Lean, unshaven, and dressed in a t-shirt, jeans and sneakers, he walked up to me and extended his hand. He was relaxed and

88

smiling. He saw me looking cautiously at his other hand, which held a selfie stick with a small camera attached.

"Oh, my goodness, I forget I'm using it half the time," he said. He placed the camera on the kitchen bench before putting out his hand once more.

"I'm so sorry I wasn't here to greet you, but nature caught us napping." He lifted up the box of diapers. "I can't believe we ran out. You'd think we'd at least be on top of the diaper supply."

"We're just so busy," said Amy. "Maybe a little too much. Why don't you boys go and talk. I'll change Rhapsody and then fix some drinks. Brad, is homemade lemonade okay with you? I promise, it's good."

"That sounds lovely."

"Come with me, Brad," said Evan. He darted back to the bench to collect the camera. "We'll go up to the office."

After climbing the stairs, we passed a couple of bedrooms and then came to a room in which a young man was sat facing two large computer monitors.

"Brad, this is Phillip, our editor. And this is where we edit the videos, or at least Phillip does. We couldn't do a daily vlog without hiring an editor. But I still edit when Phillip's not available."

Phillip stood and we shook hands. Evan passed the camera to him.

"Here's some B-roll from the diaper run," he said. "Got a good piece-to-camera about a couple of things too."

"Cool, I'll get that ingested and have a look."

"Thanks Phil."

Evan continued down the hallway, opened a door and I followed him into the home office. The room had one desk with a closed laptop on it and two office chairs. Evan pulled one out and rolled it toward me then seated himself on the other. I couldn't help but think that, so far, he was everything his YouTube audience liked about him: open, friendly, a tad absent-minded perhaps, yet purposeful.

I'd wondered, as I watched his videos, whether charisma simply came after having attained a certain degree of YouTube celebrity. Because YouTube celebrity was definitely not the same as Hollywood celebrity. Looks, artistic talent or sex appeal were not prerequisites. Being geeky or bland or possessing Average-Joe dullness were not impediments to YouTube fame. In fact, they were adored by millions because they were so much more real than movie stars. The small screen was far more democratic about who could rise to the top. Being an average person with confidence and a good idea could be all it took to become world famous and have millions of dedicated fans hanging off your every post.

Evan tapped his thighs and leaned back in his chair.

"I'm guessing you want to talk about my relationship with Luke Jameson."

"That would be a good place to start."

"You don't believe it was your client who killed him?"

"My client says he didn't do it. So if there's any evidence to prove his innocence, then I need to find it."

"And what, you're hoping to prove I killed Luke Jameson?"

"I'm not hoping to prove you did anything. I just want to better inform myself about the events leading to Mr. Jameson's death. And I do know that you didn't like him and that the feeling was mutual."

"You know that for a fact?"

"It's what I'm led to believe."

Evan tightened his mouth into a half smile. "So fire away. What do you want to ask me?"

"I understand you assaulted Mr. Jameson the day before he was shot. Is that true?"

"Yes, it is."

Evan was still looking at me in the most pleasant way, waiting to be invited to continue.

"Would you mind elaborating on why you did that?"

"Sure. In short, he crossed the line. He'd insulted me and my family too many times. He claimed we were not what we purported to be. I was sick and tired of his attacks."

"And what do you purport to be?"

"A good Christian family. One that has faults but one that lives by a bright light—the light of Jesus Christ, our savior. He's a source of great nourishment for us. He gives us the presence of mind to savor what we have. You have seen our house. It's not extravagant. It's not a mansion. And yet Luke Jameson would have everyone believe we are misleading people and are fixated on making money. He was a lapsed Christian—you know that, right?—and, as far as I'm concerned, there's no crime in that. But his public criticism of us was just so, so spiteful. I wasn't going to let his abuse go unchallenged. And I guess pride got the better of me."

"Was assaulting him the Christian thing to do?" I asked. I wasn't being righteous, I just wanted to hear how he justified his behavior.

"No. I'm sorry for my actions and for my anger getting the better of me. But when Jesus overturned the merchants' tables in the temple of God, was that an act of peace? No, it was a line in the sand, an act of self-respect, an expression of rage that has resounded for two thousand years."

"Are you saying anger can result in something good?"

"I wouldn't put it that way—but in a sense, sometimes yes. As a human condition it has a certain integrity, but it needs to be tempered, so to speak."

"Why was Mr. Jameson out to hurt you?"

"Because I was vocal about his treachery toward God."

"You mean he lapsed, and so he'd committed a terrible sin."

"Something to that effect, yes. He abandoned our Lord Jesus Christ when he should have been thanking him for the riches God endowed him with."

"What about the lapses in your own commitment to God? You know, your widely reported infidelities."

He riled a little as I said this. His lips tightened and he drew in a sharp breath.

"Of course, you have read about that. Well, as you know we handled that like everything else we do as a family—under the eyes of God. I confessed everything to Amy, and she was kind enough to forgive me. I made a promise to God that I will be a better man, a real man and not a boy seeking sinful distractions from my responsibilities. I don't like having sinned, but I have atoned, and I am a better man, a better husband, a better father. Just ask Amy."

It was clear that deep emotions were stirring within Evan's soul.

"This is hard for me to talk about with you," he continued. "But I can do it quite freely because of the healing that my wife and my family and my God have allowed me to receive."

I must admit I was convinced by his candor. But as a defense lawyer, being cynical was a tool of the trade I could never afford to abandon. I'd heard rapists tell me they were just "nice guys" at heart. I'd heard murderers protest their innocence with a torrent of Oscar-worthy lies. You just can never be certain whether or not someone is telling you the truth.

"It strikes me that while you and your family are willing to forgive your own sins, you did not extend the same generosity to Mr. Jameson. Is there a reason you disliked him so much?"

Evan shifted a little.

"Have you seen what he does on his channel and other platforms?"

I'd seen enough. You didn't have to spend too long on Luke Jameson's channel to see that he'd been living out the bad-boy dreams of teenage boys the world over. Hanging out with strippers, playing in a punk rock band, and travelling the world riding motocross bikes and surfing. Everywhere he went he had chicks hanging off him, all looking smugly into the camera like they were queens of the high life. He was a loudmouth too—firing off about censorship and internet controls with a loutish spit to his tone. To me he was barely watchable, but to others he was a hero: no less than twenty million people subscribed to his channel.

"I've seen his work, if that's what you call it," I said. "Can't say I'm a fan and I can't see what people see in him, but I guess twenty million people would disagree with me. That's a lot of subscribers, isn't it?"

"Well, yeah it's a lot, but a lot of other YouTubers have more."

"How many do you have again?" I knew already, I just wanted to see how much it bothered him.

"Two million," he said, with an attempt to inject pride into his words that didn't quite come off.

"Sounds like a lot to me. And it's enough to make a living out of?"

"Yeah, it's working out really well."

"Why do you think Jameson turned away from his faith?" I asked.

"I think he discovered that the more outrageous he was, the more money he made. But, you know, there are plenty of people out there making more than he did without selling their souls to the devil."

"Is that what he did? Sold his soul to the devil?"

Evan nodded without speaking, as if he was weighing up whether to answer with words.

"There is no question that's what he did," he said. "And look where it got him."

"You think he brought his death on himself?"

"I've got no doubt about it. To me, it's almost like God pulled the trigger."

He was quite agitated now. Something was boiling inside him, an anger he was trying hard to contain. His arms were folded across his chest and his breathing was audible.

"Are you glad he's dead?"

"I wouldn't have said that, but, because you have ... yes, I'm glad he's dead."

His mouth stretched into a rueful smile.

"Evan, where were you when the shooting happened?"

"Ah, I was wondering when you were going to ask me that. But that's where we're going to have to leave our chat."

"It's a very simple question, Evan."

"Yes, I know it is, Mr. Madison. And I've told you about as much as I can tell you, for now at least."

"What's that supposed to mean?"

He stood and gestured an arm towards the door. I got to my feet and walked past him into the hallway. He shrugged, almost apologetic.

"It means I'll see you in court, as they say," he said, waiting for the penny to drop. "Jessica said to say hi."

Damn it! Jessica Pope had secured him as a prosecution witness.

"You're an eyewitness?"

"Yes."

"So you were there at the shooting?"

"Yes."

"Well, that is interesting—you being Johnny-on-the-Spot when your hated rival is murdered."

"Some would call it fate."

We walked downstairs and back to the front door. Passing through the living room, I heard happy squeals coming from the back yard. Evan opened the door for me and held out his hand. We shook, and I stepped out onto the steps.

"Well, Evan. Thanks again. And if this case does go to trial, I look forward to you answering all my questions under oath."

"I live under oath every day of my life, Mr. Madison."

"Well, good for you."

I approached my car and hit the remote button to unlock it. As I touched the door handle, my phone rang. I fished it out of my coat pocket and was surprised to see Jasmine's name on the screen. I'd figured it was just about impossible for her to call me from her home since the coverage there was so bad. I immediately sensed that something was wrong.

"Hello, Jasmine."

I could hear her breathing hard, like she'd run up a flight of stairs.

"Brad, something terrible has happened." *What could be more terrible than having a son charged with murder?* "It's Demarco. The police say he killed another man."

"What? He's been charged with a second murder?"

"Yes, oh my God. Oh my God."

Jasmine's voice faded. I heard a woman tell her to sit down.

"Jasmine!" I shouted.

I held the phone to my ear with no response.

"Jasmine!"

Someone picked up.

"Hello?" A woman asked.

"Hello," I said. "Who's this? What's happened to Jasmine?"

"She collapsed, but she's okay. She's sitting on the pavement. I'll need to get her back inside the house."

Jasmine must have gotten herself outside somehow to make the call.

"Please, can you ask her what's the name of the second man police say Demarco killed? Please."

"Hold on." I heard her cup the phone and then ask Jasmine, "What's the name of the man who was killed?"

When I heard Jasmine's answer, it didn't register as news but rather as something dreadful that already seemed apparent.

"Sir? She said it was Toby. Toby Connors."

CHAPTER 11

On my way to see Demarco, I called Mike Bayer, the detective leading the investigation into what was now considered a double murder. I had a good relationship with Bayer, and I knew he'd be straight with me about what the cops knew. Looked like a hit, he said: the killer had finished Connors off with a shot to the back of the head. Ballistics on the two bullets buried in Connors' body indicated it was the same weapon used to kill Luke Jameson. On top of that, Demarco Torrell's DNA was found in the passenger seat of the vehicle. Hard to tell precisely, but the medical examiner's estimate was that it had all gone down the same day Jameson was shot.

"Looks like your boy saw fit to have himself a spree," Bayer said.

"It doesn't make sense," I said.

"Nothing makes sense—apart from the evidence. You better get your boy to explain what the hell possessed him to kill two people in a day. You know what this looks like don't you, Madison?"

"Looks like a mess."

"That too. But this is black gang violence crossing into white territory. Two young white men murdered by a young black gangster out to prove how tough he is."

"Now that's a convenient way to package a case."

"It doesn't need wrapping paper and a bow. Black on white hate crime. You don't think that's how a jury's gonna see it?"

"Well, I'm sure that's the picture Jessica will paint for them."

I hung up. I couldn't believe how bad this looked for Demarco.

I waited a few minutes before Demarco was brought into the visitation room. When he entered, he stood still, saying nothing.

"How you holding up?"

"Love it here, man. Big screen TVs and hamburgers. Never want to leave."

I tried to imagine what it would be like to be his age and charged with two murders. Still, I wondered, how did I know he wasn't guilty? As a defense attorney, whatever I thought was true or not didn't matter. My job was to ensure my client got a fair hearing. To Jessica Pope this must have seemed now more than ever a slam-dunk case.

"You think I did both these killings?"

"What I believe makes no difference. What I can prove or disprove is what matters. So I need details. Starting with what happened that day."

"I already told you."

"You need to tell me again and again until it actually makes sense to me. Because right now it's not looking too flash. The cops are saying the same weapon was used in both murders. They found your DNA in Connors' car. And we have witnesses swearing they saw you shoot Jameson at point blank range. So if I'm going to help you, I need a reasonable explanation for this series of events. I need to know why you apparently had a front row seat to two murders yet had a hand in neither."

"Whatever."

"What's that supposed to mean?"

"It means, if God wants to see me taken down for this, then maybe that's just karma for things I done before."

"Nothing you've done in the past is worth you taking the blame for a double homicide you didn't commit. Maybe there's something important you haven't told me yet."

He looked at me like he was done talking already.

"How did you meet Toby Connors?" I said.

"Like I told you. He was standing outside the mission. Like he was waiting for me."

"You said that God had something to do with this."

"I was pumped up. I'd just had a talk with one of the carers in the mission, and I was riding high with the love of God in my heart. She said, 'God will lead the way to your salvation, your truth, your eternal peace.'"

"Why was she saying things like that?"

"Because that's what we did. We prayed together. She wanted to help me turn my life around. And I felt that it was working, you know. I actually felt sure I was going to make a change. Man, was I right."

"Who is this woman?"

"She works at the mission."

"What's her name?"

"Fran."

"Fran who?"

"Dunno. I just know her as Fran."

"Okay, so you walk out of there all pumped up. What were you going to do?"

"Well, to be honest I was thinking about my dad a whole lot, and about how I wanted to make him proud of me."

"Okay, so?"

"So I walked out the gate and this white guy was standing there. This Toby dude. He says to me straight up, 'Hey, you want to earn a thousand bucks?' Naturally, I thought he was shitting me, or else trying to get me to offload some stuff for him. You know, drugs or something. But he didn't look like that. He looked like some white dude who had no place being in Skid Row."

"You told him you were interested?"

"Dude's offering me a grand—I'm all ears."

"And what did he say?"

"He said he needed somebody to help him out with a prank. Said it was for his YouTube channel. So I listened, and he told me what he wanted me to do."

"Which was to go find Luke Jameson at VidCon and deliver him a message."

"Right. I said, 'What sort of message?' And he said that he was some sort of big shot on YouTube who had turned against God and that he needed to be humbled."

"So you had to say, 'You've been served by God?'"

"Right. And Toby said at that point someone else was going to smash a cream pie in this guy's face. He said the dude needed to be taught a lesson in humility. He needed to stop putting sin into the minds of young people and use his celebrity for good."

"And so?"

"And so I agreed to do it. He gave me five hundred dollars right there. He gave me a pass and then drove me out to Anaheim."

"How were you supposed to find Luke?"

"He showed me a photo. One look at the hair, the face metal and there was no mistaking that guy. Toby said he'd be doing a concert, gave me the time to go and the place to wait for him."

"It all sounds pretty harmless."

"That's what I thought. And that's exactly how it played out, except—"

"Except instead of a cream pie, he catches two bullets in the chest."

Demarco nodded.

"Why didn't you run after he was shot?"

"I told you already. I just saw this dude die right in front of me, man. I felt sorry for him. I knelt beside him after he collapsed. I was in a bit of a daze, you know. I felt kind of still with all this crazy shit going around me. Then I stood up and two guys rushed me."

"Demarco, do you think you were set up? And if so, who would do that to you?"

"I dunno. Not Toby. I mean, he was just some white kid from the 'burbs."

"He seemed legit to you?"

"Yeah, on the way over to Anaheim he was talking about how this would be good for his channel, you know. He was saying that having a Luke Jameson prank video would get him a lot of views. He was lit."

"What else did he say?"

"Well, he was saying he might think of other YouTube stars he could target, that if his subs went up from Jameson, he might be able to give me more work. It was like a kind of career move for him."

"And then he dropped you off at the venue, and you walked in."

"Yeah, he said he'd meet me inside the theater."

"How was he going to find you?"

"He just said he knew where to find me and he would be there to catch it all when the lights came on."

"But you never saw him again?"

"No, the dude said he had to do something before he parked the car, then he would come in after that."

"Are you sure this Toby guy was as innocent as he seemed?"

"I may only be seventeen, but I know how to judge whether or not a dude has it in him to bury someone."

"And he didn't?"

"No man. That Toby dude was no cold-blooded killer—he was as soft as a fucking puppy."

✳✳✳

The bartender placed two beers in front of me and Jack and took my card. I was done for the day, and it was one that made me half want to reflect on my job and half want to forget it. The Varnish, a nice dimly lit speakeasy on 6th Street, seemed as good a place as any to put a little five-beer perspective on things. Around my brain swirled everything that was on the line: why I'd taken the case in the first place and how Demarco wouldn't stand a snowflake's chance in hell in the hands of a public defender. It was possible he had only a slightly better chance with me.

"Well," said Jack. "You'll be pleased to know my mission at the morgue was successful."

"That is good news. What have you got?"

"All Connors' recent messages and phone calls. Plus folders for his encrypted messages."

"He was using Wickr Me?"

"Yes."

"Is there a way to hack into it?"

"I think so. But I'm not the expert. I have a friend."

"So your other friend, the one at the morgue—sweet on you too, I take it?"

Jack took a sip of his beer and smiled.

"I just needed her to turn her back for a couple of minutes and I was done."

I didn't want to know the specifics of how he'd gotten the information off the phone. Scraping someone's phone was not legal. I could subpoena the phone records, but I was after more than that, and time was of the essence. Jack knew various ways to get the information off the device, though. If it was an iPhone, he could have used Siri to access the recent phone calls and messages. If the phone needed a fingerprint ID to unlock it, he would have simply taken Connor's thumb and pressed it onto the home button. As I said, this wasn't playing by the rules, but I needed leads and I needed them fast. I was desperate to add a ring of truth to Demarco's story because it would be hard for a jury to swallow. And if and when it came to trial, that's what would matter most— the story.

"How fast can your hacker work?" I asked.

"No one's quicker, I can tell you that. But cracking these kinds of files can take a long time, if it can be done at all."

Jack drained his beer.

"Gotta go," he said.

"Got a date tonight?"

"I do, as it so happens. Jane, the medical officer, wanted me to buy her a drink after work."

"Ha. Thought as much. Just try and keep the conversation lively or she might go cold on you."

"Very funny."

"No, I'm dead serious. They can be a bit stiff at that place."

"You need to go home."

Just then a waft of perfume hit me, and a woman's body leaned against my shoulder.

"Not leaving now are you, Brad?" said Jessica Pope. "I came here especially to see you."

"So now you found me. Jess, this is my investigator Jack Briggs."

The two of them looked at each other with mutual admiration.

"Lovely to meet you, Jessica."

"And you, Jack. Thanks for keeping my seat warm."

Jack's eyes told me he was tempted to flirt with Jessica but thought better of it.

"I'll leave you two to it."

As he made for the door, Jessica settled onto his stool.

"Dry gin martini, please," she said to the bartender before turning back to me. "You ready for another?"

I nodded.

"I'll have the same."

"So Brad, when are you going to come visit?"

"You are talking about your office, right?"

"Or my place. It all depends on whether you're interested in business or pleasure."

"It's going to have to be strictly business while we're on the same case. You know that."

"That's a shame. I understand. So long as you don't take it personally when you lose."

"I won't."

"Why haven't I heard from you yet? I've been waiting for you to come see me about a plea bargain."

"I would if Demarco is willing to plead to a lesser charge, but he's not."

"Oh, I don't want you to misunderstand me. There's not going to be a lesser charge on offer. The only thing I might be able to swing is taking the death penalty off the table. Even then, I'd first have to discuss it with the victims' families. The Jamesons are quite pious, so they may be amenable to the idea. But Toby's mother, well, I think she'd plunge the needle in herself."

"So that's it? Not that I'm bargaining."

"Brad, you know what's going on. The state would happily see more cases settled quickly with a plea. With all the budget cuts, we don't want trials choking up the courts and everyone's time. But this case is different. It's the golden child of our justice system."

"Are we talking about you or the case?"

"The case. It will be a shining light for everything that's right about the law. They want to see Lady Justice in all her glory."

"Again, it's the case you're talking about? And who's they?"

"Are you kidding? Everyone who matters, that's who. A double homicide, black on white, with criminal gang connections. Everyone from the Governor down wants your boy to go down hard for what he did."

"You've yet to prove he's guilty, Jessica."

"Well, I'll have everything riding on it. From the evidence I've seen, our case will be bulletproof."

"You have witnesses, I believe."

105

"For the Jameson murder, yes."

"They say they saw Demarco kill Jameson, don't they?"

"Yes."

"You don't have a compelling motive," I said, knowing full well Jessica believed otherwise.

"I beg to differ. Defending the honor of the Crips and winning favor with Ramon X. I'd say what he did was a pretty certain way to rise up the ranks."

"What, commit two daylight murders? That amounts to a suicide mission. It's absurd. Demarco was not of a mind to throw his life away."

Jessica looked at me, touched my face, and smiled.

"You're very sexy when you're all stirred up. I can see this boy means something to you. I've been wondering why you stepped in to take on such a loser case."

I took a sip. "His father and me. We were buddies back in the Marines. Fought together in Afghanistan."

Jessica's face softened. She only knew a little about my military experience, but she liked to listen. Or, at least she made a point of listening on the rare occasions when it came up in our conversations.

"So you owe it to the father to be the son's champion?"

"In a nutshell."

"Doesn't it matter to you if he's guilty?"

"You know that's not the question to ask."

"Then what is the question to ask?"

"Can you prove beyond a reasonable doubt that he's the killer?"

"Yes, I believe I can."

"Well, it won't be enough."

"What do you mean?"

"I mean, from my experience, in murder trials where the fate of a young man is at stake, the jury wants to walk away with a conscience as pure as the driven snow. They won't want to put a boy on death row on the strength of reasonable doubt. They want to be convinced beyond a shadow of a doubt. And I'll make sure they aren't."

As Jessica weighed my words up and took a sip of her martini, my phone buzzed. It was a text message from a blocked number.

"Demarco Torrell is innocent."

Another text arrived.

"I can help you prove it."

And another.

"Got your attention? Meet me at the Paragon in thirty minutes."

The Paragon was a sleazy downtown dive a few blocks away. I didn't have any time to waste.

"Something tells me you're about to walk out on me," said Jessica.

"Sorry, Jess. I have to go. Thanks for the drink."

"You're wrong, you know, Brad."

"About what?"

"The jury. After they hear what I've got to say, reasonable doubt will be plenty."

I hit the streets, thinking Jessica could well be right. Which was why I was so desperate for a break. Desperate enough to go meet whoever sent me those text messages despite feeling certain I was wasting my time. It was probably a set up. Someone wanting to have a laugh at my expense. A jaded cop or a bitter reporter. The chances it was for real were slim.

What the hell. If I ended up being the butt of someone's joke, so be it.

CHAPTER 12

The Paragon was a smoke-filled speakeasy with lushes at the bar and freaks in the booths. As I walked in, an elderly woman smoking a cigarette through a long-stemmed holder talked loudly to her companion—another elderly lady—about how she detested sports and craved a better class of conversation. Her gaunt face was painted with make-up, and huge jewel-encrusted rings hung off fingers tipped with inch-long nails. At the bar, the bartender was shaking the shoulder of a large man who'd fallen asleep beside his basket of wings.

"Joe, Joe. Eat your food. You should eat." A moan rose from underneath Joe's buried head. "Eat up or I'll have to kick you out."

With that, Joe's head sprang up, his eyes locking straight onto the TV screen ahead. He felt for his beer, took a gulp, and then grabbed at his wings.

I scanned the bar for eye contact and got it from just about everyone. Six strangers were checking me out like I was the only tumbleweed to roll through town. And then I remembered I was wearing a suit. I guessed some were worried I'd managed to track them down.

In the end booth a large man with dark hair combed over a balding scalp flicked his eyebrows at me. I slid into the seat across from him. The guy had the physique of Buddha. But he was not a picture of peaceful transcendence. His face was round, framed by fleshy cheeks and a triple chin. His pallid skin had a sweaty sheen and his breathing was shallow.

"You expecting me?" I asked.

"I didn't think you'd come."

"Why wouldn't I? How could I pass up on this place?"

The guy looked at me like I took him for a drunk.

"It's good for our purposes."

"Our purposes? Who are you? And what do you know about my case?"

"I'm Dino. Dino Cassinelli."

He extended a big paw towards me. We shook hands. Mine disappeared into a fleshy mitt that squeezed with machine-like strength. It was a relief when he eased off—it felt as if he could have crushed my bones at will. Dino Cassinelli. The name ran elusively around in my head.

"Should I know you?"

"Detective Dino Cassinelli."

It still didn't register, so Cassinelli proceeded to jog my memory. He told me that five years ago his career had been ticking along nicely. But then things started falling apart. He was struggling to control his weight. His wife cheated on him. A year later they split up, and she got the two kids. He drank more and more until it affected his work. Then he made a mistake that sent his twenty-year career as a detective into a downward spiral. He gave a television interview about a cold case he'd been assigned to and said the case was only getting resources thrown at it because Bob Viner, a Californian Republican Senator, had a direct interest in the case. Viner's cousin had been killed in an apparent gay-hate crime, and he had pushed the LAPD hard to make the case a priority. Cassinelli told the media that while he didn't deny the case needed attention, there were many more worthy cases affecting a lot more families that he and his colleagues should be working on. When the interviewer sought to clarify his comments, Cassinelli had basically said outright that the LAPD was working to please one powerful man rather than serving the most important needs of the public. He said he wasn't alone in thinking that.

After the interview aired, Cassinelli found himself more alone than he could have ever imagined. He was yanked off the case and given a desk job. Humiliated and disillusioned by the lack of loyalty and support shown to him, he became an outsider in the community he once thought of as family. So, Cassinelli took to the bottle even harder. But he didn't turn his mind off homicide altogether. He still maintained a keen interest in particular cases, and when he'd looked over Demarco's file, he realized something wasn't right.

"A black kid steps out of Skid Row and kills two white guys he's never met?" he said. "To me, that just didn't add up."

"Well, it adds up nicely for the rest of your colleagues."

"Yeah, I know. Listen, I don't know what you've got, but if you treat this as a case of did he or didn't he murder two people in cold blood, you're going to lose."

"And you think you can help?"

Cassinelli took a swig of beer and paused.

"This ain't no hate crime. It ain't no revenge hit. It's got nothing to do with gangs. Your boy wasn't the trigger man."

"I believe that. I want to believe that. But if it wasn't him, who was it?"

"A serial killer."

I looked at Cassinelli, thinking maybe his colleagues had been right to sideline him. Just the words "serial killer" made him sound like a crackpot with a conspiracy theory. And since word had gotten out that I'd taken Demarco's case, my inbox had been getting jammed with emails from crazies wanting to give me their two cents' worth about who was behind the killings. I'd read a few for amusement, but the humor wore off quickly. Everyone from the Ku Klux Klan to Kayne West was behind it, and every suspect had been explained away with some whack-job string theory. I felt deflated as I realized I'd been called to this bar to hear nothing more than booze-addled gibberish. But I did my best to hide my disappointment.

"You're going to have to explain this one. What, in short, makes you so sure it's the work of a serial killer?"

"This is the fourth killing in six months. All victims were prominent social media 'influencers', except for that Connors kid, of course."

"Someone's picking off famous YouTubers?"

Cassinelli gave me a blank stare that dried up my cynicism pronto—or at least made me tuck it away out of courtesy.

"Kyle Chambers, Puerto Escondido, in August. Aaron Rybka in Miami a month later."

"Never heard of them."

"Both had millions of followers, and both were regarded by some as the bad boys of the internet."

"How so?"

"There's a lot of creators out there who make a big name for themselves doing stunts. It's a proven formula to win over subscribers, mostly in the form of American kids. And then some have used that platform to play the bad boy. These two were at the viler end of that spectrum. Their YouTube channels were nasty, but on other platforms and forums they were extremely offensive.

Anything from misogyny to saying the US needed to wipe out Syria and be done with it."

"Hell, there's no shortage of keyboard warriors out there. Take a look around Washington."

"Yeah, but Washington DC is for grown-ups—these guys have a direct line to the minds of kids."

"And you're saying someone doesn't like that?"

"Someone took deep moral offense to the depraved stuff these guys were doing."

"And they decided to kill them?"

"They're cleaning house."

"You're going to have to join the dots for me."

"No, that's my point. You want to get your kid off, you're going to have to join the dots."

Cassinelli scanned the room, then reached to his side and pulled out of his briefcase a beige folder fat with documents.

"This is for you. Don't read it here."

I put a hand on the folder and slid it closer to me.

"So this will give me an idea of where to start, assuming I buy into your theory?"

"I can tell you where to start right now."

"Where?"

"Mexico or Florida. Puerto Escondido or Miami, to be precise. Take your pick."

CHAPTER 13

For my first day with Bella under the new rules, I wanted to keep it fun and simple. I suggested we ride our bikes up to Santa Monica for ice cream.

When I arrived at Claire's house, she and Caitlin were in the studio, still busy on the collection launch. It was good to see Claire doing so well. She had little time for anything else and had just broken it off with a guy she'd been dating for about a year.

Since our divorce, she'd been determined to follow her head, place her heart into her business and be the champion of her own independence. She said she feared nothing from pursuing such a life, even though I'm sure some women her age, and men, would openly fret about whether loneliness and miserable old age lay ahead.

Claire had always been an exceptional woman, and her success only elevated her—she was in total command of her life. And despite my misgivings about Bella's social media activity, I thought she was a wonderful mother. Admittedly, it did seem like her assistant was spending a lot of time as a stand-in caregiver. Still, with work based at home, Claire was never too far away.

Soon after I greeted Claire and Caitlin, I heard the happy sound of footsteps coming down the wooden steps. Bella rounded the bottom and ran into my arms.

"Daddy!"

It was a relief that she had no hesitation approaching me. We'd spoken on the phone a few times over the past few weeks, and Claire had assured me there were no lingering problems. Bella had not wanted to leave the house for a few days after the shooting, and Claire took every opportunity to talk about the experience with her. And, to her credit, Claire had eventually conceded there was some noble logic to my actions that day, but that didn't mean she'd accepted that those actions were right. Still, it was a nice reminder that Claire would stick to her word that she'd never try to turn Bella away from me.

"We should get a move on. Where's your bike?" I said to Bella.

"In the garage."

"We'll go out that way," I said to Claire.

"Where are you headed?" she asked.

"Just going to ride the Strand up to Santa Monica, grab an ice-cream and head back."

Bella did a little pogo dance of joy before racing ahead into the garage.

Claire had closed in behind us. I felt her hand on my shoulder.

"Just play daddy. That's hero enough, trust me."

She said this so warmly I couldn't object. Sometimes there was a lot of wisdom in a wife's words. Even an ex-wife's words.

I smiled.

"We'll be back about three."

"Okay. Have fun."

It was a perfect day for a ride, and because it was winter, the Strand was not crowded. It had been too long since we'd been riding together. It seemed like it was yesterday that I'd helped Bella get off her training wheels. She didn't want me to take them off, but I did. I held her seat, running behind her as she got up to speed. Then, within three yards of riding all by herself, she called out, "I don't need training wheels!" and off she went. My heart swelled to see her go. Now, four years later, she was onto her first proper mountain bike and keen to hit some trails. I'd promised her in recent weeks that we'd find one without too many hills.

Bella led, and I hung off her tail as we rode north. A few times she dropped the gears and stood up in the saddle to drive the pedals down hard and fast, shooting ahead of me with a laugh. I was impressed with how athletic she was. Bella was so much like her mother. Tall, slim and elegant, she had a beauty to her that had prompted more than a few of our friends to declare she'd be a model. I didn't kid myself—it was not just her style that was catching so many eyes on her Instagram account. She was a striking young girl growing up too fast for my liking.

But as I watched her scoot away from me, she was just my little girl, a piece of wonderment I'd always be proud of and slightly in awe of. My dad once said to me a long time ago that his children were his greatest teachers. I didn't really understand that until I'd become a father, when I was compelled to re-evaluate myself for the better and act differently. That was how I'd become an adult, to a large degree. Well, that and the Marines.

When we reached Santa Monica, we stopped at a beachside cafe and found an outside table. It was time to air what was foremost in my mind.

"So, how are you feeling? You know, about the shooting. That day and all."

I was an attorney who relied on speaking confidently before a crowded courtroom, but I was fumbling over a chat with my daughter.

116

"I'm good. Really I am, Daddy. You needn't worry about me."

"I do worry about you, sweetheart. Mom said ..."

"I was fine after a couple of days. It was a shock, that's all. I mean, I still think about it, but it's not a problem."

"Well, good."

"Mom says you're defending the man with the gun." It was clear she wanted help to understand.

"That's right, Bella. Someone's got to make sure he is not treated unfairly, and second, as it happens, he's the son of a very good friend of mine."

"Did your friend ask you to do it?"

"No sweetheart. My friend died a few years ago. But he was a very good man. Someone I admired very much. I just had to make sure for his sake that there would be no miscarriage of justice."

"Well, I guess that makes sense. But what he did was horrible."

"It's not crystal clear what happened yet, darling. That's what I'm working hard at to try and figure out. But it was a terrible thing, you're right."

"But something good came out of it."

"What do you mean?"

"Check this out."

Bella pulled her phone from the small handbag she had slung over her shoulder, then she tapped and flipped her way to the thing she wanted to show me. She turned the phone to face me. It was her Instagram account.

"Nice. You look lovely," I said, not really knowing what to say.

"No, look here. See? Check out who commented." She was abuzz with glee.

I looked closer and saw "@cicilypines" and a comment from her: "Loving your style, Bella! You're amazing!"

"Can you believe it? Cicily Pines. She's following me. And she DMd me."

"I take it that's a good thing."

"Direct messaged me. She's so cool. She said she would definitely get me a VIP pass for her next all-ages gig in a couple of weeks."

She stopped and looked up at me.

"I can go, can't I, Daddy?"

"Of course. If it's okay with your mom. She and I'll talk, but I can't see why it would be a problem. Now what are you having?"

She told me her order, and I went inside the cafe to get the ice creams. A few minutes later I returned to find a man in his early thirties wearing just shorts and runners standing next to Bella and talking to her. Immediately, I was on edge. He was a good-looking guy who was clearly aerobically fit. The sheen on his tanned body suggested he'd halted his run to talk to Bella. His dog was nuzzling her, and she was petting him. I saw Bella reach for her phone, but then she saw me and withdrew her hand.

The guy looked at me with a big smile on his face. I was inclined to wipe it off. Something just felt wrong.

Since when is it okay for a grown man to stop and shoot the breeze with a seven-year-old girl?

Was I overreacting?

"Hello, are you Bella's dad?" he asked like it was the best compliment he could pay me. The parting words of Claire echoed in my brain but sometimes as a father it seemed justified to shoot first and ask questions later. I didn't, though. I told myself to calm down, to rack my shotgun. But that didn't mean I had to be friendly.

118

"That's right. Who are you?"

He put out his hand. I was carrying two ice creams and was not about to do anything but see him off.

"My name's Steve. I'm a fan of your daughter's. She is just about the coolest thing on the internet."

I looked at Bella, handed her her ice cream, and then sat down. "We're kind of having a father-daughter moment here, Steve."

"Sure, I'll leave you be. Oh, just quickly."

Quick as a flash the guy bent down, put his head next to Bella's, and took a selfie. I saw Bella react in an instant, pulling a mock surprise face before taking a lick of her ice cream. The natural fluency of it struck me.

"Come on, Rufi," said Steve, tugging lightly on the leash. The little hound scooted after him as he jogged away. I couldn't tell if he was straight or gay, but either way he irked me. How could any of this be okay for a seven-year-old girl?

Bella saw me mulling over things.

"Daddy, don't worry. He's harmless."

She said it with such reassurance that she reminded me of Claire. My God, sometimes she struck me as being seven going on seventeen.

"Mmm, salted caramel. Deeee-liciousness. Thanks, Daddy."

Yet every bit a seven-year-old girl, pure and simple.

CHAPTER 14

"Dino Cassinelli? You can't be serious." The file Cassinelli gave me was sitting on my desk. And across my desk sat an unimpressed Jack Briggs. "The guy's a complete washout. What the hell are you talking to him for?"

"There's some interesting stuff here," I said, tapping the file.

"I bet there is. I bet it's a real pot-boiler. So who does he think is behind these killings? The Illuminati?"

"He didn't sound unhinged at all. And he was a damn good cop, Jack. Highly respected. Highly decorated. Remember the DJ Darius murder? Sat as an open investigation for fifteen years until 2009, when Cassinelli revealed that two LAPD officers were paid off to bury evidence. That kind of work, to out cops who've been in on a cover-up, takes balls and brains. Before it all went south, he was regarded as something of a cold case expert. But even since then, they found Darren Stockdale's killer on the back of Cassinelli's work."

"Darren Stockdale?"

"You know—little kid that disappeared from his front yard out in Cheviot Hills six years ago?"

"Right. But as true as that may be, that was the old Dino Cassinelli. The new Dino Cassinelli would give anything to reclaim a scrap of the dignity and respect he blew to hell. Word is he's holding onto that desk job of his by a fingernail. The guy's shot, Brad. He's like some drunk leaning over the crime scene tape offering his two cents worth on every major case Homicide has going. But it's all babble."

"It doesn't sound like babble to me."

"So what's his two cents on this case?"

"That it's the work of a serial killer."

Jack scoffed loudly. "Sorry. Please, continue."

"Reckons someone's trying to cleanse social media of its most vile stars."

"Well, they've got a hell of a job on their hands. How many have been killed so far?"

"Cassinelli says two others besides Jameson in the past six months. And there could be more."

"Oh, please."

"Let me lay it out. Last August, a kid name Kyle Chambers in Puerto Escondido. Owned a house down there and went there solo to bunker down after some controversy surrounding a phone recording in which he viciously maligned various female gamers. And a heap of his misogynistic 4chan posts were exposed along with the call."

"So he was a tool. Again, they're a dime a dozen on YouTube. Why should anyone care what this idiot said or did?"

"Because he had fifteen million subscribers. In TV ratings numbers, that's bigger than *America's Got Talent*."

"Why was he so popular?"

"In the beginning it was all about online gaming. He'd post videos of himself playing Minecraft and narrating the action. But he reveled in being a douche bag towards his opponents, especially girls. Nothing too explicit because he didn't want to be pulled off YouTube, but elsewhere he unleashed some pretty vile hate speak."

"Sexist gamer. Again, he's not Robinson Crusoe there. That pimply little world is thick with propeller heads who love hating on girls. I'm not excusing it. But it's a wider problem than one individual."

"But this guy encourages it. He sets an example for other little sociopaths to follow. And there are also suggestions he's solicited naked photos from young girls who were fans of his channel."

"Jesus. And you know this how?"

"The file. Cassinelli printed it all out. It's right here."

"How did this—what's his name?—Kyle Chambers die?"

"His hacienda was burned down. The police declared it arson."

"Anyone get nabbed?"

"Yes, a local wino is doing fifteen years for it."

"Okay, that's one dead YouTuber. Next?"

"Aaron Rybka. September last year. Miami. He was shot dead in a rented flat, and a drug dealer is doing time."

"And if this wasn't a drug deal gone bad, how does Cassinelli explain it as a hit?"

"Again, Rybka was a big success on YouTube and a loud-mouthed punk. A kind of shock jock YouTuber. Vented all kinds of bigoted, hateful, offensive garbage. He also did whacked-out stunts that earned him plenty of cash. Then he'd post videos showing himself living it up like a young Onassis. One day he's getting a Rolls Royce customized, next he's buying a luxury power boat, next he's giving a tour of the house he's building in Nassau."

"Again, that hardly makes him stand out. There are countless channels devoted to projecting their own version of *Lifestyles of the Rich and Famous*."

"But away from YouTube, Rybka also let it be known loud and clear that he is anti-Christian. Not just an atheist or Muslim or Buddhist. And he's a cheerleader for America's recent wars because, and I quote, 'the Middle East is where good Christians go to die'."

"How old were these two?"

"Chambers was 19, Rybka 18."

"Man, whatever happened to good clean fun, eh?"

"That's Cassinelli's point, though. He reckons it's a matter of morality. Someone's deeply offended by how these wicked idiots are influencing millions of impressionable young minds, and whoever that is has decided to start taking out the trash."

"A serial killer crusade?"

"Something like that."

Jack sat back and shook his head. After about a minute's rumination, he raised a finger like he'd had an epiphany.

"You know what this sounds like, my friend?"

"No. What?"

"Sounds to me like you are being thrown a bone. But I'd suggest it's one that you do not want to go chasing."

"How so?"

"They're messing with you."

"Who?"

"The cops. They want you wasting your time on unproductive leads, so they send Cassinelli over and have him pull this X-Files bullshit on you. It's a distraction. A ruse. I mean, come on. Serial killer? Burns one victim in Mexico. Shoots one in Florida.

Somehow sets up two stooges to take the fall. And then comes to LA to shoot two dudes in a day.

"It's just too ridiculous for words, Brad. But they know it's something you can't resist. They know how much you want to clear that kid's name. Do you think they don't know about your connection to his dad? Of course they know. They're watching you like a hawk. And they're scared of what you might find. So they give you a sniff of a bone that, if you chase it, is going to lead you so far off the trail you won't know what you're looking for."

I had to admit Jack had a point. Jessica had told me straight up that there was a lot of heat to get this murder dealt with promptly and emphatically. It would not be the first time authorities had resorted to sneaky or diversionary tactics to throw a defense team off the scent. I was not at all convinced that that was the case. But I'd be naive or desperate to start believing I could get Demarco off by proving someone else had pulled the trigger, and that person was a serial killer.

"Go on," I said.

"Think about it. What would we have to do to investigate this thoroughly? We'd be trying to catch a serial killer. You know how much work that would involve? A multiple murder case, and it would just be us. I dare say that's what the cops, the DA's office, I bet even the fricking Governor, would love for us to be doing right now. I mean, I'm up for a trip to Puerto Escondido or Miami any time, but shouldn't we focus on what we have in front of us? We need to keep our minds on the main job."

Jack was right. The best thing I could do for Demarco was to put all my energy into building the strongest possible case I could. First, we needed to prove he was reforming and see if we could find any corroborating evidence for the deal he made with Toby Connors. Next, I had to investigate the Christian vlogger Evan Harrington as a suspect. Who knew what other leads those investigations would unearth? Then I had to target Jessica's case—find weaknesses in her witnesses and holes in her logic. Throwing our efforts into proving what may well be a conspiracy theory risked losing all hope of keeping Demarco out of prison.

"Okay, just do me a favor, would you?" I said. "Just look into it over the next couple of days—nothing exhaustive—just when you have an odd free moment to make some calls. See if anything of interest comes up."

Jack rolled his eyes. "Sure. Whatever you say."

"Great. Now what about Harrington?"

"Well, I'm glad you asked, because the more I look at this guy the more I think he could be capable of anything."

"How so?"

"I spoke to a few 'creators' who have been doing VidCon and some of the smaller video channel events around the country for a while, and they all talk about Harrington as being an odd character with a temper. One person told me she heard him say his life would be better if Jameson was dead."

"In what context?"

"Apparently, a television production company called Twenty20 was sniffing around looking to convert a YouTube channel into a reality TV series. They spoke to a bunch of vloggers who had more than two million subscribers. The plan was to document the vlogger's life, how they made their videos and how they dealt with the public. It promised to be huge for whoever the company chose—they'd get a huge uptick in subs, which would mean more revenue from their channel, plus whatever Twenty20 paid them."

"And Harrington was in contention?"

"Oh yeah. More than in contention. He'd charmed the pants off the producers. Apparently, they had a shortlist of five, and both the Harringtons and Luke Jameson were on it."

"They'd be very different shows, wouldn't they? Wild boy versus Christian family?"

"Funny you should say that. Apparently, they entertained the idea of using both channels for the show. Word of this got back to Harrington, who hated the idea of sharing the show with Jameson, and that's when Jameson started bad-mouthing Harrington. But what Jameson was saying wasn't half of it."

"What do you mean?"

"Well, Harrington has a history. When he was in his late teens, he got charged with assault. He beat up some Arabic shopkeeper. And then after the court case was done and he'd gotten off lightly, the shop was vandalized repeatedly until the owner moved. Word is that Harrington was behind it."

"So he's a racist with an anger management problem? But what, if anything, could provoke him to actually kill Jameson?"

"Well, after hearing what Jameson was saying about Evan Harrington being a fraud, the producers dropped the Harringtons out of contention."

"When was this?"

"A few days before VidCon."

Jack's phone rang. He picked it up and then looked at me.

"It's Charlie."

"Who's Charlie?"

"My hacker. Usually I just get a text. This must be good."

Jack tapped the screen to take the call and put the phone to his ear.

"Charlie. What's up?"

There was silence as Jack listened. Then his eyebrows raised a little.

"Good work," he said. "Now you stay put ... Why? Because I'm coming over ... Now. Ahorita ... Yes, you have time to go get lunch, but be quick, you hear me? See you in twenty."

126

Jack pocketed his phone.

"News about your boy," he said. "And it's not good."

"Demarco? What about him?"

"Looks like he had probable cause."

"To kill Jameson? Or to kill Connors?"

"Both. That's all Charlie said."

For a split second I pondered the prospect that Demarco was guilty. Would that matter? Would that change anything? In a sense no. If he'd confessed to the crime, I'd still defend him to the hilt, making damn sure he got a fair trial. But there was the trust issue. This case was personal. Demarco had told me he was innocent and I was inclined to believe him. Did I actually want to find out he was lying to me? Other times I'd say no, it didn't matter. But what if Tank's son was playing me for a fool? I decided I wanted to know everything this Charlie character had. Otherwise I felt I'd be walking forward with eyes half shut.

"Well, let's go then," I said.

"Brad. Charlie doesn't deal with strangers."

"I'm writing his checks. We're practically family. I'm coming and that's final. Now let's go."

CHAPTER 15

Jack pulled up outside a white two-level house on Midvale in Westwood. I parked across the street, taking in the pretty white home framed by leafy trees, shiny green hedges and a white picket fence across the front.

This was where Jack's hacker lived? I'd expected to be led Downtown to some grimy gaming store that served as a front for a hidden room you could only access by retina scan. Jack's vagueness about Charlie's identity added to the covert mystique. He said he'd met Charlie through some dark net forum. That was the thing with Jack. On face value, you'd take him as a Hollywood player trading off his looks, smarts and charm. But Jack's talents knew no bounds. On the tech front, he was fluent not just in several types of code, but also in the language spoken in the tech business pages.

Online he mixed with the kind of people who liked to roam the recesses of cyberspace and break and enter wherever they pleased. He'd said Charlie had achieved legend status by hacking the Secretary of State's home network, emblazoning his television screen with "The blood of Syria is on your hands, Ted." Of course,

Jack was only guessing Charlie was responsible. But ever alert to the need of having good talent on standby for his investigation services, he'd managed to track Charlie down. That he did so earned him kudos with Charlie. That's why he was trusted with a face to face.

I got out of my car and walked over to Jack.

"Don't tell me your hacker lives with Aunt Polly?"

Jack smiled and shook his head. Suddenly, the angry sound of a high-powered motorbike under throttle reached our ears. Within seconds the bike appeared. A red Ducati. Its rider braked hard and steered the beast into the driveway. Once the stand had dropped, the rider dismounted and undid the chinstrap. As the helmet came off, I found myself staring at a very attractive girl who looked barely old enough to have a license. She was dressed like she fronted a punk band. Her hair was cut short, brown with white tips. Below a studded leather jacket, she wore a t-shirt and ripped jeans and a scuffed-up pair of Doc Martens. She was a mountain of attitude packed into a frame almost half my size. And right now that attitude looked ready to come down on Jack's head.

"Who's this?" she scowled. She didn't so much as nod in my direction.

"This is Brad Madison, the lawyer we're working for."

Jack was watching me to see how I'd react. He knew with the name Charlie I'd been expecting a man. An adult man. I'd forgotten good hackers could more or less turn pro by the age of fifteen or sixteen. They say you have to spend ten thousand hours on complex tasks to acquire base-level expertise. Well, these computer-obsessed, nocturnal fiends could put in eighteen hours of screen time a day, easy. And at that rate they could clock up ten thousand hours in less than two years. Charlie didn't look a day older than seventeen.

"I told you no strangers," she snapped at Jack. "I don't do face-to-face with clients. Especially not suits."

I was a bit taken aback by her insolence. "Do mommy and daddy know what you get up to in their garage, sweetheart?"

Charlie flashed me an angry, slack-jawed look. Jack momentarily put his Switzerland face on—happy to leave me to it. Then he thought better of it and intervened before I made an even bigger fool of myself.

"This is Charlie's place."

"The garage? Got it, which she rents off—?"

Jack interrupted before I could use my "Aunt Polly" line again. "No, the whole house. It's hers."

This took a second to sink in. The Avril Lavigne of the hacker world had already made enough cash to buy herself a house in Westwood.

"You need to keep this dickhead away from me," Charlie snapped.

"Easy," said Jack. "He's one of the best defense attorneys in LA."

"Did he win an award for that?"

"Yes," I said. "It's called keeping people's asses out of jail."

"Not my ass."

"Don't be so sure. Doing what you do. You might well need me one day."

She gave me an "as if" shrug. I liked this Charlie girl. But I wasn't sure she appreciated how hard and relentless the people she messed with could be. And how much they would like to make an example of someone like her by putting them behind bars for a very long time. Not everyone could expect a pardon like Chelsea Manning. While the US Government wanted to get their hands on Edward Snowden, they'd settle for some hotshot trouble maker who treated real-world law and order like grandma's house rules.

She relented and walked down a path between the house and the garage. It took no less than three keys to unlock the garage door. I figured the retina scan would be next. But no, that was it. We were in.

Inside was dark, save for the light of half a dozen computer monitors.

"Play Tame Impala," Charlie ordered her Echo virtual assistant and music began to play. Charlie dropped her pack off her shoulder and unzipped it. She took out a can of soda and a container of sushi.

"I need to eat. Sorry."

She set the food down on her main desk, tore open a packet of soy sauce and then some wasabi and mixed them in the container. She then split her wooden takeaway chopsticks, dipped in some sashimi and dropped a bite into her mouth. She nodded as she chewed, letting us know she wasn't ignoring us.

"So," she said after her mouthful. "I got some interesting stuff on Toby Connors." She opened her soda and took a sip. "I printed it out."

She handed a few sheets of paper to Jack, who started to read through them.

"Could you walk us through it?" I said.

Charlie swallowed another mouthful and took another sip before finally feeling like she'd taken the edge off her hunger.

"How much do you know about Toby Connors?" She was keying something into her computer as she talked. As I assumed it was an open question, I figured I'd answer.

"He was a guy with a very small channel desperate to make it big on YouTube. He had the very unoriginal idea of reaching that goal through creating his own version of *Candid Camera*."

"That's the top line, sure, but there's a load of fine print that indicates this guy was making the kind of enemies that will kill you."

"What are you talking about?"

I took a seat as Charlie ran through what she'd found. The data Jack stripped from Connors' phone gave a detailed account of his activities and interests. Toby Connors had nothing going for him other than his piddly little channel, she said. Besides trying to boost subscribers by pranking famous YouTubers, he'd started doing "hood pranks", ones where white guys go into poor black neighborhoods, do something provocative to get a hostile reaction, and then point to the camera and say, "It's just a prank, dude." After the reveal, everyone was supposed to end up laughing and chill, but Connors had made the mistake of pranking a gang member. Charlie had found a heated text message exchange between Connors and someone who wanted him to remove a video from his channel.

"I traced the number. It belongs to a rapper called Ramon X."

"Ramon X?"

"You know him?"

"Yes, I've already interviewed him."

"About Toby Connors?"

"No, I knew nothing about this. I was looking into his beef with Luke Jameson. This video Ramon X wanted taken down—do you know what's in it?"

"Yes. Connors took it off his channel, but it was still on his phone. This is it here."

Charlie turned to her computer and played a video showing Connors approaching a car he knew was parked in Crips turf in Pomona. You could see someone was sitting in the driver's seat of the vehicle. Connors said, "Hey, bro. You don't mind if I tag your car, do you?" And he pulled out a can of spray paint and pointed it at the door panel. The driver leapt out, grabbed Connors by the throat, threw him up against the car, and shoved a pistol into his face. Connors started shrieking, saying, "Don't shoot, dude! It's just a prank! The camera's over there. Look."

And then there was Ramon X, YouTube star with plenty of reasons to keep his image clean while he raked in the cash off his channel and music, staring at the camera with his gun stuck into some stupid white dude's face. Ramon X relaxed real quick, stashed his gun behind his back, and then saw Connors off with a smile. But it was clear he was furious.

"Jesus. Talk about a Darwin award," I said. "And Connors posted this?"

"Of course," Charlie said. "It was the type of clip that was certain to go viral. But it somehow failed to get any traction for five days and then it was taken down before Connors got to enjoy his jackpot moment and a pile of new subscribers."

"And this text message exchange—it was about this clip?"

"Yes, Ramon X was demanding that Connors take it down."

"Show me the number," I said. As Charlie zoomed in on it, I pulled out my phone and compared it to the number I had for Ramon X. It was a match. "What did Ramon X threaten to do?"

"What do you think?" Charlie said. "He told Connors straight out that he was a dead man."

I looked at the printout. It was pretty chilling stuff. What was it with these YouTubers? They were all clawing at each other like alley cats. I'd always thought YouTube was about harmless, often dumb fun. But now I was seeing behind the screen, and it was as desperate, ambitious and dog-eat-dog as Wall Street, or the ghetto for that matter.

"So it was up for five days until Connors came to his senses. When did he delete the video?"

"The day he died," Charlie said. "Actually, his phone data shows he deleted the video *where* he died."

Jack was right: Demarco's hole was only getting deeper. To the police and prosecutor, this was probable cause. They'd say Demarco was sent by Ramon X to demand Connors delete the video. Then after he did, they'd say Demarco shot him anyway.

"What else is there?" I asked.

"Well, an hour or so before Toby dropped Demarco off, he got an odd text message," Charlie said.

"What did it say?"

"'Coming now.'"

"Coming now? Who was it from?"

"The number's not in Connor's contacts. I rang it yesterday and it's dead."

"Were there any other messages or calls from this number?"

"No calls. And just one message thirty minutes earlier. One word: 'Outside.'"

"Charlie, can you find any other correspondence—in the comments sections of his videos, in a chat room, a phone call or an email—anything that could shine a light on who sent these two messages?"

"It's too vague. There's no telling what this person is referring to."

"Obviously, it sounds like Connors was meeting someone," I said. "But it could be something else entirely. Could you please keep digging?"

I was very impressed with Charlie. I was only too happy to keep paying her top dollar to continue helping me.

"Sure."

Trying to find out who sent those messages was a long shot and ultimately of questionable benefit. Every development in this case only seemed to bury my client deeper.

I thought of the promise I'd made to Jasmine. How empty it now seemed.

CHAPTER 16

I needed some air, so I walked to Skid Row from my office. I got air alright. The gusts of wind coming down Fifth Street were thick with the stench of urine. I was headed for the Los Angeles Mission to meet a volunteer who'd helped Demarco out. It was only a fifteen-minute walk from my office to Skid Row, but it felt like a journey into another world. Just a few blocks away from Downtown's high concentration of super wealth was an entire neighborhood that, economically and socially, belonged to the Third World. Here, some twenty thousand people were so cut off from society that they lived in tents on the sidewalk, using buckets for toilets because thugs charged taxes to use the public amenities. As the buildings I passed grew more decrepit and I watched a woman wheel her life's possessions around in a shopping cart, I felt for Demarco. How had he ended up here? The man I was going to see would hopefully be able to provide some insights.

I threaded through a crowd of people at the entrance and told reception I'd arranged to meet Warren Anderson.

"He's right over there," said the lady, pointing back over my shoulder.

I turned around to see a tall, big-chested black guy whose t-shirt strained to cover his biceps. As I approached, he was talking to an elderly woman, who burst into tears. Warren put his big arm around her, drew her in, and patted her back. It was like a bear comforting a rabbit.

"Don't worry, Loretta. I'm going to find her. I promise. She'll be okay."

The two separated, and the woman wiped her eyes with a handkerchief.

"Thank you, Warren."

"No problem. I love you."

I didn't know whether these two had known each other for years or whether that was just a phrase Warren used, but I could feel that it carried weight. The man was clearly genuine in his care for others.

"Warren Anderson? I'm Brad Madison," I said, putting out my hand.

A big smile lit up Warren's face. "Nice to meet you, Brad," he chuckled and spread his arms out a little. "Welcome to my office."

"Is there somewhere we can talk?"

"The street's as good a place as any. Let's go."

Warren led me back out onto Fifth Street and turned left to head deeper into Skid Row. This was not what I had in mind. I thought we'd be sitting down in his office and running through files, maybe having a cup of instant coffee from a stove kettle that whistled on the boil. Everyone on the street watched us come and go.

Warren walked as though he was among family. Every few steps he either greeted someone or someone called out to him. It was like being with a boxing champion who'd returned to his hometown to walk the hood.

"I helped that guy get off crack," Warren said, pointing at a man who'd just called out. "But unfortunately, he's back on it."

He said hi as we passed a young black woman with a lovely smile.

"She came to Skid Row a week ago," said Warren once we were beyond earshot. "Now they got her turning tricks."

Warren pointed to an old man standing beside a tent across the street.

"Joe over there. He's a vet. Suffers PTSD and just fell through the cracks."

"It's brutal, that's for sure," I said. "But how did Demarco end up here?"

"Same reason as all these other people are here. The shelter. People gotta eat. They gotta try and find somewhere off the street to sleep. And that's where we come in. I saw Demarco the day he arrived at Skid Row. But we'd met before."

"Where?"

"Pomona. I help run a gang intervention team, and we helped Demarco break away from the Sintown Crips."

I stopped.

"He came to you to get out of the gang?"

"That's right. It was a ballsy step for such a young kid. He was only just fifteen, if I remember rightly. But he was smart enough to realize where he was headed if he didn't break free."

"How hard is it to extract yourself from a criminal gang?"

"Most people assume the big hurdle is the fear of violent reprisal or being seen as a traitor. They can be factors, don't get me wrong, but the biggest issue is how that individual can cope with going it alone. He has to give up the only community he has, the only place he feels safe, the only people who ever gave him respect, and the only friends who had his back when shit got real. It's too much for most—the bulk go back."

"But Demarco was determined to get out?"

"That's right. At about thirteen years of age he'd had enough of walking five blocks out of his way home to avoid getting jumped by some gang members. So he joined the Sintown Crips. Suddenly, he was part of a tribe and had some elders to look up to."

"What changed? What made him decide to leave?"

"I think it was a few things he saw. He got busted a few times and was put away in juvie. But that wasn't it. He saw friends being shot dead right next to him. He saw women getting raped. He saw the ugly side of humanity."

"And you helped him?"

"Yeah, me and the team did. We kept in regular contact with him. He came to meetings. We had ex-gang members and ex-cons come in and try to talk sense into these kids. We organized activities in the community to try and get the kids engaged in a different way. It's not always successful, but Demarco showed promise. But then I didn't see him for quite a few months and then he turns up at the shelter."

"How long had Demarco been living in Skid Row?"

Warren smiled.

"Two days. Just in time."

"Just in time for what?"

"To be saved. If you spend more than three days here, you're here for life."

"How so?"

"It becomes apparent very quickly how hard it's going to be for you to find a way out. So you take drugs to escape, but that just seals your fate. Because then you'll do whatever you can to get drugs. You'll turn tricks, rob, steal, beg, hustle for money. Then you lose your purpose, you lose your hope, you lose your mind. You're never getting out."

"Did Demarco have a chance of saving himself?"

"You bet he did. He was more committed than ever. We found him some accommodation and he was coming here every day to pray and help out."

"He became a volunteer?"

"Sure did. And he'd just gotten a job as a dishwasher at a diner over on Grand Avenue. But he had plans."

"To follow his dad."

"That's right. I talked to him about other opportunities but enlisting seemed to be what he had his mind set on. He just wanted to get his head straight, get some money together and graduate from school."

By this time our walk had brought us back to the mission.

"Thanks for your time, Warren."

"No problem. Say, have you spoke to Fran?"

"Fran? She's the one who offered him spiritual guidance, right?"

"Yes. She's one of the benefactors of the mission. Can seem a bit uptight, but she's got a heart of gold. She spent a lot of time with Demarco. You know, supporting him in his quest to get closer to God."

"What, is she a preacher?"

"No, but she knows the Good Book better than most preachers I know. But she's a bit, how should I say, unconventional?"

"In what way?"

"She's extremely devout. Hers is a more old-school take on the scriptures. And that can make her seem a little out of touch with how most people like their religion nowadays."

"But she's allowed to provide spiritual guidance here?"

Warren shrugged. "Well, she pays a lot of our bills and, you know, she's not actually doing anyone any harm. And besides, Demarco seemed to like her."

"How so? Seems to me they'd make a very odd couple."

"I don't know. Sometimes strictness has an appealing kind of clarity to it."

He had a point.

"Well, yes. I would like to speak with her. Where can I find her?"

"She's right over there."

I looked to where Warren was pointing. There, standing in the doorway of the mission, was none other than Francine Holmes, the woman I'd met after the shooting.

"Fran," called Warren. "Fran, there's someone here who'd like to speak with you about Demarco."

The trace of a smile on Francine Holmes's face disappeared the moment she saw me.

"Mr. Madison. We meet again."

I put out my hand, and hers met mine somewhat reluctantly, if not for anything other than that a handshake seemed too familiar a greeting.

"You two know each other?" quizzed Warren.

"We've met once before. Just recently," I said.

"And fate has brought us together once more," said Francine. "How is that sweet daughter of yours, Mr. Madison?"

"She's doing very well, thank you."

"Quite the Instagram star, I understand," she said joylessly.

"How do you know that?"

"Cicily told me. She said she began following your little fashionista, and the two of them have become quite chummy."

Francine looked down and ran her palms along her coat front, as if it needed grooming. She then looked me square in the eye.

"I'm not sure how it is appropriate for such a young girl to be posting photos of herself for all and sundry to see, but then I'm not her parents. Perhaps I'm too old-fashioned."

"I'm not here to discuss my daughter, Ms. Holmes. Or whatever views you might have about my parenting. I'm defending Demarco Torrell, and Warren here tells me you had quite a lot to do with him here at the mission."

"Yes, that's true. I tried my best with that boy. I really thought he was making headway."

"What do you mean?"

"I mean, Mr. Madison, that he didn't stay the course. He strayed from the path I tried so hard to keep him on."

"Tell me about your relationship with Demarco. Please."

"For the past six months or so I saw him three or four times a week. I would teach him the Gospel and urge him to reflect on the behavior that had led him down such a ruinous path."

"You would talk about the Bible?"

"Of course. We would talk about God's word, about God's plans for us and how we would appear before the Almighty when it came time for our final judgment."

"Forgive me Francine, but I can't help but think the two of you would make a very unlikely couple. I don't say that to be rude. Would you say you had a connection with Demarco?"

"No offense taken. And, yes. I did have a good rapport with Demarco. Perhaps I was at last someone who impressed upon him that his actions had consequences and that he would have to answer for every sin he'd committed in the life God had the grace to give him. I think he, like many young men, craved discipline, even while it seemed to be something he had avoided at all cost. And the most important discipline is *self*-discipline. With God's help Demarco was beginning to understand that. But he was confused about how to apply it."

"How do you mean?"

"Well, he was intent on following his father into the armed services. We clashed on that issue, as I am very opposed to war."

"Do you mind me asking why?"

"I lost someone very dear to me in the Gulf War, if you must know. That was what drew me to the Halo Council: the fact that I could apply my faith to repairing some of the damage inflicted by conflict. I do not find war a glorious pursuit, Mr. Madison, and I expressed my disapproval of Demarco's senseless plan to enlist in no uncertain terms."

It seemed clear to me that Francine was speaking honestly. And that was good news, because with her on the stand the jury would see Demarco was genuinely leaving gang life behind. I hadn't warmed to Francine, but I wanted her on the stand.

"Francine, would you be willing to ..."

"No, Mr. Madison. I would not. And besides, you're too late."

"What do you mean?"

"I have agreed to serve as a witness for the prosecution."

I was stunned.

"Why on earth would you do that? Demarco did not commit these murders. Surely you don't believe he did. How could you turn your back on him when he needs you most?"

"I must correct you, Mr. Madison. Demarco was the one who turned his back on me."

"Are you telling me you think he's guilty?"

"Not entirely, but it's not out of the question."

My head was spinning.

"Francine, when did you last see Demarco?"

"It was the very day of the shooting."

"Did you have a Bible study meeting with him?"

"No, we only spoke briefly. A week earlier he had told me he did not want to continue our sessions. This was after I'd once again challenged his plan to enlist."

"When you spoke that day, were things amicable?"

"Yes. I wanted to be sure he understood there were no hard feelings. I told him to do as his own heart advised. I said what I had said to him many times before: 'Keep your heart open to God and He will guide you and reward you, close it and He will punish you.' And perhaps that describes what happened next—perhaps he had already closed his heart to God."

After Francine stopped talking, she held her head very still and looked at me with a kind of serene defiance. I shuddered at the damage she could cause Demarco by delivering a such a damning assessment of him from the stand.

I held my tongue for now. Because, from that moment on, I was looking forward to seeing her in court, where I could unpick that smug righteousness stitch by stitch.

"Is there anything else I can do for you, Mr. Madison?"

"No thank you, Francine. That's quite enough for now."

CHAPTER 17

Jessica Pope watched me enter her office like a cat with the cream. She'd tucked the end of her pen lightly into the corner of her mouth, as if to punctuate her self-assured smile as she leaned back in her chair.

"Careful, Jessica. You might get a hernia trying to appear so confident."

"Very funny, Brad. Good to see you again."

Over the last few weeks I'd been in touch with Jessica as we worked through various pretrial matters. Today was the last of our discovery sessions, when we exchanged the evidence each of our cases was built on. Clearly Jessica had some good news—and that meant bad news for Demarco.

"It's been a very interesting week, my friend," she said. "With every passing day it becomes clearer that we've got it right—that your client killed two innocent men and he's going to face the full force of the law."

"He wants to go to trial. And so do I."

"That makes three of us. This is shaping up to be worth every cent the public purse can spare to get justice for the families of these two young men."

"You mean to get good press for the DA with an election coming up."

"You may like to spin it that way, but take a look at what landed on my desk yesterday."

She leaned forward, tapped out a few keystrokes, and then twisted the monitor around for me to see.

I was expecting to see the video of Ramon X pulling a gun on Toby Connors. I figured the cops would have gotten that off Connors' phone by now. But I was wrong.

"This is your client, Demarco Torrell, using the phone at Juvenile Hall," she said.

My blood dropped a few degrees colder. This was not going to be good. Even before anything happened on the screen, I was already cursing Demarco for disobeying me. I'd told him to stay off the phone to everyone but his mother. I'd told him the phone room was monitored with cameras and that the phones were tapped. I'd told him it was all fair game and that the prosecution would be sniffing around for anything they could turn against him. I'd told him the case against him was strong and that the last thing we needed was for him to give them more ammo. It now seemed all my pleas had fallen on deaf ears.

Jessica turned up the volume loud and clear. It started with Demarco chatting away to a friend. He looked relaxed. He was laughing like the person at the other end of the line was cracking jokes. Then the tone got serious, and Demarco was nodding his head.

"'Preciate that, bro," he said.

"I'd do anything for Ramon, you know that ...

"I know he'll take care of me in the house ...

146

"Makes me proud ...

"I ain't got no chance of walking, I know that much ...

"But I'm counting on his support, you know that ...

"True. Well, I'm still loyal, dude. Can't make it any clearer than that, know what I'm sayin'?"

My head lowered. I knew what Demarco was doing. This was not a confession; Demarco was taking out insurance. It was a pragmatic move, and one that I knew he would consider making. As much as I understood his reasoning, I was annoyed to think he might have given up on me. I reminded myself about his faith, that he would believe the outcome of the trial was in accord with the will of God. To him, perhaps, it was not giving up; it was surrendering to the flow of a divine tide.

I sat back in my chair.

"That's not a confession, Jessica, and you know it," I said, knowing I'd be in the minority of people who'd believe that.

"Well, that's what you say. From this side of the desk, it looks like what you'd expect from a callous murderer—laughing off his crimes and looking out for himself."

I didn't want to argue.

"What else you got?"

Jessica reached for a folder to her right and flipped it open.

"There's some interesting information we extracted from Toby Connors' phone."

"What's that?" I had to pretend I knew nothing about the Ramon X video, but now I was sure they had it.

"Oh, a few things that damn your client even more, but I'll let you unpack those little presents on your own."

"Anything else?"

"We've been through most of the rest of it."

"Give me a look."

She handed the folder over to me with a slight reluctance that made me think she'd keep it from me if she could. So it wasn't all going her way after all.

I scanned through the contents and then I saw what she'd been wanting to hide. A new DNA result from Toby Connors' car. What I read snapped me out of my pessimistic mood immediately.

"Well, well, well. Isn't this interesting? There's a positive match for a second DNA sample from the car."

The match was Evan Harrington.

"You're following this up, aren't you, Jessica?" I asked.

Jessica was not so bold now. "Of course we are, Brad."

I knew she was bullshitting me.

"Jessica, this places Evan Harrington at both murder scenes, you know that, right? He's a suspect. He has motive!"

"Harrington says he was in Connors' car, but not the day he was murdered."

"So you've asked him that?"

"You bet."

She was either lying or telling a half truth. Jessica and the DA's Office had no intention of deviating from their mission to nail Demarco for these crimes. They were locked and loaded. That made me angry and all the more determined to give them the fight of their lives. They were not going to railroad my client into jail. I was going to blow their case wide open for everyone to see.

Demarco may have been willing to put his fate in the hands of God, but he wasn't out of my hands yet.

***

148

Back in the office I got a call from Jack. He'd been looking into the Cassinelli file, and by the tone of his voice, I knew he still thought Cassinelli was a crackpot. I told him to humor me with what he'd found.

"Okay, first thing is the Florida and Mexico deaths do not appear to be linked in any way, let alone to our case."

"How so?"

"Well, as you know, the one in Puerto Escondido was arson. Some deadbeat freak with a history of break-and-enters took what he wanted while the victim was in bed and then decided to torch the place."

"Why would he do that?"

"He had a reputation for being not right upstairs, and he had at least one arson charge under his belt already."

"And the other case?"

"The Miami case was, so the records tell me, a drug deal gone wrong. The victim was after a few grams of coke, and he just picked the wrong street dealer to invite to his place to do the deal."

"What happened?"

"Apparently, there was some dispute over money, and so the dealer put two bullets into the victim and took all his cash. Just the sort of shit that happens every day in that neck of the woods."

"Do we know the weapon used?"

"Yeah. Ballistics on the shells indicated the weapon was a Glock."

"Just Glock. No model number?"

"Nope."

"Well that narrows it down," I said. I was kidding. About seven thousand people a year are killed by handguns in the States, and Glocks are so popular they could account for more than half of those deaths. So to have a Glock listed without its model number was about as useful as saying the getaway car was a Ford.

"How did the suspects plead?"

"Guilty. Both of them."

"To murder charges?"

"In Miami, it was reduced on a plea bargain to manslaughter. The guy's doing sixteen years. In Mexico, the guy pleaded guilty to arson and manslaughter. Twenty years."

"So why is Cassinelli so sure they are linked, besides the victims both being internet bad boys? It hardly sounds like they were both killed by the same moral crusader. How strong was the evidence against them?"

"In both cases, there were eyewitnesses who saw the perps hanging around the respective premises prior to the deaths."

"How quickly did they plea?"

"Within days."

"What about the records of their first interviews? They must have denied it initially."

"I'm trying to get transcripts and video from the interviews. But don't get your hopes up on that front."

"Let me know if and when you get something. I can get the Mexican one translated."

"I can already tell you what the Mexican perp said, and I don't even speak Spanish: 'I had nothing to do with it. Nada.'"

No doubt that was true. Perhaps there was no great value in pursuing this line of inquiry. I couldn't let this become too much of a distraction, for one. And I was fast running out of time to find real evidence of an alternative suspect. The fact remained that Demarco's trial was going ahead. My job was first and foremost to save Demarco from a guilty conviction, not to solve a serial killing.

"Jack, if there's nothing in the transcripts, you can drop it. I can't let it run on and on as a distraction."

"Sure thing, boss. I'll let you know what comes back."

As soon as I hung up, a message appeared. I was expecting a quip from Jack. But it wasn't. It was a message from a blocked number.

"YOU KNOW NOTHING ABOUT JUSTICE! YOU'RE A FRAUD!"

Initially, the words threw me. But then I reminded myself that copping abuse for defending an alleged murderer was just part of my job. It had happened in every homicide case I'd ever taken on. A fair trial wasn't what mattered to some people. To them, Demarco Torrell was obviously guilty—so just lock him up already and throw away the key.

I closed the message. Then I left the office. I'd resume working on my strategy at home.

Sometimes it seemed I was the only person in the world who believed I was defending an innocent man. Make that an innocent boy. A boy whose life was literally in my hands. I wasn't convinced the call he'd made to the Crips would be enough to keep him alive.

My gut told me that if I didn't keep him out of prison, he'd be dead before his eighteenth birthday.

CHAPTER 18

Show me a prosecutor who doesn't like the sound of their own voice and I'll show you an empty courtroom. But before Jessica Pope had uttered a word, every member of the jury was transfixed on her.

She rose from her seat behind the plaintiff's table, touched it lightly and then set her gaze upon the jury. The awe, wonder, envy and attraction she instantly aroused wasn't limited to the jury box—I could almost feel it coming off the public benches behind me.

Yep, it was always a tough day at the office when going up against Jessica Pope. She could put points on the board even before her opponent had warmed up. And let's not pretend Judge Abraham T. Garner was immune to her charms. Don't get me wrong; this was nothing sexual. Garner simply could not help but enjoy the pleasure of seeing such brilliance in a younger generation. But then again, that admiration wasn't entirely one-sided; Judge Garner liked me too. During pretrial and jury selection, we'd worked together a lot—the three of us—and throughout the process, Judge Garner had exuded a sense of pride at being one of three impressive wheels of justice in action.

Now it was time for the fourth wheel, the jury, to come into play. And make no mistake, they were in charge now. It was all about them. Jessica and I would be battling to get them to not just see things our way, but to believe things our way with all their hearts.

"Last year, July 6, the lives of two young men were callously cut short," Jessica began. "Their murders were not opportunistic. They were planned. Both were shot at point blank range. Both saw the face of their killer. And that face, the evidence will show, belongs to the man seated there—the defendant, Demarco Torrell.

"Let me state some basic facts. These are not theories or opinion. This is what we know without a shadow of a doubt. The defendant was apprehended standing over the dead body of Luke Jameson after he had been fatally shot. The murder weapon was lying on the ground close by. Gun powder residue was found on the defendant's right hand. The defendant was seen in an altercation with Mr. Jameson just moments before he died. These are the facts. No one, not the defendant nor his learned attorney, will contest their veracity.

"Then we have Toby Connors, a young man who, the evidence shows, was fatally shot not long before Mr. Jameson was gunned down. Ballistics testing shows that the weapon used in these two murders was the same. The defendant was the last person seen with Mr. Connors before he died. His DNA was found in Mr. Connors' car.

"Another fact: when the defendant was caught, he was in possession of a pass assigned to Mr. Toby Connors. He used the VidCon pass of the first victim to get to the second.

"I expect you will hear some erudite and impassioned words from the defendant's attorney. I know he will try and convince you that the same indisputable facts I have just given you do not mean that his client committed two first-degree murders.

153

"The man behind that desk will ask you to believe that black cannot only be white, but it can be gray, blue, red and every other color in between. But ladies and gentlemen of the jury, as this trial proceeds, I urge you to resist being distracted by the power of words—I urge you to always hold firmly onto the power of facts.

"And the facts show that this defendant embarked on a ruthless plan to kill. A plan so cold and calculating that I think it is entirely fair to call it an assassination. And once armed with all the facts of this case, I'm sure you will overwhelmingly draw the same conclusion. The defendant had the motive, the means and the nature to carry out these two most heinous crimes.

"The question that needs to be addressed, naturally, is why. What drove the defendant to commit such senseless acts of violence? The short answer is pride, ego and evil.

"You will hear that the defendant is a member of the Sintown Crips. They are a criminal street gang that survives off two fundamental activities: violence and crime. Now the counsel for the defendant will tell you to believe he is a 'former member.' But we have evidence to indicate he committed these murders in the name of the Sintown Crips and that gang's most famous member, a man by the name of Ramon X.

"As you might expect from a gang member, Ramon X has a lengthy criminal history and a stream of violent convictions to his name. He also happens to be a rapper and a YouTube star. He once counted Luke Jameson as a friend. But then they fell out, after which Ramon X made public threats against Mr. Jameson's life. You will also hear that Ramon X threatened the life of Mr. Connors, who had embarrassed Ramon X on YouTube. So both victims had upset Ramon X so deeply that he wanted them dead.

"What does this have to do with the defendant? Well, the fact is we have a confession. You will see it with your own eyes and hear it with your own ears. The defendant, while being held at Juvenile Hall for these two murders, boasted to a gang member friend about the killings and then sought assurance that he will enjoy protection from his gang once he is imprisoned.

"The facts tell us the defendant carried out two cold-blooded murders to restore the dubious—no, non-existent—honor of his gang. There is no honor in that gang, at least not the kind of honor that any decent, self-respecting citizen of Los Angeles holds dear.

"Now I want to tell you something about the two men killed. You may or may not have heard of Luke Jameson, but he had forged an extremely successful career as a vlogger on YouTube. Every day he posted a video to his channel, and every day millions of people enjoyed watching those videos. His senseless death has left an immense hole in the hearts of his mother Helen, his father Richard, his sister Kate, his brother Randy and his girlfriend Margot. They all are suffering a degree of heartbreak we could hardly imagine. They were proud of Luke, they loved him, and now all they have left are memories.

"Toby Connors, the first to die on that horrible day, was pursuing a passion he wanted to convert into a career. He had his whole life ahead of him. He too was loved dearly by his parents and his girlfriend. But their lives have been changed forever. They have had to deal with unbearable grief. But their pain is all the more acute for the sheer senselessness of Toby's death.

"Members of the jury, no amount of jail time can bring back the lives of those two young men. The perpetrator of their callous murders, the defendant, deserves to feel the heaviest impact of the law. Anything less than the death penalty would be a slap in the face for the family and friends who are yearning for justice.

"Thank you for your service to the community. You have been given a great burden, but it rests on worthy shoulders. I know you will make the right decision. And that is to find the defendant twice guilty of murder in the first degree."

Throughout Jessica's statement, I scrutinized the faces of the jury. She'd made the perfect start. Delivered a powerful, coherent story. Told it in clear, resonant language. She stuck to the facts, unlike some trial lawyers I know. And, also unlike some lawyers I know, she never talked down to the jury. While she spoke, I'd paid particular attention to four jury members.

Before the trial we'd spent three days on voir dire, conducting interviews to reduce a field of fifty-two potential jurors down to twelve plus four alternates. Within that core dozen were four who, I believed, would be the hardest for me to win over.

First there was Juror #1: Stacey Callahan. White. Thirty-five-year-old mother of two. She worked as a receptionist for an auto parts chain. During voir dire, she'd responded dutifully to every question, contemplating it earnestly before replying. She'd said she was aware of the case, declared she hadn't yet formed a judgment on Demarco Torrell's guilt or innocence, and insisted she'd be able to put everything she'd heard prior to the trial aside and deal only with what was presented in court. I'd have gotten rid of her using a peremptory challenge, but by the time we'd interviewed her I'd used up twenty already. Yes, that's right—twenty times I'd had to strike out a witness on the grounds I believed they wouldn't be able to judge this case without bias. That may sound like a lot, but there was a young man's life at stake, and I was doing all I could to ensure the prosecution didn't get a head start.

Then there was Juror #4: Holly Myers. White. Twenty-two. Bright and assertive. I'd actually called a peremptory challenge to remove her, but Judge Garner hadn't allowed it. My objection was that Ms. Myers had admitted to subscribing to Luke Jameson's channel. But she said she was subscribed to more than a hundred channels.

"Just because I subscribed to his channel doesn't mean I was in love with him," she said to me. "Are you in love with Alicia Florrick because you like to watch *The Good Wife*? Or do you necessarily think Charlie Sheen is an okay guy just because you love watching re-runs of *Two and a Half Men*?"

"She's got you there," Judge Garner said with a wry smile, enjoying every moment.

I had to concede she did. So she was in. But because of the way she handled herself so confidently, I picked her as a person who'd be quite influential in the jury. I sensed she'd back her conviction and urge others to follow. I also figured once she'd made up her mind, she'd be hard to flip. I believed she could swing the case one way or the other. And my inclination was that she would lean more toward Jessica than me.

Juror #6 was Mark Carnavan. White. Forty-two. A plumber from Century City with a wife and two teenage boys. My bet was that he'd be biased against Demarco because he'd naturally sympathize with the deaths of two young men and seek justice for their families. But he'd said he had many black friends with sons and he wouldn't approach the trial on race lines. That said, I remained concerned that I'd have a tough time winning him over.

Now let's be honest. The difficulty I faced was not just the perceived leanings or attitudes of any particular jury member. Jessica had a very strong case, and I knew she'd lay it out brilliantly. And while I'd be pulling out all the stops to sink her argument, I simply knew that when people were presented with a convincing story by the authorities or law enforcement or sitting governments, they by and large tended to accept that what was told to them was the truth. And that's how I saw Mark—someone who was comfortable trusting authority.

Juror #12 was Don Gretler. White. Sixty-four. There was nothing specific I feared about Don. He just seemed to be someone whose life was so far removed from Demarco's that I suspected he might lack empathy.

But despite my reservations about these four, I didn't want any of the alternates riding the pine to be subbed in. My feeling was that the insertion of any of one of them would weaken my chances. So beyond the challenge of winning the argument on the evidence at hand, I also had to hope like hell that none of the standing twelve jurors would have to excuse themselves.

157

When I stood to make my opening statement, I adopted a relaxed posture. It was a fine line between projecting overconfidence and honesty. Obviously, I was going for the latter. Given the voir dire process, the jurors and I were, if not familiar with each other, at least acquainted. In the interviews, I'd taken care to never be pushy, argumentative or ingratiating, something Judge Garner would have jumped on in an instant. Any attempt to get overly familiar with a juror—probing for mutual friends, common interests, or shared humor—was also out of line. And don't think I didn't practice my tone of voice, my posture, facial expressions, and the movement of my hands in the mirror at home. It might sound vain, but I don't care—everything I did had to work in my client's favor. Everything. Every breath, every movement, every small action or reaction. My client was the one on trial, but I was too—or at least under constant review.

The start of a trial. My client against the odds. If I lost, he'd go to a prison where men were waiting to kill him. No pressure.

"Ladies and gentlemen of the jury, I'm going to make this very clear from the outset. You should acquit Demarco Torrell. Why? Because although the prosecution will no doubt make a convincing argument, it's an argument built on the misrepresentation of the facts at hand.

"The prosecution told you the facts point to Demarco Torrell's guilt. But that's true only if you line up certain facts and look at them in a certain way—that is, the exact way the prosecution wants you to.

"The question you must ask is why on earth would my client commit these murders? The prosecution has rather luridly portrayed Demarco as an assassin. They say he was avenging some slight against a gang member Ramon X.

"But the fact is that the defendant had left the gang life behind. That took courage. He reached out for help. That took courage. He conceived of an honorable future for himself by joining the military. That took courage.

"Out of the gang life. Out to shape a better future for himself. Out to do his late father proud. That's what Demarco Torrell had achieved. So you will have to ask yourselves, why would he throw all that away by killing two men in broad daylight?

"The prosecution will have you believe that because Demarco Torrell's DNA was found in the car of Toby Connors, he must have killed him. And that because he was the last to speak with Luke Jameson, he must have killed him.

"But I'm here to tell you someone else committed these murders. I wish I could stand here and tell you who that person is, but I can't. My client happened to be in the wrong place at the wrong time. Twice. They say lightening doesn't strike twice, but I'm sorry to say it has for my client.

"Believe me, I know what the sum of evidence looks like when pieced together by the prosecution, and I can see the appeal of buying into their theory. But you have to remember that their story is only a theory.

"They say Demarco shot those men, but no one saw my client holding a gun. That's a fact. No one saw my client shoot Mr. Jameson. That's a fact. Demarco made no attempt to flee the scene of the Jameson murder. That's a fact. He was observed crouching over the dying man. That's a fact.

"As for my client's DNA being found in Mr. Connors' car, he has never denied being in the vehicle. He had a very good reason to be in that car. Then there is the fact that my client was found wearing a pass registered to Mr. Connors. Now the prosecution has put two and two together to say my client killed Mr. Connors. But I will show you that this is not what those facts actually add up to.

"Let's get to the heart of this—for my client to be guilty, he would have had to be hell bent on murdering two individuals come what may. This would have to be the work of a fanatical madman, a cold-blooded killer on a suicide mission. Demarco Torrell is no such thing. I will show you he is a young man of honor. A young man who had the sense and self-discipline to make profound changes in his life for the better. Who among us can say we did the same at such a young age?

"Unfortunately, his will to better himself was what got him caught up in this dire mess.

"I agree that this looks like cold-blooded murder. But there is a dominant narrative here that the media is already indulging in—the hysterical notion that Demarco is the face of a sinister threat to us all—black criminal gangs.

"But there is another even more compelling narrative—it's called the truth. It wasn't hate or revenge or gang pride that led Demarco Torrell to the Anaheim Convention Center that day. It was the most simplistic of things—doing something for a buck. Toby Connors offered him a thousand dollars to take part in what he was told was a prank, an attempt to humiliate one of YouTube's biggest stars. 'Help me get a pie-in-the-face video of Luke Jameson for my channel,' Toby told Demarco, 'and I'll give you a grand—half now, half later.' To Demarco, this offer was like a gift from God—a sign from the Almighty that he was on the right path.

"But your responsibility is not to swallow the alluring perceptions crafted by others. It is for you to craft your own perceptions, using all the facts and the abundant common sense you possess. And I say again, try to resist any effort to trick you into thinking this is a simple crime of hate and vengeance.

"I urge you to put yourself in Demarco Torrell's shoes. Would you, could you walk out onto the streets and commit such a terrible crime? To find Demarco guilty, you will have to convince yourself he had a motive so powerful that he was willing to throw his own life away to see these two men dead. I don't think you will be able to. Demarco Torrell could no more have carried out these terrible murders than you could have.

"I am honored to be defending Demarco against these charges. There is no greater service of the justice system than to ensure that innocent people are not sent to prison. This is your earnest duty—

to resist the efforts to paint an evil picture of my client. Because to accept them would be serving the opposite cause of justice.

"The bedrock of justice is the presumption of innocence. You must presume Demarco Torrell to be innocent. It is the task of the prosecution to convince you beyond a reasonable doubt that he is guilty. The prosecution has the burden of supplying proof.

"Beyond reasonable doubt. This is the highest bar our legal system sets. If you believe the balance of guilt is more than half—that you mostly think the facts indicate he's guilty—you must find him innocent. If you think there's a seventy-five percent chance he's guilty, you must find him innocent. If you cannot say beyond reasonable doubt that you think he is guilty, then you must acquit him. Thank you."

As I spoke, I was encouraged to find the jury well engaged. None of them sat back or slouched. No body language betrayed a resistance to my words—no one folded their arms, stole a yawn behind cupped hands, or let inattentive eyes stray anywhere else in the courtroom. I resumed my seat behind the defense table feeling boosted. I gave Demarco a look of encouragement.

"We can win this," my expression urged. "We're going to win this. I'm sure of it."

And that's what I truly thought. Against all odds, I was going to win this case. I allowed myself a brief daydream of seeing the weight lift off Demarco's shoulders, Jasmine's tears of relief, the satisfaction of honoring the memory of Tank. It was a wonderful feeling, but premature.

I smacked the indulgence clear from my mind.

It was game on.

CHAPTER 19

Jessica Pope began with the eye witnesses. First in line was seventeen-year-old Mandy Alvarez. Dressed in a light blue sweater with thick glasses, braces and black hair in pony tails, she was a picture of virtue. And that meant a potential angel of doom for Demarco. Having seen her original testimony, I knew the crux of her story. But I believed there were holes that needed prying open.

After Alvarez was sworn in, Jessica stood and walked her through some background. Then she began establishing her credibility as an eyewitness.

"Ms. Alvarez, please tell the court where you were on the morning of July 6 last year."

"I was attending VidCon at the Anaheim Convention Center."

"Were you there alone?"

"No, I went with a bunch of friends, school friends. We all had three-day passes."

"And you were particularly keen to see Team 5MS perform, is that right?"

"That's right."

"Could you please explain what Team 5MS is?"

"It's a group of ten YouTube stars who have more than five million subscribers—hence the name 5MS. They come together to perform at events like VidCon. You know, they put on a show for their fans."

Alvarez came across much cooler than her sweet little girl looks suggested. She was confident. She didn't hesitate a second before answering. She looked at Jessica the entire time, sitting up straight, hands in her lap. I could see why Jessica had wanted her on the stand first and would no doubt want her there a good while—the jury would swallow her every word.

"What kind of shows?"

"It's a mix of stuff—music, talks, interviews, dancing. It's awesome."

Alvarez couldn't help but shudder with excitement.

"Was this event what you were looking forward to seeing most?"

"Yes."

Snap. Just like that, that joyful vibe evaporated. Alvarez was now as solemn as a tombstone.

"Ms. Alvarez, walk me through the lead-up to the shocking event you witnessed. When did you enter the theater to see Team 5MS?"

"I knew they'd be late. They always are. Luke in particular. I mean, he's the real star. He put the crew together—it was his idea—the guy is a genius, but he's always late. It's like his thing. And he makes a grand entrance from the crowd. So I waited to try and see him come in and then follow him."

"And did you see him enter the theater?"

"Yes, I did."

"At what time?"

163

"It was just before twelve-thirty. He was about half an hour late."

"How could he just walk in without being noticed?"

"Everyone was already inside the theater waiting for the show to begin. Well, there were a few stragglers. But he could just walk straight in. And it was totally dark inside. That's what he asks the production crew to do—to turn off every single light except for the exit signs, of course."

"What about cell phones?"

"Everyone's told via the PA to keep them off until the show starts. It all adds to the excitement."

"Okay. I get the picture. Now, did you see Luke Jameson approach the theater entrance?"

"Yes, I did."

"Was anyone else near Mr. Jameson?"

"Yes, I saw a person a few steps behind him."

"Is that person in this court?"

"Yes, he is. Right there."

Alvarez pointed at Demarco.

"For the sake of the court record, I'll just confirm that the witness is pointing at the defendant. Ms. Alvarez, what happened next?"

"Luke kind of jogged up to the entrance then went inside."

"And what did you see the defendant do?"

"He kept right behind Luke and followed him in."

"Did you see any words being exchanged between the two men?"

"No, not then. My impression was that they didn't know each other."

"What did you do once Mr. Jameson walked past you?"

"I followed him into the theater."

"Did you speak to him?"

"No, I didn't want to out him. I just wanted to see him surprise everyone."

"Then what happened?"

"I followed Luke inside, but that man over there was between us. He stuck right behind Luke. It was very dark, so I stayed right behind that man, and I could sometimes see Luke's back as he made his way through the crowd. After a minute or so we'd worked our way up to within a few yards of the stage, and that's where Luke stopped. So I stopped."

"Was the defendant there?"

"Yes, he was standing between me and Luke, so I worked my way around him so I could stand next to Luke."

"And that's when you heard the defendant address Mr. Jameson?"

"Yes."

"Please, tell us what you heard."

"The defendant kept trying to get Luke's attention. He was like, 'Yo, dude. Yo, dude.' He was saying it loud again and again. I turned around but I couldn't see too well because it was so dark."

"Then what happened?"

"The defendant was saying stuff like, 'What goes around comes around, bro. You're gonna have to pay. You're gonna have to pay. You've been served by God!' Then finally Luke turned around. And that's when he shot him."

"You saw him shoot Luke?"

"Yes, there was a flash of light that lit up his front. Then the gun went off again. And then everything went crazy."

Alvarez was in tears now. She brought a handkerchief up to her eyes and took a few deep breaths to collect herself.

"Please, when you're ready, tell us what you saw," said Jessica.

"Luke collapsed. He just dropped to the floor."

"Sorry to interrupt but how can you see if it's so dark?"

"Well, it wasn't pitch black. There was a small amount of light so that after your eyes adjusted you could make out some things. And then after the shooting some people put their phone flashlight on."

"Okay, please continue."

"Everyone started pushing and screaming as they tried to run away. People were shouting out that someone had a gun. I could hear someone shouting, 'Get down!' Others were screaming, 'Run!' But no one was sure where the shots had come from, so people were trying to escape in every direction."

"What did you do?"

Alvarez began to sob.

"I ran away. I was so scared. That's all I could hope to do—to get away before I got shot. I didn't want to die."

Jessica paused to give Alvarez time to collect herself.

"Mandy, can you tell the court who shot Luke Jameson?"

"Yes. It was him. That man sitting there."

"You are pointing at the defendant Demarco Torrell, is that right?"

"Yes. That's right. He's the one that shot Luke."

"Thank you, Mandy," said Jessica. "Nothing further from me, Your Honor."

I stood and waited for Jessica to resume her seat before I stepped out from behind the defense table. I knew Mandy Alvarez's witness statement word for word, as I did for all the prosecution witnesses disclosed during discovery. Jessica had done a good job. She'd pretty much prompted Alvarez to reproduce her statement verbatim. But I'd flagged a few points about her testimony. Now it was time to raise them.

I'd be lying if I said I didn't enjoy this part of being a trial lawyer. I wondered what Jessica had done to prepare Mandy Alvarez for my cross-examination. Nothing less than thorough, I expected.

"Ms. Alvarez, I don't have too many questions for you. First up, you say you saw my client Demarco Torrell shoot Luke Jameson, right?"

"That's right."

"I just want to be absolutely sure we are clear on where you were standing when the shooting happened. Were you standing in front of Mr. Jameson, or beside him?"

"A bit of both—I was standing just in front of his left shoulder."

"And there was no one else standing between you and Mr. Jameson, is that right?"

"Yes."

"How tall are you, Ms. Alvarez?"

"I'm five six."

"Five six. Right. And from the records, we know Luke Jameson is six foot one. So you're seven inches shorter, would you agree?"

"I guess so. That sounds about right."

"Okay. Now, was your shoulder touching Mr. Jameson's body?"

Alvarez shifted a little. The suggestion of physical intimacy, however nonsexual, between her and her idol made her self-conscious.

"At times, yes."

"To be precise, the back of your right shoulder was coming into contact with his upper left arm. Does that sound right?"

"Yes."

"Was Mr. Jameson indicating in any way that he was aware you were touching him?"

Alvarez blushed a little.

"No, I don't think so. It was a concert. You expect to bump into the people around you."

She flashed a guilty glance at Jessica. She knew she was not meant to elaborate. She straightened, mentally telling herself to be more careful.

"Ms. Alvarez, were you turning your head to look at him?"

"Yes. From time to time."

"At the time of the shooting, which way was Mr. Jameson facing?"

"He was facing away from the stage."

"So he had turned around to talk to my client, is that right?"

"Yes."

"Before any shots were fired, did you know Mr. Jameson had turned around?"

"No, I did not."

"He didn't bump you as he did so?"

"No."

"You didn't feel his body touch yours?"

"No."

Alvarez shifted a little uncomfortably. Good. She was no longer the rock-solid little figure the jury had been presented with under Jessica's Q and A.

"Objection, Your Honor!" Of course, Jessica was on her feet to defend her witness. "How is this relevant to the case?"

Judge Garner gave me a look of thinning patience.

"Get back on track quickly, counselor. Overruled. Please answer the question, Ms. Alvarez."

"Yes, Your Honor. No, I did not feel any contact with Mr. Jameson to indicate he had turned around."

"So you turned around when you heard him talking to my client, is that right?"

"Yes."

"Would you say you heard everything that was said between my client and Mr. Jameson?"

"I can't say for sure. But I think I caught most of it, like I said before."

"In your pretrial testimony, you said you were sure you had heard the entire conversation. Is that not true?"

Alvarez squirmed.

"Upon reflection, I can't say I heard it all—but I know I heard a good deal of it."

"And you turned around because you heard raised voices, is that right?"

"Yes."

"You say Mr. Jameson sounded like he was angry with the defendant, is that right?"

"Yes. They were angry at each other."

"And what did you see immediately?"

"Just after I turned around two shots were fired, and I saw the face of the defendant light up."

"Even though it was dark, you are sure it was him?"

169

"Yes."

"Thank you, Ms. Alvarez. You have stated the defendant looked angry. Now, remember when I asked you your height and we compared it to how tall Mr. Jameson was?"

"Yes."

"Can you please help the court understand your field of view? You have said you were standing just in front of Mr. Jameson to his left before you turned around. Did any part of Mr. Jameson's body obstruct your view of the defendant when the muzzle flashes went off?"

"Yes, his shoulder. I could just see over his shoulder."

"Did you have to stand on tippy toe to do that?"

"No."

"Could you see the defendant's hair?"

"Yes."

"Could you see his eyes?"

Alvarez hesitated like she had to think carefully about her answer.

"Yes."

"Are you absolutely sure you could see his eyes, Ms. Alvarez?"

"Yes, but it was quick."

I could almost hear Jessica groan.

"Could you see his nose?"

"No."

"His mouth?"

"No."

"His chin?"

"No."

"Right, so from two split-second glimpses at the defendant's eyes, you have testified that he looked angry. Are you sure you want to stand by that assertion, Ms. Alvarez? Because this is the defendant you're talking about. This man sitting right here. And you're sure he looked angry?"

Alvarez paused longer than ever. But she decided to stick to her guns.

"Yes."

"You're certain about that? Are you sure he didn't look shocked?"

No answer.

"Are you sure he didn't look shocked rather than angry, Ms. Alvarez? Because if he is innocent, then my bet is that he would have been as shocked and surprised as you were. Are you sure he didn't look shocked, Ms. Alvarez?"

No answer.

"Please answer the question, Ms. Alvarez."

"Yes, I'm sure. He looked angry," she said, almost apologetic.

"So you expect us to believe that having never met Demarco Torrell, and going by a fleeting glimpse of his eyes, you can tell whether he looked angry, as opposed to confused or incredulous? Do I need to remind you that this young man's life is at stake, Ms. Alvarez?"

"I don't know," she murmured.

"What's that, Ms. Alvarez? Please speak louder."

"I said I don't know," she said, her head bowed. "I can't be sure."

"Are you saying that upon reflection you are not certain my client looked angry?"

"Yes, that's right."

"Now, Ms. Alvarez, did you see any other faces lit up by the muzzle flashes?"

"Yes, a couple."

"Did you recognize any of them?"

"Yes. One of them was Evan Harrington. And there was an older guy I'd never seen before."

"For the benefit of the court, could you please let us know who Evan Harrington is and why you would recognize him so readily?"

"Um, he's another vlogger that I follow. He posts daily videos about family life. He has a lovely wife and two adorable kids."

"Thank you. And what was the expression on Mr. Harrington's face when it was lit up by the muzzle flash."

"I don't know. Not happy, I guess."

"Not happy. That can be taken so many ways. What do you mean? Sad? Angry? Hateful? Resentful? Confused?"

"His face looked kind of blank."

"Blank. Did you have a better look at his face than my client's?"

"Yes, he was standing right behind me. I could see his whole face."

"What about the other faces you saw?"

"There were a couple of others, I guess, but I don't remember any details about their appearance."

"Would you say there were a few people all standing close enough to shoot Mr. Jameson in the chest at point-blank range?"

"I guess so. But that's not the way it looked."

"But it's possible that it was not my client who pulled the trigger, isn't it?"

"I guess so. Yes, it's possible."

"Ms. Alvarez. You did not see the gun at all, did you?"

"No, I did not."

"So you cannot be one-hundred percent sure that my client was the shooter, can you?"

"No, I guess I can't."

"Nothing further, Your Honor."

I turned back to take my seat at the defense table. I was heartened to see Holly Myers busily taking notes with raised eyebrows. Anyone with a mind to apply their judgment impartially had reason to doubt the veracity of Mandy Alvarez's testimony against Demarco, as well intentioned as it may be.

I was quite pleased with where things stood. I saw Jessica Pope working hastily through her papers. I expected her to come out guns blazing.

She didn't disappoint.

CHAPTER 20

I've seen countless people sworn in. Some are matter of fact, they understand it's part of the process, like walking through an airport scanner. Most are respectful and earnest. They believe the oath they recite holds profound weight, and they're willing to be honest to the full. Placing a hand on the Bible is now optional, but if it were still mandatory, you might as well have used a case of beer instead of the Good Book for all some witnesses' words are worth.

Naturally, Evan Harrington elected to use the Bible for his swearing in, and I have to say I've never seen someone put such piety into the act. No one in the courtroom doubted that he wanted them to know his promise ran soul deep—but his overdone display just got everyone asking the same question from the outset: is this guy for real? I snatched a look at Jessica Pope and could see her wishing he'd tone it down. But I was pleased—he'd unwittingly planted the seed of distrust from the get-go.

Jessica was not going to let that endure. She would soon make sure that Evan Harrington impressed the jury as being highly relatable and utterly convincing.

Harrington sat looking at Jessica, calmly waiting for her to begin questioning him, priest-like in his gentle, patient smile.

"Mr. Harrington, could you please tell the court where you were on the day of the shooting?"

"I was attending VidCon."

"In what capacity?"

"My wife and I have a YouTube channel that is quite successful, and as a convention for YouTube creators, VidCon gives us a chance to connect with our fans in person. There were appearances and a couple of panels we were invited to sit on."

"And how did you come to be at the scene of the shooting?"

"Well, I was interested in seeing the Team 5MS show, so I went along. I went inside the theater like everyone else and found a place to stand up near the stage."

"And did you know you were standing right behind Luke Jameson, the star of the show?"

"I had no idea he was there until the man next to me started trying to get him to turn around."

"Is that man in the courtroom today?"

"Yes, he is. He's sitting right over there. The defendant, Demarco Torrell."

"You are in no doubt that he was the man you saw?"

"No doubt whatsoever."

"Mr. Harrington, can you tell us precisely what you saw unfold inside the theater?"

"Well, like I said, the defendant was trying to get Luke to turn around. Luke was trying to ignore him, hoping he'd stop, I guess."

"Was the defendant being friendly?"

"No, he was being pushy to the point of aggression. He was persistent. It seemed he wasn't going to stop until he got a reaction from Luke."

"And did he get a reaction?"

"Yes. Luke turned around. He seemed very annoyed but was trying to stay cool. I think he didn't want his cover blown to spoil his grand entrance."

"What did the defendant say to Mr. Jameson?"

"He was talking about karma. You know, like what goes around comes around. He said Luke was going to have to pay—for what, I don't know. And then he said, shouted really, 'You've been served by God!' Then the gun went off."

"Would you say the defendant's tone was threatening?"

"Yes, I would say that."

"Tell us, please, what happened next."

"Well, like I said, the gun went off. It was incredibly loud. Then there was another shot."

"What was your reaction?"

"I didn't really react. My eyes were just drawn to the light created by the shot."

"And what did you see?"

"I saw Luke kind of bend forward."

"And what did you see then?"

"I saw the gun."

"You saw the gun?"

"Yes."

"Do you know who was holding the gun?"

"Yes, ma'am, I do."

"And who was it?"

"It was that man there—the defendant, Demarco Torrell."

I felt the jury turned its gaze as one towards Demarco, who sat dead still next to me. I took the opportunity to show solidarity by leaning towards him, saying, "It's okay. He's got to answer to me too, Demarco."

"He's a liar," said Demarco through gritted teeth. He was behaving just as I'd told him to—impassive. I doubted the jury even noticed his lips move.

"Are you absolutely sure you saw the defendant Demarco Torrell shoot Luke Jameson?" Jessica said.

"Yes."

"It was no accident?"

"No way. What I witnessed can only be described as cold-blooded murder."

"No more questions, Your Honor," said Jessica. And with that she swaggered back to her table and sat herself down.

I began talking as I rose. "Mr. Harrington, you and the victim Mr. Jameson were very familiar with each other, weren't you?"

"We knew each other, yes."

"But you were not friends, were you?"

"No, we were not," he said.

Harrington looked relaxed. Obviously, Jessica knew she was taking a slight gamble by putting him on the stand. She had a trade-off to consider. On the one hand, she had a witness who was prepared to testify that he'd seen my client pull the trigger. On the other, that witness had a history of violence that could not be entirely whitewashed by his born-again devotion to God.

She would have known about his past assault and his hostile relationship with Jameson. But I was betting she was unaware of

177

the fact that the television production company Twenty2o had abruptly dropped the Harringtons from contention for their reality show project. Something told me Harrington had not shared that with her. To me, he seemed too eager to incriminate my client. And that told me he was hiding something—that either he knew the real killer or was the killer himself.

"Would it be fitting to describe your relationship with Mr. Jameson as a feud, Mr. Harrington?"

"That's a bit strong, but we didn't like each other."

"That's one way to put it. Mr. Harrington, you believed Mr. Jameson was out to destroy your career, isn't that right?"

"No, I wouldn't say that."

"Did he ever speak about you negatively in public?"

"Yes."

"Did he accuse you of being disingenuous about how you presented yourself to the public and your fans?"

"Yes, he did. He said my faith was an act to win subscribers."

"He also said you had cheated on your wife, didn't he?"

"Yes. But that was public knowledge. I had an affair on Tinder, but I made amends to my wife and to God, and we have worked hard to move on with our lives."

"The day before Mr. Jameson was shot, you assaulted him. Is that true?"

"I confronted him and it got physical."

"Is it true you confronted him because you thought he had cost you the chance to star in your own reality TV show?"

I heard Jessica move. She didn't know where I was going, and she didn't like it.

"Yes, that is true."

"Up until a few days before the shooting, you and Mr. Jameson were both being considered as subjects for a reality television show, weren't you?"

"Yes."

"And then you were told by the production company that you were no longer being considered. Did they tell you why?"

"No, they did not."

"But you knew why they dropped you, didn't you, Mr. Harrington?"

He shifted uncomfortably, caught between the compulsion to lie and the commitment to tell the truth.

"Luke Jameson had been telling them lies—he was slandering me so he would get the show."

"And that made you feel angry, right?"

"I was very upset."

"And so you confronted him at VidCon?"

"Yes."

"You actually tried to attack Mr. Jameson, but you were restrained. Is that true?"

"Yes."

"It was at that point that you verbally threatened Mr. Jameson, right?"

"Yes."

"What did you say?"

Harrington hesitated. Ashamed, he looked at me darkly. He obviously hadn't thought I'd find out.

"I have it from various sources what you said, Mr. Harrington."

"'You're dead,' I said."

"And the day after making that threat, you just happened to be standing behind him when he was shot dead. And now you swear that the person next to you was the one who pulled the trigger."

Jessica was on her feet. "Objection, Your Honor. The witness is not on trial here, and the police have thoroughly investigated Mr. Harrington's relationship with the deceased."

Harrington couldn't stay quiet.

"I wasn't the one with gunpowder on my hands, was I?! How do you explain that?!" he yelled, looking at me with fierce defiance.

"Order," said Judge Garner. "Mr. Harrington, control yourself, please."

That last outburst cut some shine off my cross-examination but I didn't believe all my work had been undone. I wanted to prove Harrington had the motive and opportunity to kill Jameson. Doubt. Doubt. Doubt. I needed to plant as much as I possibly could into the jury's mind. And to that end, I felt it was mission accomplished.

"No further questions, Your Honor."

CHAPTER 21

"Your Honor, I'd like to call Detective Michael Harrison Bayer to the stand," said Jessica Pope from behind the lectern.

She seemed a shade off her game. Maybe because she wasn't as far ahead of me as she'd hoped. Still, she and I both knew that while I'd chipped some credibility off two of her key witnesses, the ledger still weighed heavily in her favor. Any natural sympathies for the state's cause would only be aided by the fact that the jury would never hear from Demarco himself.

As in most murder trials, the defendant would not be testifying. The reason is simple—you don't want him to tarnish your case with a poor showing on the stand. You can't let the trial be about the defendant; you have to keep it focused on the fallibility of the prosecution's case. And Judge Garner had played his part in maintaining that aim—he made it clear to the jury that they should not interpret Demarco not testifying as being a sign of guilt. So, if anyone was going to put daylight between my case and Jessica's, Detective Bayer was it.

A single look at Bayer and you might take him for an accountant, or a back-office public servant. He was slim and dealt with going bald by cropping short whatever hair was left. His face was long and clean shaved. His skin was almost colorless, and his eyes were big and set deep in their sockets. They peered at the world through thick square-framed glasses. But if you'd ever heard the man chide an unthinking officer for accidentally fouling up a crime scene, you'd know that this unassuming package bore the confidence and authority of a standout leader. I knew good detectives twice Bayer's size who'd come up short if measured against him.

Jessica got Bayer's details and service record out of him. A police officer for a decade before becoming a distinguished investigator, Bayer had been decorated for bravery and was widely renowned for cracking tough cases. With those five-star credentials served up for starters, Jessica moved onto the main course.

"Detective Bayer, you have led the investigations into these two murders. Are you convinced they are connected?"

"Absolutely."

"How so?"

"Well, for starters the weapon. Glock 17. Our tests show the same gun was used to kill both Mr. Connors and Mr. Jameson."

"You can be sure of this?"

"I have utmost faith in our firearms analysis unit. And their testing showed the same gun was used to commit both murders."

"You mean your ballistics team?"

"Yes. We had all the key pieces of evidence we needed to determine that the same handgun was used in both murders. We retrieved the gun and two shells from the first murder scene—that is, where Mr. Jameson was killed. And we retrieved two bullets from the bodies of each victim. Our ballistics technicians were able to conclusively show that the same weapon was used in both murders. It's all there in the report."

"Did you conduct a fingerprint search on the weapon?"

Jessica knew that I was going to bring this up and wanted to steal my thunder. The truth is, prints were hardly ever retrieved from handguns.

"Yes, we did."

"Did you find any fingerprints on the weapon?"

"No, we did not."

"No fingerprints on the murder weapon? Isn't that odd, considering the weapon was dropped by the shooter and recovered by the authorities at the scene."

"We rarely get latent fingerprints from a handgun. Only in about five percent of cases are we able to do that, and this case wasn't one of them."

"Why? Because the shooter was wearing gloves?"

"No, not at all. It has to do with how handguns are made, the conditions they are used in, and how they are stored on the body."

"Could you please explain that for the court?"

"The best way to get fingerprints is off a smooth surface, and handguns have very few smooth surfaces. The handle and trigger are textured or marked to enhance grip. On the Glock 17, even where you load the magazine is not smooth, again to aid the user's grip."

"So it's no surprise that no prints were found on the murder weapon?"

"Like I said, if we only relied on that kind of evidence, ninety-five percent of the gun crimes we crack would remain unsolved."

"Detective Bayer, the murder weapon—this Glock 17—it had its serial number scratched out. Why would that be?"

"To ensure the weapon can't be traced back to its owner. It's what most criminals do when they purchase an illegal weapon."

"Is it easy for someone to get hold of a weapon like this?"

"Depends on the person. Average Joe on the street, not so easy. You need to have a contact in the black market to buy a weapon like this."

"What about a member of a criminal gang such as the Sintown Crips—of which the defendant was a member—how hard would that be?"

"Trading in illegal firearms is what gangs like the Crips do. They can get a Glock, or even an assault rifle, as easy as they can get a pack of smokes."

"How do you know this?"

"Ma'am, I've been working the streets of Los Angeles for about twenty years. I've dealt with a lot of gang crime and arrested more gang members than I can remember. I've seized too many weapons to count from gang members' dens, their cars, their person. These guys are swimming in guns."

"Detective Bayer, in your vast experience, what does this case look like to you?"

"To be frank, it looks like a double hit carried out by a member of the Sintown Crips."

"Why would the defendant do such a thing? He claims to have left that gang."

"Objection, Your Honor," I said. "This calls for the witness to speculate on the hypothetical actions of the defendant."

"Sustained," said Judge Garner.

"Detective Bayer, from your experience, how hard is it for gang members to leave their criminal organization?"

"I'd say it's near impossible. A lot of guys make that claim, but very few can actually live up to it. The truth is that most gang members who try to leave their gang—whether it's the Crips, the Bloods, whatever—end up back in the fold and back on the streets, back to a life of crime."

"It's a hard environment to extract yourself from?"

"The only way I've ever known a gang member to leave is by getting killed."

"Detective Bayer, you have interviewed the defendant at length as well as many witnesses. Why do you believe Demarco Torrell set out to kill both Toby Connors and Luke Jameson?"

"In short, our belief is that it was a revenge mission carried out by the defendant on behalf of a prominent gang member."

"Can you name this prominent gang member?"

"No, I cannot. That remains an active investigation."

"Okay, without naming names, can you tell us why you believe these two men were murdered?"

"Sure. A few weeks before his death, Mr. Jameson made a video mocking a fellow YouTuber who is, we believe, a current member of the Sintown Crips. Mr. Connors also upset the same gang member by posting a YouTube video of a prank he played on this person."

"I'd like to play the latter video for the court, Your Honor, exhibit number two-three-seven," said Jessica before turning to address the jury. "The face of the man Detective Bayer has been referring to has been blurred to hide his identity."

The court monitor came to life, and Jessica maneuvered the touchpad of her laptop to bring the clip up before she hit play. Jessica paused the video as Connors approached the car, and asked Detective Bayer to explain what reason Mr. Connors had to attempt a "hood prank." At the end of the video, Jessica resumed her direct examination.

"Detective Bayer, why is this video relevant to this case?"

"Several reasons. We believe this video cost Toby Connors his life."

"How so?"

"The person in that clip who put a gun to Mr. Connors' head is a member of the Sintown Crips. After Mr. Connors posted this clip to his YouTube channel, he received death threats from people who wanted him to take it down."

"We have some of those threats on the screen now. Jurors please look at the monitor. These are the comments or threats that you investigated, aren't they, Detective Bayer?"

"Yes."

"Can you please read them for the court?"

"Certainly. 'Your choice bro—take it down or die.' That has a gun emoji on the end there. The second reads: 'Yr dumb white ass gonna pay for this shit. U dead.' The third reads: 'Fucking with the Crips gonna cost you your life.'"

"Were you able to determine whether these threats were real or not?"

"Some were very real. We identified two users making these threats as associates of the Sintown Crips. That line of inquiry is part of the ongoing investigation I mentioned earlier. But there were a few social media platforms on which Mr. Connors was threatened."

"Did he take these threats seriously?"

"We interviewed his girlfriend. She told us he thought they were genuine, but he didn't want to take the video down until it had gone viral."

"Is this video still live on Mr. Connors' channel?"

"No, it is not. It was taken down."

"It was deleted from his channel?"

"Yes."

"When?"

"The day he was murdered."

"Detective Bayer, do you think it's possible more than one person was responsible for both murders?"

"It is possible but for that to be true, they would have had to exchange the gun at some point. Now that could be a sale in which the defendant purchased the gun off someone else. Or perhaps another gang member shot Mr. Connors and then delivered the gun to the defendant. But, given the facts we have at hand, the eyewitness accounts, and the background to these murders, it is highly unlikely anyone other than the defendant played a role in the fatal shootings of Mr. Connors and Mr. Jameson."

"You're saying the defendant Demarco Torrell killed them both?"

"Objection, Your Honor!" I called. "Leading the witness. And it calls for speculation."

"Sustained," said Judge Garner.

"Okay, I'll rephrase," Jessica said. "Is there any evidence the defendant killed both men to avenge the honor of a criminal street gang?"

"Yes, there is. We heard the defendant confess to his crime."

"Who did he confess to?"

"A fellow member of the Sintown Crips."

"But the defendant claims he had left the Sintown Crips."

"Yes, I know. But we secretly recorded a telephone call he made to a member of the Sintown Crips while being detained in Juvenile Hall. In that telephone call, he laughs off the murders and seeks assurance that he will be looked after in prison."

"Let's play the tape—exhibit number two-zero-nine."

I watched the jury's reaction to the video carefully. It was as bad as I'd expected. After the clip was finished, many of the jurors looked at Demarco in a way I hadn't yet seen. I could see their impression of him had hardened. It was now not only plausible, it

187

was almost irresistible for them to regard this seventeen-year-old black boy as a cold-blooded killer. Jessica had driven a nail into Demarco's coffin that I feared could not be pulled out.

"No further questions, Your Honor," she said.

The jury now had a clear story in their heads as to how and why Demarco Torrell killed two men. They may still have been wondering why would he commit murder in a place where he was almost certain to be caught. But it was likely that pure imagination was providing them with an acceptable answer to that question. None of the jurors had ever set foot in a troubled black neighborhood plagued with gang violence. A diet of TV crime shows, movies and news would have them think Demarco's alleged behavior was all very logical—that a young black man would decide to throw away his life to avenge the honor of his gang. Hell, they could remind themselves of the stories they'd heard about Tupac or 50 Cent. To them, this was just what life was like in America's black concrete jungles—all a senseless blur of drugs, crime, guns and rap music.

If I had any hope of winning this case, I had to, with all my power, dispel these myths—starting right now with my cross-examination of Detective Michael Harrison Bayer. A chink of doubt in Bayer's armor—that's what I needed to expose. And I knew he was fully prepared not to give me an inch.

"Detective Bayer, where was the body of Mr. Connors found?"

"In a vacant lot a few blocks away from the convention center."

"What are we talking in distance? A mile?"

"Yes, about a mile."

"And Mr. Connors was found dead in the trunk of his car?"

"Yes."

"And it is your belief that my client Demarco Torrell was the person who shot him?"

"Yes."

"And you posit that Mr. Connors deleted the video featuring the former Crips gang member under duress, at the point of a gun while in the car park, yes?"

"Yes."

"And you believe that Mr. Connors' phone was used to delete the video post from his YouTube channel?"

"Yes."

"And the data retrieved from Mr. Connors' phone provided the exact time the video was taken down, right?"

"Yes."

"Do you know what time the video was deleted, Detective Bayer?"

"Yes."

"Can you tell the court, please?"

"Twelve twenty-six PM."

"Twelve twenty-six."

"Now I'm going to ask you to read something for me. This is a printout of the entry records for VidCon." I handed Bayer the sheet. "Do you see the entry highlighted there in green?"

"Yes."

"What time does that say?"

"Twelve thirty-one."

"Do you know what that is, Detective Bayer?"

"No. But I figure you're about to tell me."

"Yes, I am, Detective Bayer. That five-digit number corresponds to the pass my client used to get into VidCon. So, according to your theory, Demarco Torrell shot Mr. Connors and then got himself to the convention center in five minutes. Or else he was in two places at the same time."

"Who said he went by foot? Another gang member probably drove him."

"Right. This sounds like quite a professional arrangement—a rapid two-kill assassination carried out by an LA street gang. You are convinced that that is what happened?"

"Yes. Do I have to remind you that the Sintown Crips are a professional criminal organization?"

I pulled an image up onto the screen.

"Detective Bayer, please look at the map I have here. Exhibit one-four-eight. You have seen this before, haven't you?"

"Yes."

"What is it?"

"It's a map of Toby Connors' movements using his GPS data."

"Right. So the global positioning system in his phone leaves a kind of breadcrumb trail of his movements, isn't that right?"

"Yes."

"Now my client has told you in a statement that Mr. Connors engaged him to help shoot a prank video of Luke Jameson, didn't he?"

"Yes."

"He told you he was paid five hundred dollars up front and promised another five hundred after the prank, is that right?"

"That's what he told me."

"Sounds like an offer too good for anybody to refuse, let alone a seventeen-year-old kid living on the streets, am I right?"

"Objection, Your Honor!" cried Jessica. "Calls for speculation from the witness."

"Sustained. Next question, please counselor. And try to keep it related to what the witness might know or have seen."

"Certainly, Your Honor. Detective Bayer, my client told you he was driven to the convention center by Mr. Connors?"

"Yes."

"And he said Mr. Connors dropped him off at the center, saying he was going to park the car and that he would meet him inside, is that right?"

"Yes."

"If you look at the path marked on the map, doesn't it lend plausibility to my client's version of events? Mr. Connors passed by the convention center before proceeding to the location where he was shot, isn't that right?"

"Yes but ..."

"My client didn't need to walk to the center from the vacant lot. He did not need a lift because he was never there. This is the more likely interpretation of this GPS data, is it not?"

"There are many possible stories we can weave to match that map—but yes, your client's story does bear some resemblance to what that map tells us."

"Right, but instead of accepting what pure, unbiased logic dictates, your preferred interpretation is to claim that my client pulled off a double hit that Jason Bourne would be proud of?"

"Objection!"

"Sustained."

"No further questions, Your Honor."

CHAPTER 22

I wouldn't say the room chilled when Francine Holmes entered, but there was no doubting that her presence changed the atmosphere. She walked to the stand with a rod-straight spine and sat wearing an expression of fearless poise. Her dress looked like something out of the fifties, as did the double string of pearls. A large silver brooch—a dove, as far as I could make out—was pinned on one side. Her make-up was applied with the lightest of touches, and not a strand of hair was out of place. Everywhere was Sunday School for this woman, and her ever-present duty was to teach.

I bet Jessica could hardly wait to get started on the establishment details. Francine told the court she'd known Demarco for about a year. She'd met him at the Los Angeles Mission where she worked part-time on a volunteer basis. She highly valued her role there as a spiritual guide. She considered it her calling to help the less fortunate find prosperity of spirit through God. And that salvation only came one way—through deep meditation on the scriptures. In her other role as philanthropist, she was a member of the Halo Group, an organization that sponsored young stars who were good role models. When asked why the Halo Group did this, she said America's youth was being swamped by poor exemplars who had nothing to showcase but greed, lust and avarice. She said this was happening in a parental blind spot—the internet. The world of social media was taking over television as the gateway to the minds of young Americans, but adults seemed oblivious to their responsibilities when it came to policing what their children were exposed to.

Francine couldn't help but look at me when she was saying this. *Jesus, couldn't she take her morality wig off for one second? No doubt about it—I'm a lost cause. Hell's got a bed of nails with my name on it.*

With Francine's impeccable virtue established, Jessica moved on to Demarco.

"Ms. Holmes, what were your impressions of Demarco Torrell when you first met him?"

"He was very troubled, but that was understandable. He was trying to take a better path in life, and that was proving to be extremely difficult."

"How so?"

"Demarco was only sixteen, but he had already been a street hoodlum for almost four years, so he told me."

"Did he open up to you?"

"Well, yes. Eventually. Someone at the mission suggested he meet with me. They thought I could help him find the strength to change his life for the better."

"What did he tell you he wanted to change?"

"It took a while for us to have that kind of conversation. Initially, we would meet for thirty minutes or so. I would talk to him about the importance of living a good life and tell him he was courageous for attempting to break away."

"From his gang?"

"Yes. He had joined a gang intervention group that had helped steer him away from that life."

"And he had left the gang life behind then?"

"I'm not sure, to be honest."

"What makes you unsure?"

"Well, sometimes I would not see him for a week, but then he'd return and be evasive about where he had been. It's my belief he'd been visiting his thug friends in Pomona."

"So you don't think he had left his gang?"

"I don't believe so, no."

"What happened when he came back to you at the shelter?"

"We would start all over again. Each time he seemed to trust me more. And I got to learn more about his life and his dreams."

"And what were those dreams?"

"He wanted to become a Marine, just like his father. That's what he told me."

"And did you encourage him to do that?"

"No, I most certainly did not."

"Why not?"

"Because I have devoted my life to peace. I have no faith in war. This is a deeply personal issue for me, and I have spent a large part of my life trying to repair the damage done by war."

"How so?"

"I have done a lot of development and rebuilding work in Afghanistan, where Americans have been fighting for more than a decade. Our organization tried to build hope from the rubble."

"So you could not support Demarco in joining the armed forces?"

"No, but I suggested he should get his head and heart in the right place before he made such a big decision, and the way to do that was to follow the word of Jesus Christ our Lord and Savior."

"What about when you last saw the defendant—how was he progressing toward his hopes and dreams?"

"He had ceased to progress, I hate to say it. He had regressed. Perhaps worse than ever."

Demarco hissed quietly next to me. "Lying bitch," he muttered. I had to admire his restraint.

"Could you elaborate, please?" said Jessica.

"I feared I was no longer able to get through to him."

"Why not?"

"He was avoiding me at the mission. Then he told me he did not plan to continue our work together."

"What was your reaction when you heard Demarco had been charged with murder?"

Francine paused and looked at Demarco with pity.

"I have to be honest. I felt extremely disappointed. Heartbroken, even. But I cannot say I was surprised. I'd tried my best, but it can be extremely difficult, if not impossible, for leopards to change their spots."

"Did you believe you had lost Demarco to the gang again?"

"Yes."

"Nothing further, Your Honor."

I put a hand on Demarco's shoulder.

"We get a say in this too," I said quietly.

I stood up and looked at Francine, who returned my gaze with quiet expectation. I'd like to say that I proceeded to find a crack in her armor of virtue, but that's not how it went down.

196

"Ms. Holmes, you told the court Demarco no longer wanted to continue the work he was doing with you, is that right?"

"Yes, he made that very clear."

"And do you think he could have broken free from his past and established a productive future for himself without your spiritual guidance?"

"I believe that it would have been almost impossible for him to succeed without deep spiritual conviction."

"Don't you mean your particular flavor of spiritual conviction?"

Francine had not expected me to interrupt her, and my challenge was taken as an insult. Her attempt to hide that fact with a smile failed.

"It is my view that anything less than the most earnest commitment to God would see Demarco fail," she said with forced composure. "And I think I have been proven correct."

"What you think and what you know are two very distinct matters, Ms. Holmes. We are not here to indulge in your speculation."

Francine stiffened, clearly not used to being reprimanded. But my point was made for the jury's sake, not hers.

"What I mean, Mr. Madison, is that it is like an alcoholic trying to dispense with the bottle once and for all. It is no accident that the twelve-step program is in essence a pathway of spiritual commitment—a contract you make with God. When suffering is at its most acute, the helping hand needs the strength of the Almighty if we are to be saved, or to save ourselves."

"You say that, but other social workers were very happy with Demarco's progress, weren't they?"

"I don't know, Mr. Madison. I do not wish to speculate."

"Nice try, Ms. Holmes. But it is not speculation to reveal the nature of discussions you had with fellow volunteers about

Demarco's welfare. And it is my understanding these discussions took place every week, isn't that right?"

"Yes, but I did not involve myself in the relationships he had with other people."

"That's not what I'm asking. Did anyone at the mission express the view that Demarco's progress was encouraging?"

"No, not that I can remember."

"You are under oath, Ms. Holmes."

"I do not need reminding of that, Mr. Madison. I can only repeat that I made no business of Demarco's relationships with others."

"Did you consider yourself to be essential to Demarco's salvation?"

"Yes. I'm not saying it had to be me personally. But I was the only person striving to help him develop his spiritual and moral discipline. Maybe someone else could have played that role, but at that time and place, only I was in the position to guide him to success."

"Ms. Holmes, until recently you were a key donor to the Los Angeles Mission, is that right?"

"Yes, Mr. Madison. It's one of several causes I support."

"And recently you were in discussions to become a board member, yes?"

"That's right."

"Why did those discussions break down?"

"I wouldn't say they broke down. I'd say they resolved in a way that was agreeable to all parties."

"You had attached a number of conditions to your board membership, isn't that right?"

"A few."

"You wanted more say in how religion was to be offered at the mission, didn't you?"

"I believed there was room to change things for the better, and I expressed that belief very clearly."

"But the other board members obviously did not see things your way. And they refused your demands, didn't they?"

"We agreed to disagree."

"But their refusal to bend to your wishes upset you, did it not?"

"It did not bother me in the slightest."

"But immediately following this falling out with the other board members, you stopped funding the mission, didn't you?"

"That was something I'd been considering for some time. I help a lot of charities, as I have said, and I thought it was time to sow my seeds elsewhere."

"Seems to me you were sulking, Ms. Holmes. You couldn't get your way, and so you discarded what up until that moment was something you considered to be a very worthy cause."

"Objection. Counsel is testifying!" called Jessica.

"I did no such thing!" Francine said.

"Sustained," ruled Judge Garner.

"I'm almost done, Your Honor," I said. "Ms. Holmes, do you still work at the mission?"

"No. I have decided I have better things to do with my time."

"Funny you should say that. My client also decided he had better things to do with his time as well. Is he going to hell for turning his back on you, a disciple of God, Ms. Holmes?"

"Objection!" cried Jessica.

"Your Honor, I think it's a fair question that points to a double standard this witness may be applying to my client in a case upon which his life depends."

"Overruled," said Judge Garner. "Ms. Holmes, please answer the question."

"Yes, Mr. Madison. I'm sorry to say that I firmly believe he is going to hell."

I turned back to my table.

"No more questions from me, Your Honor."

I took my seat with mixed feelings. Although I'd taken Francine Holmes down a peg or two, I hadn't made up enough ground on Jessica. Things still looked grim for my client, and everybody knew it. Me, the jury and, of course, Demarco. Before they took him away, he grabbed my forearm.

"I want to take the stand," he seethed.

"Demarco, I understand you feel that way, but I'm telling you it would be a mistake. We need to stick to the plan."

"And that is?"

"You know what the plan is. We make it all about the prosecution's case. They have to prove their case beyond reasonable doubt. And my job is to make it clear as day that they have fallen short of that standard."

"It looks like I'm screwed."

"You're not screwed, Demarco. But if I put you on the stand, it will only take one microscopic bad impression for the jury to turn on you for good. If the prosecutor gets a rise out of you, if your frustrations get the better of you, if you just get so fed up with people assuming you're bad that you decide to show them just how fucking bad you can be, then your case is lost. There'd be no coming back."

"But if I'm going down, I want to have my say. Just sitting here is killing me. Listening to that bitch lie about me like that. How can she do that? No more just sitting here and taking it, man. I want them to hear me out."

"Taking the stand and having your say is not the same thing. Remember our mock trials? You know where it will go if I expose you to the prosecution."

As part of our preparation, I'd already taken Demarco through a mock cross-examination. Within three questions, he'd been pinned, having to defend himself against his prior deeds, that phone call, his gang connections. And he hadn't reacted well. His emotions were so raw.

Demarco stared at me, his reservations still intact.

"Demarco, we need to keep the jury sympathetic towards you. Without that sympathy they won't want to stand up for you, they won't want to protect you, because they will no longer care about you. I hate to say it, Demarco, and it sounds so wrong, but this trial is not about you, it's all about the jury."

"It's hard. It's like you're telling me to go down without a fight."

"I'm fighting for you."

"But you ain't winning and you know it."

"I'm not losing either. Hang in there, Demarco."

✳✳✳

"Madison!" Someone shouted out from behind as I left the court. "Hey, Madison! Wait up!"

I didn't want to wait up for anyone. I was heading straight back to the office with a mountain of work to do. Tomorrow I'd be calling my first defense witness, and I needed to make sure I was on top of my game. Just about every second of the day I was telling myself, "This is Tank's kid, his only son, and if you don't save him, he's dead." Not exactly desk quote material, but it sure as hell kept my motivation throttle up.

I turned around and groaned at the sight of Dino Cassinelli. He'd moved twenty yards or so at a hurried pace, but it was enough to leave him gasping for air. As he faced me, I detected a slight heaviness in his eyelids. He looked drunk.

"What do you want, Cassinelli?"

"What the hell are you doing, Madison? Did you bother to follow any of my leads at all?"

"Your leads? What are you talking about? I went through the files you gave me. My investigator checked out those two deaths, and guess what? There was jack shit to suggest they're connected— to each other or to this case. Nothing."

"Then you need to get a new investigator."

"And you need to get a new ear to bend. I don't have time to indulge in the ravings of a..."

"You think this is some batshit crazy fantasy of mine? Is that what you think?"

"Cassinelli, I'm busy. I've got a man's life to defend. What do you want? Make it quick."

"The Puerto Escondido case. Kyle Chambers. The kid who died in the fire. Did your guy look into that?"

"Yes, he did. It was exactly as it seemed. Arson and manslaughter. The perp got twenty years."

"Go deeper."

"Why don't *you* go deeper and bring me something other than X-Files BS. You do understand I'm defending a man on two murder charges, don't you? If you were going to be of any use to me, I needed your help weeks ago."

Cassinelli bowed his head and suddenly stumbled to his right. I grabbed his shoulder.

"Are you drunk?"

Cassinelli kept his eyes lowered. "Course not."

"I can't believe it. You're loaded."

"Doesn't change the fact that I know I'm right. This ain't about your boy. It's about something bigger, something messed up."

I bent my head in towards him and lowered my voice, keeping the tone calm and considerate.

"Cassinelli, you need to give me something I can use. Otherwise you're just in the way. You understand?"

His face was knotted with indignation. He dug into his pocket and pulled out a crumpled piece of paper.

"This is the one guy I know down there that speaks English," he said, unraveling the paper. "I've been trying to find someone to trust, so it's taken a while."

"And?"

"And he's telling me what I'm telling you. Gunshots were heard before the fire. Two. The family next door told the cops that's what they heard, but the cops ignored it. The family's statement is gone. All that's left are statements about the fire and a confession from the perp."

"But if the perp shot the guy, why didn't he confess to that? Why just confess to arson?"

"He never knew about the shots. The family said they heard them about an hour before the fire."

"So?"

"That means someone else killed Chambers."

"And?"

Cassinelli suddenly looked almost sober.

"And the killer pinned the murder on this guy—a bum off the streets. And no one doubted this bum was guilty of any charge the cops threw at him. Sound familiar?"

***

As I walked to my office, I called Jack.

"Yo," he answered. "What's up?"

"I need you to go to Mexico."

"What, now?"

"Yes, now. Why, you busy?"

"Well, if you call heading up to the Napa Valley with a hot Swedish girl for a couple of days busy, then yeah. I'm flat out."

"Are you on your way there now?"

"No. I'm going to get Elsa then head to Santa Monica airport to pick up a whirlybird a client's kindly lent me."

Apart from everything else he had going for him, Jack had gotten his pilot's license while in college. And through his work, he seemed to have acquired several wealthy friends who were only too happy to let him borrow their helicopters every now and then.

"I hate to ask, but is there any chance you could push your date back a couple of days?"

Jack sighed.

"Jesus, Madison. I won't have access to this chopper in a couple of days."

"Hire one and send me the bill."

"Forget it. What's in Mexico, anyway? Don't tell me—chasing up more bullshit from that Cassinelli clown?"

"We need to know more than we do, Jack. That's the truth," I said. "Can you go check it out?"

"No sweat. I'll head to LAX now. Then I'll call Elsa and get to hear every Swedish word for 'asshole.'"

When I hung up, I saw I'd received another message from a blocked number.

"YOU'RE GOING TO LEARN WHAT REAL JUSTICE IS. I'M GOING TO TEACH YOU."

Jesus, these morons were tedious. Copping crap from vigilante trolls was one downside of my job I particularly disliked. By operating in the court of the people, I was subject to the court of public opinion. And I'm not talking reasonable public discourse—in the media I got an equal mix of backers and critics. And even then there was a byline attached, so I knew who was taking swings at me. But these anonymous, threatening texts were somehow more personal, and sinister. They were such utter cowards. Just once, I thought, I'd like one of these gutless grubs to come out of his stinking hole and address me face to face.

Oh yeah, that would very much make my day, punk.

CHAPTER 23

Now it was my turn. I had to lodge an immovable object in the mental path leading every juror to conclude Demarco was guilty. The first such obstacle was the giant of a man named Warren Anderson. And on his heels would be Elroy Franks and Loretta Valentine—two other witnesses Warren had found for me who agreed to testify that they'd seen Demarco having an amicable conversation with Toby Connors outside the shelter before walking off together. Both would be saying it was Connors who approached Demarco, corroborating Demarco's story and dispelling the notion that Demarco had vengefully hunted Connors down.

Warren walked to the stand like he walked the streets of Skid Row: nothing to fear, nothing to hide, and plenty of good will to share. He oozed integrity and strength of character. I was sure that when the jury heard what he had to say, they'd see Demarco Torrell in a compelling new light.

"Mr. Anderson," I began. "You know my client Demarco Torrell. Please tell the court how you two came to meet."

Although he had the build of a weight-lifter, Warren's body was perfectly relaxed. No macho posturing.

"Sure. I work with a gang intervention group called Exodus. We help kids escape street gangs before they stay long enough to ruin their lives. On top of that, I do some volunteer work down at the homeless shelter, the Los Angeles Mission. I developed a relationship with Demarco through both."

"What's your role at the shelter?"

"I act as a mentor and counselor to the men and women who turn up. They've all got nothing but they all need something, be it a meal, accommodation, clothing, addressing their drug issues, proper medical care, finding work, that sort of thing. It's a long list."

"So they come to the mission and you try and help them out as best you can?"

"That's about it, yes."

"And you don't get paid for this work?"

"No, it's on the house." Warren broke into a modest smile, almost imperceptible. I was glad his eyes stayed locked on me and he hadn't turned to the jury with that smile—it could have hit the wrong note. As it was, the jury seemed to be lapping Warren Anderson up. I didn't have to turn my head to know they were drawn to him.

"And Demarco was one of those people who just walked in the door and you decided to help?"

"Yes."

"When did he arrive at the Los Angeles Mission?"

"It was January 12, 2016. A Tuesday. About two-thirty in the afternoon."

"Why do you remember this so distinctly?"

"We'd met before when he'd come to Exodus and joined in a few activities. But when he walked through the mission door, I knew he was desperate. He was one fall away from being lost to the streets for good. There was something about Demarco that reminded me of myself."

"How so?"

"He was in deep trouble but still searching for a way out. A good way out. I was in a similar predicament when I was his age—deep in a life I wanted out of. I know firsthand how tough it is to transition from the street to what we all call a normal, productive life. It might not sound like much of an achievement, but to me it's the arc of an astronaut. So I went up to Demarco and asked what he was doing at the mission. He said what everyone says at first— he was hungry. After that he was hoping to find a bed off the streets."

"You got to know Demarco very well, didn't you?"

"Yes. That day we had a basic conversation and he got something to put in that empty belly of his, but I offered my help. I offered him an ear. I told him things about myself that he didn't already know, and that helped him see I was someone who understood him, that I was someone he could trust."

Jessica was on her feet.

"This is all very warm and fuzzy, Your Honor," she said, "but is there any chance the court can hear some specific information relating to the double murder we're here to rule on?"

This was a weak objection to make—Jessica was merely trying to trigger a sense of skepticism in the jury's collective mind.

"Overruled." Of course it was.

"If the prosecutor doesn't mind," I said, "I'd like to continue establishing the witness's credentials in speaking to the defendant's character and state of mind. Mr. Anderson, please tell the court why Demarco felt like he could trust you?"

"I was once a gang leader. Where exactly in LA is not important. I got put away in juvie for assault, for robbery, for drugs—I did all

208

the right things to build the wrong future. But I got out. So I knew how hard life was for Demarco and how hard it was going to be."

"What was so hard?"

"Leaving a gang is not easy. Intervention groups like ours do their best, but without enough family and community support, those kids don't get traction on new ways to live. More often than not they are alone, and to fight their way up from the very bottom of society is just too much."

"Why did Demarco want to abandon gang life?"

"He'd been locked up in juvie twice. He'd seen some bad stuff on the streets and he saw where he was headed. But for him to decide to leave was a huge call. In juvie, he'd paraded his tattoos with pride. He got into fights with rival gang members. And when he got back home to the gang, he had more cred."

"The gang was his family?"

"More than that. It's about identity and self-worth. For kids like Demarco, the gang is the only place where they are embraced by a community. They build up their self-esteem through the eyes of the gang. Their measure as young men is shaped through the eyes of the gang. It's a hard rite of passage, but for a scared young kid getting mugged to and from school, it can become a clear path to follow—one that offers safety, power and pride."

"But also a pathway to prison."

"Exactly. It took me two years to make a clean break from my gang. Demarco was six months into his journey when he came to the shelter, and he was doing it pretty much all by himself."

"Is that unusual?"

"Not so much in that he was doing it alone, but he had the rare determination to stick it out, even if it meant ending up on Skid Row fighting for a tent, fighting off people trying to steal the shoes off your feet, fighting to stay off drugs when some crackhead blows meth smoke in your face just because he knows you're trying to get clean."

"How many people escape this cycle?"

"Hardly anyone. If you end up on Skid Row and do not find a way out within three days, you'll spend the rest of your life there. That's the way I see it, based on my own firsthand experience."

"What happened to Demarco once you'd established a relationship with him?"

"He was pretty much moving forward, forming new ideas of what his life might become. He was enjoying his chats with Francine and getting the kind of spiritual strength he needed. It's such a huge leap to make, you basically can't do it without committing yourself to a higher power. That provides a source of encouragement, guidance and love. And he was tracking pretty well. I'd helped him find accommodations, and he was about to start a job."

"What was the job?"

"Washing dishes in a diner over on Grand Avenue."

"It sounds like he was making progress. Francine, Ms. Holmes, told the court that Demarco had turned his back on his faith. Is that what happened?"

"No. He just outgrew her approach, I think. I mean, she can be Old-Testament tough, and I guess I was kind of someone who advocated a gentler, if no less committed, approach to finding his true self-esteem, as opposed to the false version built by gang machismo."

"Mr. Anderson, did you see Demarco on the day of the murders?"

"Yes, I did."

"Where?"

"At the shelter. We chatted for about ten minutes."

"Did you notice anything unusual about Demarco's demeanor that day?"

"No, he seemed fine, just the same. He was asking me about education, about how to go about getting his high school diploma."

"Realistically, this goal was out of his reach, wasn't it?"

"I've seen many people come into the shelter off Skid Row and wander straight back into it to spend the rest of their lives there. Skid Row's as hard to escape from as a gang is—even harder. But Demarco was smart. He had been doing a lot of reading in juvie. He was self-educating. Do you realize how rare that is? Anyway, to me, he had the will, the brains and the outlook to make something of his life."

"Can you imagine him walking out of the mission that day and killing two people he had never met?"

"That is the last thing I would have expected him to do. Fall down and return to the gang? A long shot. Descend into drug addiction? Maybe. It's happened to stronger wills than his. But to go and kill two people? That's just crazy. He had a point to prove to himself."

"What was that?"

"I think deep down he just wanted to be a young man his father would be proud of."

"Thank you, Mr. Anderson. Nothing further."

I allowed myself a glance at the jury and was pleased to see that, as a whole, they were deep in thought. I just had to keep giving them something to think about.

Jessica was watching them too. And she got to her feet with a will to put an end to this Warren Anderson love-fest once and for all.

"Mr. Anderson, you say the defendant was determined to make a different future for himself, right?"

"Yes, that's right."

"Did he have any money?"

"No. But he was about to start a job, like I said."

"Had he enrolled in any class, any form of education whatsoever?"

"No."

"You said trying to extricate yourself from a gang is most likely going to end in failure, right?"

"Yes."

"And you say getting out of Skid Row is even harder, right?"

"Yes, the challenges are different, but I believe it's a true statement."

"So Demarco Torrell is some kind of superman, is he? By your reckoning, he was facing double near-impossible odds to fix his life, wasn't he?"

"That doesn't mean it can't be done."

"But realistically, the overwhelming odds were that he would have gone back to what he knew—a life of crime."

"That doesn't mean those odds can't be beat."

"And Demarco Torrell was that extraordinary?"

"I think he was exceptional, yes."

"Well, the facts are that he was with two men that day who are now dead, and he was found with five hundred dollars in his pocket."

"I know that."

"Where did this money come from?"

"I have no idea."

"That's a lot of money for someone like the defendant, wouldn't you say?"

"Yes."

"A defendant who is well versed in the art of robbery, assault, theft and intimidation, a defendant who faces Everest-sized odds of living a crime-free, drug-free, gang-free life, walks out of a Skid Row mission without a dime in his pocket. Yet an hour later, he has five hundred dollars in his possession. Wouldn't the most logical deduction be that Demarco Torrell just accepted that going straight was way too hard?"

"I can see why you might think that, but I had a lot of faith in Demarco."

"But during the time you knew him, the defendant did relapse, didn't he? He returned to his gang, didn't he?"

"Those visits were very brief—just a few days."

"But the truth is the defendant walked out on you and went straight to the Sintown Crips. Isn't that a reflection of where his loyalties lie?"

"No, it's not like that at all. Demarco still had a lot of respect within the gang."

"And yet as the court has heard, the defendant boasted about the murders and talked up his gang pride."

"That was foolish of him, but it was purely for self-protection."

"The purpose of the defendant's visits to the gang was to seek readmission, wasn't it?"

"That's not what he told me."

"But he could tell you anything, couldn't he? He could tell you anything he thought you wanted to hear. And might a condition have been placed on the defendant that to re-enter the gang, he'd have to perform a high-risk criminal task to demonstrate his loyalty?"

"That is a far-fetched theory."

"But it's not uncommon. You must know that you don't just walk back into a gang and resume your place as a trusted member—you have to pay a cover charge, so to speak. That's how it works, isn't it?"

"No, not always. But even if it was true, there's no gang I know of that will send you on a suicide mission to prove your loyalty."

"We don't know for sure, do we? But what we do know is that after this meeting between the defendant and the Sintown Crips, two people who deeply offended the gang, two people who received death threats for insulting them were murdered. And the defendant just happened to be with both of them shortly before they died. The pride of the gang was restored with their deaths. And then we hear the defendant boasting about how he had defended his gang's honor."

"Demarco had no reason to throw his life away."

"Maybe that's not how he saw it—maybe he came to realize that loyalty to the gang was all he had, was all that mattered. Maybe he thought he was going to get away with it."

"Objection!" I yelled. "Counsel is testifying."

"Sustained," said Judge Garner.

"He's not like that," said Warren. "As I said ..."

"No further questions, Your Honor."

I know I can't read minds, but sometimes expressions speak a thousand words. And what I saw in various members of the jury was a light-bulb moment, one that told me they felt they'd reached a decision with which their conscience was comfortable. And that decision was bad for Demarco. If they retired to consider the verdict right then and there, I had no doubt they'd have returned within thirty minutes to find Demarco guilty. Jessica knew it too. Her pretty face radiated with a self-satisfied grin.

But she had not won yet. I wasn't done.

Court broke for the weekend. I had a brief chat with Demarco and told him to keep his chin up. Then I left the building.

Monday would be a triumph, I was sure of it. At least, I could counter the image Jessica had just left the jury with. I'd have two witnesses from Skid Row who'd testify that they saw Demarco and Toby talking in a very cordial manner.

On my way to the car, my phone rang. It was Jack. News from Mexico already? He did move fast.

But whatever optimism had propped me up was about to be knocked out from under me.

CHAPTER 24

"Jack, what's up?"

"I'm in a shithole town and we are shit out of luck."

"Talk to me. Where are you exactly?"

"I'm in sunny Oaxaca. The guy who got done for the Kyle Chambers murder is in the local slammer, a.k.a. Pochutla Prison."

"Right, you got a name?"

"Oscar Sanchez, and up until the day he was nabbed for killing Chambers, he was just a local wino."

"Have you spoken to him? What's his story?"

"Hear me out. After I got down here and picked up my translator, I paid a visit to the cops, because the case was processed and tried in Oaxaca. Then we headed straight to the prison. And the guard we spoke to, a young guy, told me no one's allowed to talk to Oscar Sanchez."

"What? They deny visits to prisoners?"

"No. Only to Oscar."

"Why's that?"

"Special orders, it seems. But my translator took up the fight. He asked how much cash I had and then threw the guard enough pesos to get five minutes with Sanchez. We were told to come back at one when most of the other guards would be taking their siesta. Said he could get us within shouting distance. That was the best he could do."

"Not the ideal way to conduct an interview, but I'll take it."

"There was no interview."

"How come?"

"When we got back to the prison Sanchez was on his way out."

"On his way out? He was released?"

"Yeah. On a stretcher. Someone shivved him right in the heart."

"He's dead?"

"I'm afraid so."

"You think it was to keep him from speaking to you?"

"I'm sure of it."

"What about the young guard? Did he tell you what happened?"

"He's wasn't there. Another guard, who was older and very unfriendly, said he'd gone home."

"Gone home or sent packing?"

"I asked when the young guard would be back and the new guy gave me this evil smile and said, 'Maybe never.' Then he told us we had to leave or else some terrible misfortune would befall us."

There was silence for a few seconds while I processed Jack's news.

"Okay, let's go with the serial killer theory for a minute. How would he know we're looking into this murder?"

"Maybe he left a bunch of cash and some standing orders—like, if anyone from the US comes wanting to have a chat with Oscar Sanchez, get rid of him."

"You think?"

"The cops were just as hostile as the old guard. They told me not to go to the prison. They said it was not wise for a gringo to come into town asking the wrong kind of questions."

"So what's next?"

"I'm at the airport. My flight's in an hour."

"Okay, thanks Jack. Talk to you later."

I hung up the phone and put it in my pocket. It rang immediately. It was Warren.

"Warren, what's up?"

"Bad news, I'm afraid, Brad."

"What happened?"

"Elroy Franks is dead," he said. "He was shot in his tent last night."

Warren's voice labored under the weight of sadness. He'd told me Elroy and Loretta had only agreed to come forward because they felt indebted to Warren for all the help he'd given them.

"Jesus. I'm so sorry, Warren. Why did this happen? Do you have any details?"

"No. To me it looks like he died precisely because of what he was going to do for us on Monday."

"Are you sure?"

"No one saw a damn thing. But Elroy had no quarrel with anyone. He had nothing to steal, and there was nothing anyone had to gain from his death. The fact that someone wanted to keep him silent is the only thing that makes sense to me."

218

"What about Loretta?"

"She's gone. Running for the hills and we won't ever find her."

We were screwed. Another innocent victim terminated. And this on top of Oscar Sanchez's death. Dino Cassinelli's theory was quickly becoming the most plausible explanation of so many events. But for me, his serial killer story came in at a distant second to my main crisis—all of a sudden, my defense of Demarco Torrell was dropping down an elevator shaft.

"Warren, my case is screwed without these witnesses."

"I'm sorry, Brad, but Elroy's death must have put the fear of God into Loretta."

"When did you last speak with her?"

"A couple of days back. I told her I was testifying, and she was still eager to help."

"Did she say anything else about what she saw that day?"

"Funny you should say that, because she told me something had popped into her head that she hadn't mentioned before."

"What was that?"

"She said that just before Demarco and Toby Connors met, she saw Toby standing on Wall Street just round the corner from the shelter's entrance. She said he was talking to some guy in a black car."

"What kind of car?"

"A shiny new black Lincoln."

"What else did she say?"

"She said Toby was talking to a bald man in the back seat. She thought he was in his sixties, but she couldn't be sure. But she said this man's face was all sunken in—skull-face, she called him."

"Damn. And she's definitely flown the coop?"

"She could be anywhere, Brad. She was initially from Frisco, still has a daughter there, but that doesn't mean she headed home. She could be halfway to Kansas for all I know."

"Warren, this has just about knocked the legs out from under my case."

"I understand that and I'm sorry."

"Not your fault. You've done so much for me. Thank you. And I'm truly sorry about Elroy."

After I hung up, I walked half-dazed back to the office. I didn't even hear what Megan said to me as I made my way to my desk. I was going to lose this case. Demarco Torrell was going to prison—sitting on death row wondering when those Mexican gangsters would come for him. The only things I had left were one last witness and a closing argument.

Could that last witness be enough to scrape our case over the line? I sure hoped so. It was ballistics expert Dick Sanders. And by the time I was done with him, every jury member would have good reason to doubt Demarco's guilt.

CHAPTER 25

I had to walk behind the plaintiff's table to get to the lectern. I copped a lungful of Jessica's perfume as I passed. It was almost a tactical weapon. There was barely a man on the planet she could not distract from his purpose. But that could have just been me interpreting everything she did as a ploy. She kept her head down, busying herself with paperwork. There was a hint of a smile. She was nothing if not cocky. I knew already she didn't think my firearms expert could sway the jury my way. But maybe her smugness wasn't just a front. Could I somehow be playing into her hands even as I felt poised to deliver the telling blow? That was exactly what she wanted—for me to doubt myself.

I snapped out of it. I couldn't let her mind games get the better of me.

I stood at the lectern directly opposite my expert witness on the stand. Dick Sanders was someone you would not look twice at on the street. Average height, average build. But he looked fit—the kind of guy who puts in a five-mile run every morning before shaving, donning a freshly ironed shirt and a well-cut suit, kissing his wife on the cheek, and patting the dog on his way out the door.

He'd impressed me as a guy who might never wow you, but who could nonetheless engender trust in anyone who gave him the time of day to talk. And that was why he was here. To talk about his profession—ballistics. Oh, and there was also the fact that he'd written a few papers pouring cold water on the idea that ballistics experts could match spent bullets to a particular gun with a high degree of accuracy.

I cast a glance at the jury and almost regretted it. Doing that could sometimes come across as needy. But there was no question I had their attention. Most were looking at me with pens and pads poised. Remarkably, they all seemed as fresh as the first day. And I got a familiar sense of why I love being a trial lawyer. Yes, it had taken a lot of training and preparation to get here. But there was always the sense that the job was a high-wire act—one loaded with the prospect of success or failure. I felt the adrenaline charge my body and sharpen my mind.

I used the first ten or so questions to establish Sanders' cred. Ten years in law enforcement, five years with the FBI, and another five with a private consultancy firm he'd established with a partner. His was a small business, but it meant he didn't have to travel as much as he had in the FBI and got to spend more time with his growing family. Over his career he'd gone from lab technician to highly respected ballistics expert—a reputation that kept him in demand, particularly as an expert witness in trials such as this.

"Mr. Sanders, have you studied the police ballistics report asserting the same gun was used in both murders?"

"I have."

"Would you have reached the same conclusion as they did?"

"I would not be so confident in saying it was the same weapon."

"Why is that?"

"Well, I would be reluctant to draw the same conclusion as their GRC data."

222

"GRC data? What is that?"

"Gun rifling characteristics data. You see, each firearm has what's called rifling, or grooves etched into the inside of the barrel to get the bullet to spin. They improve the bullet's aerodynamics in flight and hence improve its accuracy. Those rifling marks end up cutting distinctive grooves—or striations—on the bullet as it passes through the barrel."

"In essence, it's like a fingerprint?"

"Yes, but I hesitate to use that analogy, because it is not always possible to be that precise."

"How so?"

"Well, weapons like the Glock are all rifled the same way, and the striations are not as distinctive as some people, particularly those who make TV shows, would have us believe."

"Is this an accurate way to tell if the same weapon was used or not?"

"I would say it is a guide at best. It would be safer to say a similar weapon was used rather than the exact same weapon. And the job of matching is made harder by the fact that the bullet can be damaged by the objects it comes into contact with after it has been fired—like human bone or other materials it ricochets off."

"Did the bullets examined in the murder cases of Luke Jameson and Toby Connors have other extraneous markings not acquired from the rifling of the barrel?"

"Yes, that is why I would be more cautious in attributing both murders to the same weapon."

"Mr. Sanders, do you know how many Glocks there are in circulation in the United States?"

"It's hard to say exactly, but from my experience there are probably hundreds of thousands of Glocks in circulation in this country."

"That would be both black market and legal?"

"Yes."

"And how many would be in circulation in California?"

"Tens of thousands, I'd say."

"And in Los Angeles, where the bulk of the state's armed criminal activity is conducted?"

"You'd be talking thousands."

"You're sure about that?"

"If all the Glocks in circulation were legal, getting your hands on one would be as easy as getting an Uber."

I turned towards the jury, ensuring I wore an expression of serious thought.

"So how did the police tie the same weapon to these two murders?"

"They entered the information they had into the GRC database—it's all LAPD data—then they tested the weapon and found the striations were the same."

"They narrowed it down?"

"Yes, by noting how close the striations are together, they can determine how tight the rifling was on the firearm. And they can tell if the bullet came from a weapon whose rifling twisted left rather than right."

"So it's a process of elimination?"

"That's right."

"And although the markings on the bullets in these two murders were similar, you'd hesitate to say they were fired from the same weapon?"

"Yes."

"Why?"

"Because the data does not prove the bullets came from a Glock, let alone the same Glock."

I heard the jury to my right breathe in sharply in unison. This was good.

"Mr. Sanders, are you saying it is possible the bullets may have come from two different weapons?"

"Yes, it's even possible a firearm other than a Glock could have fired the bullets in the Connors killing."

"So different makes and models of guns can leave similar markings on a bullet?"

"That's right."

"But what about the marks left by the firing pin on the casings?"

"Well, the LAPD ballistics team naturally tested those to confirm that the shells they'd found were fired by the gun recovered at the Anaheim Convention Center."

"What about the shells found at the Connors murder scene?"

"There were no casings recovered at the scene of Toby Connors' murder."

"Right, so the LAPD's claim that the same gun was used in both murders is based mostly on the markings left on the bullets."

"Yes, that's right."

"But you do not share their certainty?"

"No. As far as matching the murder weapon goes, the LAPD's ballistics testing puts both killings in the same ballpark, but not on the home plate."

"I see. Now Mr. Sanders. Another piece of evidence being used against my client is the fact that gunpowder residue was found on his right hand. The prosecution has argued this is evidence he fired the weapon."

"Yes, I know."

"But my question is this: if I have my right hand out in front of me and someone fires a gun in close proximity to my hand, would you expect to find gunpowder residue on my hand?"

"The short answer is yes. Gunshot residue particles escape a fired weapon at high velocity and travel in many directions because they exit the weapon from every opening. So if you had an exposed hand in the vicinity I would be surprised if gunpowder residue was not detected on it. It would also be found on your clothes and your face."

"And if there were other people in close proximity to the fired weapon, would gunpowder residue have been found on them too?"

"If they were standing within a few feet, they'd almost certainly have gunpowder residue on them."

"Demarco Torrell was the only person tested for gunpowder residue following the Luke Jameson murder. Does this prove he shot Mr. Jameson?"

"Absolutely not."

"Nothing further, Your Honor."

As I walked behind Jessica and back to my desk, she almost ran into me in her haste to get to her feet.

"I have some questions, Your Honor. If I may."

Jessica placed some documents on the podium, shifted them to her liking, then gripped the edges lightly on either side and took a breath. She was projecting a slight regret at it being her task to cast dispersions on my expert witness. A shot of dread ran through me. That feeling I'd had just before I questioned Sanders had been right. She did have something up her sleeve. But she was not about to carry out a swift demolition, she was going to string it out a little.

"Mr. Sanders, I am intrigued that you have such a divergent opinion from the official ballistics findings. But I guess I am not surprised. You mentioned, or at least Mr. Madison mentioned—I can't recall—when your distinguished career was detailed for the benefit of the jury that you used to work for the very same ballistics unit whose report you are now discrediting. The LAPD's Firearm Analysis Unit."

"Yes, that is correct."

"And you worked in that unit for three years before moving on to the FBI. Is that correct?"

"Yes."

Sanders did not seem at all bothered by this line of questioning.

"And before you left you were one of several forensic scientists working in the Firearm Analysis Unit. That's true, is it not?"

"Yes, it is."

"What was the official reason you left this position?"

"I beg your pardon, ma'am?"

"Was I not clear? Sorry, I shall ask you more directly: why did you leave the Firearm Analysis Unit?"

"I was keen to work for the FBI. They were hiring, and I wanted to work in their cutting-edge labs."

"I see. Now, Mr. Sanders, can you please take a look at the ballistics report made by the Firearm Analysis Unit for the Luke Jameson case."

"Okay."

Jessica handed Sanders a document.

"Could you please read to the court the name of the person who signed that report on behalf of the team."

"Yes, certainly." Sanders was suddenly looking uneasy. I could see his breathing had gotten shallow. What did Jessica have on him? I'd been through Sanders' employment record. Jack had vetted him, quizzed his LAPD contacts about him, and nothing had come up. Nothing but a minor disagreement, a misunderstanding with a female colleague.

Sanders cleared his throat.

"Melanie Crofts," he said.

Jessica nodded her head. Suddenly, I knew I was done. I could see her tilt her head slightly in my direction. She knew I was hanging off her every word. The entire courtroom was. I was now kicking myself for putting Sanders up there, even before I knew what Jessica planned to expose.

"Yes. Melanie Crofts. Now, Mr. Sanders I find it very interesting that you should seek to, how shall I put it, challenge the weight of Ms. Crofts' findings. Because this is not the only time you have contested her findings. In fact, I have three papers here written by you on the subject of ballistics. And in all three you single out the work of Ms. Crofts as being faulty, misleading and in some cases even speculative."

"That was nothing personal. It was just—"

"Nothing personal?"

"Objection. Your Honor, this is supposed to be a cross-examination. The counselor should be directing questions to Mr. Sanders about this case and I've yet to hear her ask one."

"Sustained. Counselor, please get to it."

"Certainly, Your Honor. Mr. Sanders, you left the Firearm Analysis Unit under some controversy. Your departure followed a series of incidents in which you acted inappropriately towards Ms. Crofts. Isn't that right?"

Sanders was looking extremely uncomfortable now. He knew where this was going. I, however, was still in the dark. I could only hope it didn't destroy his credibility outright.

"That's not right, actually. I left of my own accord."

228

"Yes. That is the official version. You tendered your resignation and it was accepted."

"That's right. It has nothing to do whatsoever with—"

"But the court should know that Ms. Crofts had made a series of complaints against you. One stated you were making unwanted advances, another cited verbal abuse and another complained you exposed yourself to her. Now these were all suppressed because Ms. Crofts did not wish to destroy your career. And so your superiors sent you on your way with a glowing reference, didn't they?"

Sanders' head was lowered in shame.

"Mr. Sanders?"

"Yes, that's right."

This was a disaster. For a second I fumed at Jack, wondering how on earth he'd missed this. But then I figured the DA probably warned the LAPD brass that we'd come looking into Sanders and wanted to make damn sure Jack's contacts closed ranks on him.

"And shortly after you left, Ms. Crofts was promoted to team leader, an advertised position that you had unsuccessfully applied for. Is that right?"

Sanders just nodded.

"Please answer the question, Mr. Sanders."

"Yes, that's right."

"And following that, you sent her an abusive text message."

"I was drunk at the time. It doesn't mean that I—"

"And yet you claim you have no axe to grind with Ms. Crofts and her team's findings?"

"Yes. Yes, that's true. This in no way means I am questioning her work just for the sake of it."

"I'm not sure how you can expect us to believe that, Mr. Sanders. You made unwanted sexual advances toward this woman. You tried to intimidate her, and you abused her when she got the job you wanted. I find it hard to believe you were or have since remained impartial to Ms. Crofts and her work. In fact, I would say you bear a severe grudge towards her."

"That's not true."

"Let's address your findings, shall we?"

Her hatchet job was done. Now, having destroyed his character, she was set to destroy the value of his testimony. It was a clinical demolition job.

"Mr. Sanders, I'll make this brief. But let's compare the findings of Ms. Crofts and her team with your review. From the LAPD's standpoint, we have a killer who was caught with a Glock handgun that was used to murder Mr. Luke Jameson at the Anaheim Convention Center. And, just a few blocks away, the man who gave the defendant a ride to the venue was found dead in his car, having been shot by, the LAPD contests, the same handgun. Two murders that were most likely committed within about an hour of each other. The LAPD's ballistics tests show us it was the same handgun and most likely the same killer.

"Whereas you argue that this is all but a coincidence, that the LAPD team's ballistics work is flawed. You say that while it could have been the same weapon, we should not conclude that it was the same weapon, even given the similar striations on the bullets, and even given the defendant was, in all likelihood, the last person to see these two dead men alive. Instead of the LAPD's fine forensic work leading us to a killer, you say it does no such thing. Ms. Crofts is a highly respected forensic scientist, as I'm sure you know. Are you sure you are not letting personal grievances cloud your vision, Mr. Sanders?"

Sanders raised his head. No matter what came out of his mouth, there was no way he could overcome the damning impression Jessica had created of him. He was a wreck.

"I reject that wholeheartedly," he said unconvincingly. And not one person on that jury believed him.

"I thought you would say that. Nothing further, Your Honor."

Judge Garner looked at Sanders pitifully.

"Thank you, sir. You may step down."

I sat there for a few moments. Demarco was sitting silently beside me, waiting for me to do or say something to turn it around. But I had no cards left to play. I stood and addressed Judge Garner.

"The defense rests, Your Honor."

I sat down again, turned to Demarco and tried to offer him some encouragement before they took him away. I gathered up my documents and left.

I only had one last thing to offer—my closing argument.

CHAPTER 26

Jessica Pope came dressed for her closing argument in a dark, let's-get-down-to-brass-tacks pant suit. Her hair was pinned up, her earrings plain and modest, and her expression dour. She wasn't going to let anything soften her kick-ass delivery. Beholding Jessica Pope in this frame of mind was like admiring a caged tiger or a stalking wolf—you were content to be in awe from a safe distance. That's how everyone regarded her at the moment, from judge and jury to the trial-weary press corps: everyone was all ears.

"Ladies and gentlemen of the jury," Jessica began. "I want to thank you for the time, thought and effort you have put into this trial. I know how grueling a juror's experience can be, and I know how heavily the weight of justice lays on your minds when it comes to reaching a verdict, even in the most one-sided of cases. But if you wish to carry out your duty to this court, to this country, to the very name of justice, you must find the defendant guilty of first-degree murder on both counts."

Jessica took one step closer to the jury and rested her left hand on the lectern, as though it was the comforting touch on the shoulder of a grieving friend. It conveyed Jessica's capacity for empathy without her saying a word.

"Remember, this trial is about salvaging justice from the ruins of tragedy. It's about giving two grieving families something positive to carry forward into the future, even as they struggle to cope with heartache borne of the past. They need to know that their community will help bring to justice the person responsible for killing their loved ones in cold blood. They need to know that this murderer will be held accountable for his horrendous deeds and be punished with the clear and full might of the law.

"For let's not muddy the waters, as the defense has sought to do. This is a clear case of preconceived murder. The defendant set out with cold and cruel intentions to kill two men that day. And he did so with the unfeeling purpose of an assassin. And that, members of the jury, is how we should see him—as a cold-blooded assassin.

"We know that the defendant was with both victims in the last moments of their lives. We know that he had a reason to kill them both, and we know that the same weapon was used to carry out both murders—again, something the defense's attorney has sought and failed to create confusion over. The defendant was present at the second killing, and his DNA was found at the first. And when piecing together the facts, only one narrative stands up. Only one narrative rings true. Only one narrative provides us with a full understanding of what happened that terrible day.

"This man, the defendant, is a member of one of Los Angeles' most notorious gangs. By all accounts, he did have a change of heart and tried to leave but failed and sought to return to the fold. We know that there is a strong link between the two young men who were brutally slaughtered and the gang to which the defendant belongs. Both had dared to offend a criminal gang member and both ended up paying for their indiscretions with their lives.

"If you think murder is an overreaction to insult, you do not know gang culture like I know it. Rival gang members have been cut down merely for wearing the wrong color, for simply looking at someone the wrong way. To use a cliché, it's a jungle out there. And the defendant brought the lawlessness of that jungle to the Anaheim Convention Center and wreaked terrible havoc.

"While teenage girls and boys turned up to see their YouTube idols, he turned up with a handgun to commit murder, to take a life and to leave hundreds of others scarred by the shock and memory of the events they witnessed.

"The defense has said it makes no sense. They said if he was guilty, why didn't he run? Well, we may never know, because the defendant will not testify. Rather than present compelling evidence to prove his client's innocence, the defendant's lawyer has sought merely to pry loopholes in the prosecution's case. And I am convinced, as I'm sure you must be, that he has found none.

"I urge you not to be swayed by semantics, not to be deterred by distractions, not to be sidetracked by sleights of hand. It is your duty to weigh up the truth from all the facts we have presented to you, and to that end you must find the defendant guilty on all counts."

Nothing Jessica had said was a surprise. She'd kept beating down on the same note—that Demarco's guilt was the most logical conclusion any sane person could draw. And because I'd been unable to present the jury with an alternative suspect, I now had to try once again to embed in their minds the idea that Jessica's story just didn't stack up.

"Members of the jury, I follow an address to you that was downright misleading," I began. "It was a case of big hammer, small nail. My colleague from the prosecution desk was not subtle in her argument. I urge you to set her fevered argument aside, because in this case, as in life, there is nuance. There is gray between the black and white. And in between the few islands of cold, hard facts that have been laid before this court, there are wide expanses of open sea. The prosecutor would have you leap over these large gaps—join the dots, if you will—in order to swallow her heavily contrived version of events. And that is something you must remember. The prosecutor's version is but one of many that can be drawn, yet she has presented it to you as the absolute truth.

"I am defending a man accused of murder. But I am fighting for the same vital principle that the prosecution claims to have a monopoly on—justice. What is justice? Is it to find *the* guilty party? Or is it to settle for *a* guilty party? Will that do? Will that truly serve as recompense to the families of the victims?

"Members of the jury, I wish I could tell you who murdered these two men, but I can't. What I can tell you, though, what I have *shown* you, is that it was not Demarco Torrell.

"Please put your minds in as neutral a frame as possible and ponder why on earth my client would carry out what would effectively amount to a suicide mission. One day, he suddenly decides to kill two men, one in a very public place, and then he does not even attempt to flee? I mean, come on. Here are some facts the prosecutor's closing argument failed to reference or simply chose to ignore. It seems to my learned colleague these facts are merely inconvenient truths.

"Demarco was not a gang member. He had left the Sintown Crips. He had achieved something remarkable, something that exhibited an extraordinary amount of willpower and courage—he abandoned the security of a criminal gang and embarked on a life of an everyday citizen. Can you appreciate how much guts that took? He was determined to follow in the footsteps of his beloved father—a brave Marine who died serving his country in Afghanistan.

"He accepted five hundred dollars as a step towards that life. When Toby Connors offered Demarco that money to help out on a job, it was more than a lottery win: it was a sign from God. Demarco went along with it—he believed he was being paid to help make a prank video for YouTube. He did what he was paid to do. He made his way to the Anaheim Convention Center and delivered that message to Mr. Jameson.

"But then things went horribly wrong. And he found himself watching a young man die right in front of him. And what did he do? Did he run? No. Hundreds of others ran. Did he choose to save himself from the shooter? No. He stayed with the victim. Did he show the cruel instincts of a cold-blooded killer? No, he displayed the compassion of an empathetic human being.

"The truth here is not some simple grab at the lowest hanging fruit—which is what the prosecution is begging you to accept—it's something far more complex and, to this point, obscure. Because there were three victims that day—the two men killed and my client, who is a victim of circumstance. You would be making a grave error if you believe justice will be served by finding him guilty. Please do not oversimplify this case. Please do not err on the side of convenience because the whole truth cannot be known at this point in time.

"To find my client guilty, you must do so having dismissed every element of reasonable doubt that I have presented to you. In all good conscience, you surely cannot do that. You must not condemn this young man because there is no one else to blame. He is due justice just as much as the victims are.

"If there is any reasonable doubt in your minds, then you must acquit. You must clear Demarco Torrell of these wrongful charges. You must find him innocent even though that comes at the price of many unanswered questions and the absence of having the right target for righteous blame. Please, do not succumb to the temptation to scapegoat an innocent man. This court, this state, this country deserves better than that. Thank you."

I turned to take my seat and cast a glance behind the defense desk out into the spectators' gallery. I almost stopped in my tracks at the sight of Jasmine Torrell. I could not believe she had made it to court. She was there all right, in a wheelchair, holding an oxygen mask to her face. As she looked at me, tears rolled down her cheeks. I sat down and put a hand on Demarco's shoulder.

"Your mom's here," I said.

Demarco swiveled around immediately. He smiled, and she broke down into sobs.

"Love you, mom," he said before the guards took him away.

CHAPTER 27

One night passed. Then another. But at a few minutes past ten o'clock the following morning, I was notified that the jury had reached a verdict. I dashed back to court. I was just getting through the security scanner when I heard the elevator doors open behind me. As I grabbed my briefcase, I felt a light tap on my shoulder. It was Jessica Pope. She looked at ease if not entirely relaxed. We'd both done all we could, and we knew it was all out of our hands now. Save for appeals, of course.

"Two hundred bucks says it's mine," she said.

I looked at her. She had her jaw cocked playfully, daring me to take the bet. On other cases I might have been tempted, but not this one. Yes, we were both just doing our jobs, but this case was personal for me. What I wanted beyond my own professional score-keeping against Jessica Pope was to prevent Demarco Torrell, my friend Sherman's only son, from being put in jail on a convenience of evidence. The delay in the jury's decision gave me confidence that they'd balked long enough to acquire the wisdom not to convict my client. It would be sweet to take that two hundred off Jessica, but I wasn't interested.

"Not today. But you're being mighty sporting for someone who's about to lose."

"That's what you think. Word is there's been only one hold-out since the jury retired. That's holding out against eleven guilty votes, in case you were getting your hopes up."

How did she know that? Or was she bluffing?

"You've got a mole in the jury room?"

"No. But it comes from a very good source. You know jurors. They can't help themselves when someone offers them the chance to get their frustrations out. Particularly when they're locked up in the jury room just wanting the ordeal to be over so they can finally go home."

It was true that the longer deliberations continued, the more likely expediency and self-interest were to become deciding factors in a jury's decision. But I doubted Jessica's account was true. I still believed it was a better sign for me than her that they'd taken so long.

We walked past dozens of people crowded outside the courtroom and entered. A few minutes later the jury appeared. Demarco was brought in, and we exchanged little else but a greeting. I had to admire the strength with which he kept himself together. Then Judge Garner emerged via the rear door and took his seat.

The courtroom fell silent.

"Members of the jury," said Judge Garner. "Have you reached a verdict?"

The foreman of the jury, Mark Carnavan (#6), got to his feet. He held a slip of paper in his hand.

"We have, Your Honor."

He lifted the scrap of paper and read:

239

"On the crime of murder in the first degree of Mr. Luke Jameson, we the jury find the defendant Demarco Torrell guilty."

My heart sank. A muffled roar rose from the spectators' gallery. I reached out and gripped Demarco's shoulder.

"On the crime of murder in the first degree of Mr. Toby Connors, we the jury find the defendant Demarco Torrell guilty."

This time, the spectators dispensed with their prior restraint. Several people shouted out "Yes!", as if their team had scored a touchdown. Others began hugging each other while shedding tears of sorrowful joy and relief. It was so jarring to see people revel in a decision that condemned the life of a young man I believed was innocent.

Demarco was crestfallen. Tears welled up in his eyes, but then he shut them down by sheer will. He was not going to let anyone see him cry. I took him in my arms and hugged him close. I had to raise my voice to make myself heard above the crowd as I spoke into his ear.

"This is not over, Demarco. This is not over. We are going to appeal this decision and we are going to win. You hear me? This is not the end. I promise you."

Demarco nodded his head silently.

"Thanks, Mr. Madison," he said the words so quietly I had to read his lips. "Thanks for trying."

The guards came for him.

"Rot in hell, you monster!" someone shouted.

"You'll make somebody a nice girlfriend, faggot!" cried another.

I swiveled around to face the culprit, but all I saw was a crowd of people jeering at Demarco as he was led away.

I packed up my things and went to march out of the court. Jessica was standing at the rail and swung the gate open for me.

"Good thing you didn't take the bet."

"Go fuck yourself," I said as I swept past her.

By the time the elevator had dropped me to the foyer, my blood had cooled. I stepped outside the Clara Shortridge Foltz Criminal Justice Center into a scrum of reporters and cameramen.

"What did you make of the verdict?" someone asked.

"I harbor no disrespect for the jury—they did their job admirably. But today they got it wrong. This has been a miscarriage of justice. It is not the end of this case."

"So that means you'll be appealing?"

"Yes. I will most certainly be filing an appeal."

"Is that fair on the victim's families, Mr. Madison?"

I wasn't going to answer that. I was done talking. I began pushing through the pack and eventually broke free. I walked back to my office at a brisk pace, deep in thought.

Yes, you bet there would be an appeal. And yes, I would win it. But would Demarco live to see its benefit? How long could he survive in prison? Lethal injection wasn't an imminent threat. Guys sit on death row for decades. But Demarco was going to be sent to live among murderers who planned to kill him. Once inside San Quentin, the "rest of his natural life" could amount to just a few days.

CHAPTER 28

As fair-minded as Superior Justice Abraham T. Garner was, he was never inclined to go lightly. But there were no light options available to him—it was either life without parole or death. And Judge Garner chose death. His reasoning was that the jury had found Demarco guilty of two calculated, senseless murders, for which warranted the highest order of punishment. That Demarco was still a teenager didn't matter—in an adult court, age could not be used as a mitigating factor. Judge Garner was moved to say that it took a particularly evil mindset to do what Demarco had done and that he deserved no leniency. He added that the victims' families had not requested the death penalty be removed, and he hoped they felt their cry for justice had been satisfactorily answered.

Demarco was a mess following the sentence. He just crumbled from within. As much as I tried to console him, my efforts were in vain. In the end, he'd fared no better than if he'd gone with a judge-appointed public defender. Again, I impressed upon him that I'd be filing an appeal, but we both knew that would remain a hollow promise until I had fresh evidence.

After a few hours back at the office, I headed to Seven Grand, a retro whiskey bar, to drown my sorrows. I quickly got onto cask strength scotch—110 proof, the kind of stuff that tastes like paint thinner to the uninitiated—and it was going down like honey. I told the bartender to keep the bottle handy to save him having to slide the ladder along and climb up every time I wanted a refill. And I was going to want plenty of refills. As I took my fourth drink in hand, Jessica Pope sat down beside me.

"I knew I'd find you here," she said. She was a completely different being to the one I'd seen in court. Totally at ease, gentle even, and smoking hot. I knew this version of Jessica Pope well and, normally, I liked it.

"What are you doing here? Have you come to gloat over your win?"

"No," she smiled. "You were wise not to take that bet. But how about buying a girl a drink?"

She had that playful look in her eye. But I was cold on her. I'd never had trouble separating my work life from my personal life, but she'd just gotten my innocent client the death penalty. For me to just set that aside would have been psychopathic.

"Sure, what are you drinking? There's some nice whiskey here if you've got the stomach for it."

"No thanks. I'll have a mint julep."

"I didn't take you for a southerner."

"Who says you need to be? It's my favorite."

"Okay then." I caught the bartender. "Can I get one mint julep for the belle of the ball here?"

She smiled as she watched the barman, a handsome hipster in beard, waistcoat and white shirt, make the drink. She looked like she was of a mind to consume both the drink and its maker.

"Look who's hot to trot," I said.

"Wouldn't you be? Sorry to rain on your parade, but today I can feel good about my job. Maybe next time it'll be you who's walking on sunshine."

The bartender placed the drink in front of Jessica. She raised it at me.

"No hard feelings?" she said.

Our glasses clinked.

"The better man won, I guess," I said.

"Don't be an asshole. The better lawyer won."

"Touché." I threw my drink back and signaled for a refill. "I have to hand it to you, Jess. You nailed me with the Sanders material. My investigator had a feeling everything was not what it should be, but his contacts at LAPD assured him we had everything there was to know about his background."

"Of course they did. I made damn sure you never got a look at the internal complaints Melanie Crofts filed. I needed that to destroy his credibility."

"Well, you sure did that."

Jessica leaned her head towards me, her blond hair tipping down her right side.

"Come on," she scoffed. "Don't make like you were cheated. I did what I had to do. You would have done the same. You and I both know that to most people ballistics can be as much about guesswork as precise science. But thanks to *CSI*, the public thinks matching bullet to gun is as precise as fingerprinting or DNA testing. I for one am not about to rob them of that delusion."

"The shoe will be on the other foot someday," I said.

"I don't doubt it. But I wasn't just doing a job—your boy killed those two men, and he got what was coming."

I had to admit I did feel like the only person besides Jasmine who still believed Demarco was innocent.

244

"He didn't do it, Jessica."

Jessica leaned in closer still. "I have to give it to you, Brad. You're nothing if not loyal. But if the murderer is still out there, where's the evidence? If you want to prove you're right, get your spurs on and come up with something solid. But there's nothing out there, am I right?"

I didn't want to tell her about Cassinelli and how Jack had chased his tail trying to put meat on that bone. I shook my head. She was right: we'd gotten nowhere. But I didn't want her to know that.

"We're getting close, Jessica. So enjoy your victory, because it's going to be short-lived."

"You know what you sound like?"

"What?"

"A sore loser. I didn't prosecute that case because it fell in my lap and gave me some cheap thrill. You think I could sleep easy thinking I'd sent an innocent young man to his death? Our case was solid. Don't be pouting because yours wasn't. You had your chance to offer a reasonable alternative, but there was none. Where is this mystery killer of yours, Brad? Something tells me it's all in your head."

"Maybe you're right."

"You can't even tell whether you're in denial or not. Can you?"

I let that one slide and took another sip.

"Didn't think so," continued Jessica as she downed the remainder of her mint julep and stood up. "Thanks for the drink."

After she'd gone, I polished off the remainder of the bottle, got an Uber back to my place, and fell into bed.

***

245

The next sound I heard—the next one that registered, anyway—was my phone. It was a call that carried news I never wanted to hear.

As I reached out in my drunken haze, the phone stopped ringing. But seconds later it started up again. I lay on my back and let it ring out. The device was on the far bedside table, out of reach. I tried to summon the energy to roll over and switch it to silent but couldn't move.

It rang again.

"What the hell!" I shouted. I heaved my legs up, swung them over to the other side of the bed, and sat up. The whiskey in my gut swished around sickeningly. For a moment, the urgent need to vomit took hold. I remained still and it subsided. The phone started ringing again.

"My God, what is it?!"

I grabbed the unit and pried my eyes open to look at the screen. It was Claire. The phone fell silent again. I could see from the calls icon that she'd called eleven times already. A jolt of panic hit me—I must have done something severely wrong or forgotten to do something important. *Had I drunk called her last night and abused her? Had I sent her a text?* The shot of anxiety sobered me a little. The phone rang again. Claire again. I hesitated before finally tapping the green button.

"Hello?" I said groggily.

"Brad! Brad! Where have you been?!"

I perked up quick smart. Claire sounded like she was in trouble.

"Why, what's up?"

"I've been calling you all morning."

"Why? What time is it?" I snatched a glance at my watch—it was just past midday.

"Brad. It's Bella ..."

"What?" I said. "What?!"

Claire was struggling to find her words.

"It's Bella …"

Oh fuck. Don't tell me.

Claire was in tears.

Oh, Christ!! Is this that call?! Is this where I'm told my darling child is dead??

Claire could barely get her words out.

"What's happened, Claire?!"

"Bella's missing."

"What do you mean missing?!"

"She was out with Caitlin and she just disappeared."

"I don't understand. What do you mean?"

"Caitlin took Bella to Abbot Kinney to return some goods I used for a shoot."

My mind went blank.

"Caitlin. Who's Caitlin?"

"My assistant. She took Bella with her to Sota …"

"Sota, what's Sota?"

"A fashion boutique—Scandinavian. Caitlin went there with Bella to try something on and when she came out, Bella was gone."

That useless bitch!

Volcanic anger erupted from within me. I felt compelled to lash out, hurl abuse at Claire. *What kind of imbecile could allow this to happen? What kind of mother entrusts their seven-year-old daughter to the "care" of some air-brained teenager?* It took all I had to keep those thoughts to myself.

"When did this happen?"

"About ninety minutes ago."

"Has she called?"

"She didn't take her phone."

"Where are you?"

"I'm on Abbot Kinney. I've been walking up and down the street looking for her."

"Have you called the cops?"

"Of course, but there's no urgency from them. They figure Bella's most likely just strayed and will return without incident. But this isn't like her at all. She wouldn't just run off."

Just then, my phone pinged with a message. I pulled it from my ear to check who it was from.

"Hang on, I just got a message," said Claire.

"So did I," I told her.

The number was withheld.

"Who's yours from?" she said.

"I don't know. It's private."

Suddenly dreading what I would find. I tapped on the message. That's when I heard Claire scream.

"Oh my God!! Oh my God!! Bella!! Bella!! No!" She was screaming hysterically.

I was muttering much the same thing to myself. I was dazed. Shocked. The image I saw ripped my insides out. My body went cold and feverish.

It was a photo of Bella. She was seated in a car, unconscious, with tape over her mouth and her arms bound at the wrists.

"CALL THE COPS OFF NOW OR I'LL SLIT HER THROAT!"

CHAPTER 29

I don't know how long it took before I was able to resume a coherent conversation with Claire. Once my head began clearing, I wanted answers. But nothing she could give me was enough.

"Claire. Claire!"

"Yes?" she moaned.

"You need to tell me exactly what happened. Every detail that you know."

She muttered to herself, breathing deeply, trying to haul her mind back from the depths of horror and fear. Finally, she began to get some words out.

"Like I said. She was with Caitlin."

"Where?"

"Caitlin had to return some product to three stores on Abbot Kinney. We'd just finished a photo shoot and there were clothes, handbags, and other stuff to return. The stylist was in a rush, so Caitlin offered to take the items back for her. I was busy tying up loose ends, and Bella asked if she could go."

"How old is Caitlin?"

"Eighteen. She minds Bella all the time, Brad. You know that."

"I don't know that. How could I? I know next to nothing about this Caitlin girl other than the fact that she's your minion. So I won't pretend I'm reassured by her taking responsibility for the care of our seven-year-old daughter."

"You never said anything before."

I breathed in deeply. Anger shot through me with a violent pulse. It was all I could do to stop myself from exploding verbally. About the only thing that kept me in check was the fact that some part of me was aware of my need for payback. I hadn't forgotten her reaction to what I did at the VidCon shooting. I could feel all that indignation in my emotional mix. But it would be a cheap shot to unload on her.

"What would it have mattered if I had said so, Claire? Seriously. Let's move on. What time did they leave?"

"It was about ten-thirty. They were only going to be a half hour or so, then Bella was due to have a play date with her friend Zoe. Oh, God. I have to call Jennifer."

"Jennifer?"

"Zoe's mom."

"That can wait. Back to Caitlin and Bella. So they head up to Abbot Kinney."

"Yes, yes. Caitlin said she parked behind MTN, that Japanese restaurant, fed the meter and took the goods to the stores. Bella helped her carry some of them in. She went to three shops, returned the items, and then Caitlin decided she wanted to slip into Sota to try on a dress ..."

"Don't say it like you're excusing her!"

"I'm not! She thought she would only be ten minutes and that it wouldn't be a problem."

250

"Jesus Christ, that little—"

"Brad. She's beside herself. Can you imagine?"

"Right now, I don't really care how she feels. She feels dreadful? Good. I hope it's eating her alive."

"It's eating *me* alive! Anyway, I sent her home. She needs to be with her parents right now."

"Yeah, well she has that luxury, doesn't she?" I was on my feet, running my hand over my head, trying to think through a thousand things at once. *How could this have happened? Who would do this? Why would they take Bella? Was it because of me? What do they want?*

I tried to stay rational and calm, but it was taking a supreme amount of physical, emotional and mental effort.

"Go on. What happened next?"

"She said there were only two other people in Sota besides her and Bella—the manager and an assistant. The assistant took her to the changing room while Bella waited. Caitlin said she left Bella looking at some clothes displayed on the floor. She said the manager told the assistant she was heading out back to the store room, letting her know she had the run of the place. Caitlin said she was in the changing room for five to ten minutes."

"Five to ten minutes? Why so long?"

"She took in three dresses. She tried the first two on and didn't like them then tried on the third. That's when she stepped out of the fitting room and couldn't see Bella anywhere."

"She just disappeared? Just like that? Bella would not have just wandered off by herself."

"Caitlin said she searched the store and then began to panic. The assistant saw nothing, heard nothing. But Caitlin said when she came out of the fitting room the assistant was tucked away in the back corner of the store checking her phone."

"Right."

There was a pause of a few seconds that only invited the dread consuming us to grow more potent.

"Brad, what are we going to do?"

"Well, we don't know where this person is. He, I'm assuming it's a he, told us to call off the cops. Can you do that? Then you'd best head back home. I don't know if he's just buying himself time or whether he is actually still in the area. Either way, we can't risk it. We need to be seen to be cooperating with everything he demands."

"I'll tell the cops we found her."

"I know that will be hard but, yes, I think that's what we have to do. I'll see you soon. I'm coming over."

"Brad, I'm so sorry."

"It's not your fault," I said, even though I felt it was all her fault. "We'll get her back."

"How?"

"That's what I'm working on." I hung up and immediately called Jack.

"What's cooking, boss?" Jack answered.

"Jack, it's an emergency. I need you over at Claire's place right now. And tell Charlie to get there too. Tell her she's on the clock as of now."

"What the hell's going on?"

"Someone's kidnapped Bella," I seethed. "And we are going to hunt that son-of-a-bitch down."

∗∗∗

Claire didn't notice me as I crossed the lawn and came into her house. She was seated at the kitchenette bench at the far end of the studio. She looked crushed, her eyes heavy and reddened by tears drawn from the depths of her soul. Hearing my footsteps cross the polished concrete, she lifted her head and got to her feet listlessly. We hugged. She put her head against my chest. I rubbed her back slowly.

"We will find her, Claire. I promise."

"How?" she said, forlorn. "She could be anywhere."

I knew she hadn't given up hope, even though the most natural thing in some sense was to abandon hope. Someone had our daughter somewhere, and they meant to do her harm. Right at this point in time, we were utterly powerless. The rage within me sought to hurtle me in all manner of directions. But it also felt like a hollow, aimless power—like punching the headstone of someone you yearned to hold warm in your arms again. And yes, every ghastly thought had crossed my mind—even the prospect that Bella might already be dead.

"We'll find a way."

Just then the doorbell buzzed. Claire and I released each other.

"That'll be Jack," I said. "I asked him to come."

"What if we're being watched?"

"For all they'd know a friend's come to visit. We need all the help we can get."

Claire nodded.

"I'll let him in," I said.

Upon seeing Claire, Jack wrapped her in a big hug, then held her back at arms' length with two hands. He tilted his head to make sure he caught her eye.

"Right now, we have a little time," he said. "This has only just begun. As horrible as that sounds, it also means there's hope. She is still alive. Whoever has Bella will be sending us another message soon. They must want something."

"You mean a ransom?"

"Maybe," Jack said.

"Why? Why would they do this? Why would we be extortion targets? We're not rolling in money. It doesn't make sense."

"God only knows."

Claire suddenly realized there was another person in the room. She stepped aside from Jack and looked at Charlie. The young hacker was wearing straight-legged jeans covered in holes. Her skinny legs were—as usual, I figured—planted in Doc Martin boots. And with her spiky hair, various face piercings, studded leather jacket and white tank top without a bra, Claire must have been wondering if some aimless Venice waif had followed Jack in off the street.

"Claire," I said. "This is Charlie. She's part of the team that's going to help us find Bella."

"I don't understand."

"Charlie is a hacker," I continued. "One of the best. Without the cops to help, it's just us against that asshole. And if we want to track him down without him knowing, Charlie here could well be the key."

Charlie didn't bother saying hello, nor did Claire for that matter. They just stared at each other.

"Who said it's a he?" said Charlie.

I shook my head. We were running on the assumption that it must be a man.

"You're right," I said. "We have no idea who's behind this. We don't know if it's a man or a woman. We don't know if it's an individual or a gang."

As I said these words, my mind began to run through potential suspects. Could this be the work of the Sintown Crips? Was this payback for failing to get Demarco off the murder charge? Ramon X has my number. It would not have been hard to have me followed and discover I had a young daughter who could be used as an easy target, a pawn in a brutal payback scheme. But would they do something like this? Would they get their revenge this way? Wouldn't they come straight for me if they thought I had to pay for my failure? My brain was swirling, my sense of reason an aimless mess.

Suddenly my phoned pinged. Claire's did too. She picked hers up off the bench top. Then she looked at me.

"I don't want to look," she said. "Brad?"

Everyone was looking at me. I pulled my phone out and read the message.

It was another image of Bella—gagged, eyes open, looking utterly terrified. I felt the blood drain from my face. All the air was sucked from my lungs. I could barely breathe. As much as I steeled myself to try and conceal the intensity of my distress, I couldn't.

Claire's hands went to her mouth. She briefly lifted them away to speak.

"What does it say?"

"It's another photo of Bella. She's alive," I said. That was one way to put a positive spin on it.

"God help us, Brad. What is it?" said Claire.

I could feel my lips trembling. I opened my mouth slowly. Then read the words as though they were being forced out of me.

"It says, 'Instagram this, mommy and daddy.'" I didn't tell them the words were followed by a string of emojis—the ones crying with laughter.

I handed the phone to Jack. Claire could no longer resist the urge to see Bella. But as soon as she saw the phone, she let out a moan of despair. It was the most heartbreaking sound I'd ever heard, the soul-deep cry of a mother's anguish.

But my sympathy for Claire at that moment was short-lived. The reins that had held my anger in check suddenly fell away as it dawned on me what this was all about. I could no longer bear to stay silent, to stay neutral, to pretend like this was some kind of freak accident that we—no, Claire—had nothing to do with.

"This has to be about Bella's Instagram account," I said, glaring at Claire.

"We don't know that, Brad," said Jack trying to intervene in what he saw coming.

"What else would it be?!" I shouted. "Some twisted son-of-a-bitch has found our seven-year-old daughter on Instagram. Our little girl posing this way and that for all the world to see." I was walking slowly towards Claire as I spoke, my words rising in volume. "What did I tell you, Claire?! How many times did I tell you it was not right to make our child a public figure with this social media bullshit? But oh no, Brad. You don't understand. It's good for her. She loves it. It's no more dangerous than walking the street! Isn't that what you said?!"

"Brad, I told you I had control of ..."

"You had control of nothing except the money you made off her! You only cared about the increase in sales she generated for you. This was never about her. It was about you and your bullshit, your shallow fashion, your vanity and your greed. You lapped it up. And what did I say? What did I say about there being sickos out there? I warned you that there could be consequences. But what was my opinion worth? What was my concern worth? Nothing!"

Claire was rendered speechless by my verbal assault. I wasn't done.

256

"How many perverts were tuned into our daughter's life? Creeps that *you* allowed in. Well, Claire. This is the consequence. Some sick maniac has our daughter, and God only knows what he's doing to her right now."

Jack stepped in between me and Claire, who was in tears.

"You bastard! Shut your mouth!" she screamed.

Jack grabbed both my shoulders as he stood in front of me.

"Brad. Brad. You need to calm down. We still know jack shit about who's behind this. We don't know why they've taken Bella. I know you're pissed, but this ain't right, buddy. What we need to do right now is strip out the emotions and get our minds on the job. What can we do to get your daughter back?"

As my rage subsided, I couldn't get an image out of my mind: the man with the dog at Santa Monica. I tried hard to remember details about him. His facial appearance. His clothes. His dog. It was all too vague. Then I remembered he'd taken a selfie.

"The guy from Santa Monica! Jack, my phone," I said. As soon as it was in my hands, I tapped through to Instagram and began scrolling down the photos in Bella's account.

"What are you doing?"

"There was a guy who approached Bella when I'd gone to buy ice cream. He took a selfie with her. Here he is!"

Jack came beside me to check out the pic.

"Steve Bartis," Jack said before reading the comment Bartis had posted. "'Love you, Bella Madison. Microfashion's It Girl!' Go to his page."

When I tapped through, it was clear Bartis was a very active user. He had almost two-hundred thousand followers. I Googled his name and up came a link to his website.

"Looks like he's a personal trainer to the stars," I said.

"And he sure as hell doesn't look like someone who's going to kidnap a seven-year-old girl," said Jack.

That wasn't going to deter me. I found the number and called it. I didn't even know what I was going to say. As the phone rang, I felt a growing sense that what I was doing was absurd.

"Hello?"

"Hi, is that Steve Bartis?"

"Yes, it is. How can I help?"

The voice was friendly and a little out of breath. I could hear he was outdoors. He must have been in the middle of a jog or something. Seeing an unknown number, he probably expected a potential new client to be on the end of the line. I knew then and there that I was way, way off. What was I actually going to say to him? "Remember me? I'm the angry dad from the beach. My daughter Bella's missing, and my bet is you're the sick bastard who's taken her!" Thankfully, I thought the better of it.

"Look, I'm sorry. It's nothing. I've got to go."

I hung up feeling stupid and useless.

After a few seconds, Charlie's voice broke the silence: "What was the name of the store?" I'd become oblivious to Charlie's presence. She'd taken a seat on the sofa and had placed her laptop on the coffee table. She was busy typing as she spoke. No one replied to her.

"What's the name of the goddamn store!?"

"Sota," Claire said, her defeated voice rising just above a whisper. "S-O-T-A."

"What are you doing?" I asked Charlie.

"What no one else seems to be doing—trying to find your daughter. Does she have a phone?"

"Yes," said Claire. "But she left it here."

"That's unfortunate," said Charlie. "Her phone would be traceable."

Dejected again—it was like being punched hard in the face.

Charlie turned back to her laptop and resumed typing. "Give me your phone," she said. I assumed she meant me. I walked over to her.

"The kidnapper's number's blocked, in case you were thinking about tracing it," I said.

"I am thinking about tracing it. Give me your phone."

"You can trace a blocked number?"

"I can."

"I thought that was impossible."

"You thought wrong."

She took my phone and held it in one hand while working the keyboard with the other. After two minutes she handed it back to me.

"Now yours, please," Charlie said to Claire.

Claire walked over and gave up her phone. A few minutes later Charlie was done.

"I've installed a trap on both your phones. Essentially, the call system has now been rerouted so that when the next message arrives, the ID blocker that the kidnapper is using will be rendered ineffective, and we'll be able to see the number."

"And then you can trace it?" I asked.

"Any phone can be traced if you can read the number. It's not even a hack—cops do it every day."

"What else? What else can we do?"

"Make yourself useful. You can put the kettle on. Black tea for me, please."

I stood there unmoved. Charlie lifted her head.

"You do know how to make tea, don't you?"

I was disarmed. My emotions were swinging wildly between manic and placid at every turn.

"Yes, of course."

I turned to go.

"And by the time you're done, hopefully I'll have the footage we need to see who we're dealing with."

"The footage?"

"Yes. I'm hacking Sota's CCTV cameras, and any others I can find in the vicinity."

CHAPTER 30

Watching Charlie work her laptop and phone was like watching Senna drive. The software she was running was being operated at warp-speed. My extreme anxiety had not abated, but I was relieved to have Charlie on board.

I'd spent the past ten minutes apologizing to Claire for all the horrible things I'd said. My apology was accepted, but that hadn't made the hurt evaporate. It was like I'd been too eager to even the score after she'd chided me for leaving Bella at the shooting. On both counts, we'd only succeeded in giving each other fresh wounds that needed time to heal.

Jack had joined us to work through what little we had and try to find a clue as to who was behind this. But we were getting nowhere. No hint or connection stood out. The three of us fell into silence for a while until Claire broke it.

"How did they get my number?" she said. "It's my private cell. My business cell is listed on my website. It's the one I give out to everyone in the industry. But my private number is strictly personal. Would that mean it's someone I know?"

"Not necessarily," said Jack.

"Why not?"

"Have you been to a store lately that sends you a text receipt?"

Claire thought about it.

"Yes. When was it? Tuesday. I was at Jackman's Hi-Fi." Claire took up her phone and began scrolling through her text messages. "I bought Bella a pair of headphones. The woman at the counter asked me if I wanted her to send me the receipt by phone. I said yes and gave the number to her. Here it is. Tuesday, eleven seventeen."

Claire looked up from her phone sadly.

"It's quite possible you were followed," Jack said. "If they were standing nearby, they would have heard you give out your number."

"I think I'm going to be sick." Claire launched out of her chair, bent over the kitchen sink and heaved into it. I put my arm over her shoulders and held her hair out of the way.

"It's not certain that's what happened, Claire," I said. "It's just a possibility. There are many things about ourselves that we give away without thinking."

I grabbed a tea towel to wipe Claire's mouth and got her a glass of water. "Here, rinse with this."

She drank some water, swirled it around in her mouth, and spat it into the sink. Then she turned her back to the counter and leaned against it. She looked exhausted but not frail. Like me, she'd pulled herself back from the brink of going to pieces and was now tapping her inner reserves of fight.

One thought that had come and gone was whether the text messages I'd received during Demarco's trial were at all related. Like I said, it was pretty much standard for me to be subjected to such vitriol when defending an alleged killer. But maybe I was wrong to dismiss them.

"During the Torrell trial, I was getting some hateful text messages," I said.

"You never told me about that," said Jack.

"I know, because it's not unusual. Every time I defend a murder charge, a troll gets my number off my website and starts abusing me. Most often it's more than one, so Demarco's case was below average in terms of trolling."

"What did these messages say?"

"Just the usual—that I had a warped sense of justice. The gist was that I was a reprehensible human being. That sort of thing. Like I said, it's just the daily coffee and bagel for a defense attorney."

"Show them to me," said Jack.

I found them on my phone and handed it to him.

Jack read them out aloud: "'You know nothing about justice! You're a fraud!' 'You're going to learn what real justice is. I'm going to teach you.'"

Jack looked like a teacher I'd deeply disappointed.

"You should have at least flagged these, Brad. This last one is a threat. This could be the kidnapper."

"It happens all the time, Jack. Both are blocked numbers. We can't even say for sure that they both came from one person."

"But it sure looks that way—the theme is the same—that he wants to school you in the meaning of the word 'justice.' And he likes to keep the caps lock on."

"But the messages we got this morning were directed to both me and Claire."

"True, but I'm not sure that proves these earlier messages are not connected."

Jack was right. And that's what Claire was thinking. Suddenly there was a possibility that this was not about Bella's Instagram activity at all but that it had something to do with Demarco's trial. Given that we were both licking our wounds, Claire had the grace to not throw this revelation in my face.

"Let's bring it back to square one again," said Jack. "What does this person want? We don't know his motive, but it perhaps stems from Bella's Instagram activity or Brad's trial. No demands have been made of either of you so far. No money. No grievances expressed. Nothing to indicate this is payback or punishment—something directed at either or both of you. And then there's the possibility that taking Bella was the sole objective."

"If he wants something, he'll have to tell us soon, you'd think," I said.

We all stewed on the same thought—what a deeply vile thing it was to hope for the chance to understand the motive of the person who'd taken your daughter, who could be doing unspeakable things to her at this very moment. But a motive against Claire or me meant at least there was hope we could pay some kind of price to get our daughter back. The worst thought was that, if getting hold of Bella had been the kidnapper's objective, then there was nothing to be asked of us, that all this waiting was just giving time to a sadist who had no intention of sparing our daughter.

"Maybe we should go to the police," said Claire.

"No," I shook my head. "We don't know where this person is or what capacity they have to monitor us. Whatever we do must be in the shadows."

"What is it we're doing exactly, for God's sake!? We're sitting around the kitchen like little lost mice while our daughter is in the hands of some maniac!"

Suddenly, Charlie's voice rang out again: "Do any of you recognize this woman?"

264

The three of us rushed over to Charlie and crowded around her laptop.

"This is footage from inside Sota," she said.

It took a second to distinguish the make-up of the black-and-white video. But then it was clear—the legs of pedestrians passing the store front crossed the top of the screen. Two women, Caitlin and the sales assistant, were standing near the bottom right corner. Both spun around and walked out of frame. At that moment, the figure of a young girl emerged from behind a clothes rack positioned to the left. There was no mistaking her.

"Bella!" Claire and I said in unison. It was the saddest way we'd ever said her name. We both spoke softly, as though by some miracle we could reach her, reassure her.

The silent footage was haunting to watch. For us, it was a horror movie in the most visceral sense. The camera's field of view took in perhaps one-third of the shop. We watched as Bella touched an item of clothing, pulling the material toward herself.

A woman appeared at the doorway. She just stood there, her head was not in the shot, and she did not move to enter the store. Then she bent forward to address Bella and her head came into frame. My heart pounded. I recognized her. At least, I thought I did.

"Charlie, stop," I said. "Can you enhance her face?"

"Do you know her?" asked Claire breathlessly.

"I'm not sure." But when Charlie cropped in, all doubt left my mind. I knew her all right.

"My God," I said. "It's Francine."

"Who?"

I felt light-headed and weak, like all the blood was draining out of my flesh. Every bit of me felt like I'd seen a ghost. I leaned in closer to the screen. "Francine Holmes. She was a witness in the trial."

"Which trial?" asked Claire.

"Demarco Torrell. She buried him in court. She's a scary religious type. She'd have enjoyed watching him burn in hell." I tapped Charlie on the shoulder. "Keep playing."

Charlie zoomed out and hit the play button again. Francine addressed Bella without moving an inch from her position at the door. They spoke for a few seconds, and Bella took a step towards her. Then she began to jiggle on the spot excitedly. Francine raised a finger to her lips. Bella clasped her hands together. Francine beckoned her. Bella shot a glance towards where Caitlin must have been, in the fitting room, and then scurried over to Francine. As Bella reached Francine, the woman put an arm around her and escorted her out onto the sidewalk. They walked straight to the curb, their bodies rising out of the top of the frame. They stopped where a black car was parked. As the rear door opened, Bella's feet jumped up and down. Then suddenly Bella's body fell into the car, like she'd been yanked hard. Francine got in and the door closed quickly behind her. The footage then showed the car pulling away from the curb.

"Oh my God. Oh my God," repeated Claire. "Who is she? Brad, who is that woman?"

I told them everything I knew about Francine Holmes. How she was there to "rescue" Bella at the shooting. How she all but chided me for being a bad father for abandoning Bella. I told them she was a patron of Cicily Pines and other wholesome YouTubers and had promised Bella the opportunity to meet Cicily in the near future. I told them how she'd been a religious counselor at the Skid Row shelter, where she'd bonded with Demarco Torrell until he displeased her. I told them she reserved a barely concealed wrath for Demarco, as though his choice to be independent of her was a sinful betrayal. I said I was prepared for her to be unfavorable towards Demarco at the trial, but she'd been downright vengeful.

266

But as to the most important question about Francine Holmes, I had no answer. Why had she taken Bella? Surely the reason was not purely to harm her. Given the open contempt Francine had for my parenting skills, I figured it must be about me. But Claire was being targeted too. Was this an act of deranged, righteous punishment for our parenting choices? From my experience with Francine, that kind of made sense.

"If anyone's going to be a moral crusader, it would be her," I said, thinking out aloud.

"What do you mean?" asked Claire.

"She's a fanatic. I've seen how she turned on Demarco. She was happy to see him sentenced to death for turning away from her. There is a terrible, hateful streak of retribution in her."

"But what have you done, what have *we* done, to earn her wrath?" said Claire.

"I don't know, but maybe she loathed us as parents—me running off, Bella's social media profile—and decided to teach us a lesson."

"But that's absurd. Some wicked witch has taken my baby because she's decided I'm a bad mother?!"

Jack came over and said what I was thinking but dared not to articulate.

"You're right. It does sound absurd. But there may be a serial killer carrying out some kind of a moral crusade."

"Serial killer? What the hell are you talking about?" Claire struggled to believe things could be even worse than she had imagined. She looked at me.

I had to step in.

"During the Torrell case, we got a tip-off that the Anaheim murder could be the work of a serial killer. His targets were supposedly social media stars who were leading America's youth astray."

"Oh my God. You knew this and this is the first I'm hearing about it?"

"We looked into it, Claire, but it just seemed preposterous. We were told about two other killings, but we could not find any links between those murders and the ones Demarco Torrell was accused of. In the end, I had to set it aside and focus on Demarco's defense."

"And now?"

"It's still just a theory. But now we have Francine Holmes, a vengeful moralist, who has taken our daughter after openly condemning her social media activity."

Claire was speechless as thoughts of the deepest horror set in. Desperate to think up a clue, I reran the events of my first meeting with Francine Holmes. And I realized something: she wasn't the killer.

"Francine Holmes didn't shoot Luke Jameson," I said. "I can tell you that now. We were in the queue for Cicily Pines when we heard the shots, and she was standing a few yards away from us."

Claire freed herself from the torrent of negative thought to speak, uttering her words as she stared into mid-space.

"Cicily Pines," she said. "I bet that's how she got Bella to go with her. That witch told her Cicily was in the car."

I thought about it. Of course, she was right. The way Bella suddenly broke into an excited dance on the spot. The way Francine had hushed her. Bella's indecision—caught between staying put in the shop and meeting her idol—had been visible until the prospect of meeting Cicily won out. Just as Francine Holmes must have suspected it would.

But Francine wasn't working alone. Someone else pulled Bella into that car.

The car! The black car.

I rushed over to Charlie.

"Charlie, I want to get a look at the car. Can you go back?"

Charlie pulled the footage back to where the door closed and the car pulled out. It took just a second to identify the make.

"Black Lincoln," I said and turned to Jack. I'd passed on to him what Loretta had seen in Skid Row. Now we were both thinking the same thing: Dino Cassinelli's serial killer theory was fast morphing into devastating fact.

"What does that mean, Brad?" Claire said. "You know something—what is it?"

For more than a few seconds I hesitated.

How could I tell the mother of our little girl that I was now certain she was in the hands of a serial killer?

***

Claire took the news in grim silence. It was as though hope itself had been exposed as a wicked, hollow sham. For a few moments she appeared to surrender to the hideous forces driving her to despair. She was beyond tears. The distraught words she uttered were barely audible. I sat next to her and held her like a child. I told her everything we knew about the suspected serial killer, everything we'd been told. In time she found the traction needed to haul her emotions back from the brink. Her whole countenance steeled, her eyes too, as she began to imagine the person bringing this torture upon us.

I detailed to everyone the reports we had from Skid Row, that a bald man sitting in a new black car—a Lincoln—had been seen talking to Toby Connors in the minutes before he met Demarco Torrell outside the mission. I told her his facial features were so gaunt that one witness had described him as having a skull-face. I

269

told her about the two other murders in Florida and Mexico where, we believed, destitute men had been set up to take the blame. I also told her about Dino Cassinelli and his efforts to get me to believe his crazy theory.

"Where is this Cassinelli?" Claire said.

"I don't know."

"He's a cop, right? Can you trust him?"

"Yeah, he's a disgraced cop, which is partly why it took us so long to take him seriously. But now I trust him completely."

"So he should be on the team," Claire said.

She was right.

"Call him. Now," she ordered.

Cassinelli answered after one ring. I was relieved he sounded sober. He remained silent for the most part while I explained what was going on and detailed what we knew of the suspect.

"What do you want me to do?"

"We're trying to identify the man that Francine Holmes seems to be working with."

"You got a photo?"

"We don't even have a name."

"I'll get you an image," he said.

"How?" I reminded Cassinelli no one could know what we were doing—one false move could prompt my daughter's death. He said he understood perfectly.

"You remember the first witness in the trial, the one who claimed Torrell was the trigger man?"

"Yeah, Mandy Alvarez," I said.

"That's the one. Now she said she saw Torrell's face lit up by the muzzle flash. She said she saw Harrington. But she also said she saw another guy's face, an older guy."

"How do you know all this? I didn't ever see you inside the courtroom."

"I followed it closely, Madison. I read all the transcripts."

"So you'll go see Mandy?"

"Yeah. I'll be in touch."

Cassinelli hung up. I was left on the line thinking maybe all this could have been prevented if I'd put my faith in him months ago.

My phone rang. It was Cassinelli again.

"Dino, what's up?"

"I forgot to mention something I thought you should know."

"What's that?"

"You know Kyle Chambers, the kid who died in the fire down in Puerto Escondido?"

"Yeah, we followed that lead and the perp got knifed before we could ask him any questions."

"Well, months ago I was trying to get hold of the kid's mother. But after her son's death she went traveling, I guess to restore some faith in humanity. She went completely off the grid—trekking in Nepal or Bhutan or something like that. No email, no phone. You couldn't reach her with a fricking carrier pigeon. But I kept on calling her, and a couple of weeks ago she finally got back to me. So I went and spoke with her."

"And what did she say?"

"She was adamant that her son didn't die because of that fire, and she said she can prove it."

"She can prove it? How?"

"The poor lady didn't have the money to fly her kid's body home, and he hadn't taken out any insurance, so she had to have him cremated in Mexico and she brought him back in an urn."

"The poor woman."

"But when she went through customs something set the scanner alarm off."

"What?"

"There were two bullets in the ashes."

CHAPTER 31

Bella had been gone for three hours. I couldn't sit down or stay put, as though the mere act of moving was productive and any moment of stillness was surrender. And that's what was killing me: the intensity of my despair being outweighed by futility.

We'd discussed whether or not I should call Francine and decided that would only alert her to the fact that we were onto her. We had to track her down undetected. So that meant more waiting in the midst of an acute crisis in which every second counted. My mind raced at light speed but only crashed into walls. Every effort to conjure up a lead from the depths of my brain ended at the same dead end: we had nothing to act on. How could you get closer to someone when you didn't know where they were? And with every wasted second, my little girl moved further out of reach.

I had to force myself to shun any mental images of her present condition.

Straight after my call to Cassinelli, I'd asked Jack to begin reviewing everything in Cassinelli's file as well as his own follow-up inquiries. It was no conspiracy theory now. A connection between the four killings could give us a vital clue.

There was no telling whether Francine was the brains behind Bella's kidnapping. But we knew she had company. From the footage we saw, the way Bella had been snatched and pulled into the car, we suspected a man was involved. And, in all likelihood, her partner in crime was the bald-headed man seen talking to Toby Connors.

While Jack was on the case work, I'd asked Charlie to drill down on Francine Holmes.

I was hoping like hell that these two channels of inquiry might interconnect and reveal once and for all exactly who we were dealing with.

Claire walked up to me wiping tears off her cheeks.

"Cicily Pines started following Bella on Instagram," she said. "Bella was beyond excited. Then they were trading comments. It was a dream come true for her. Cicily was very sweet. Bella was so excited but kept a cool head at the same time. It was one of the first signs I recognized that our little girl was maturing as an individual, the way she was able to 'keep it real' as they say. Why would she think there was any harm in ducking outside to see her?"

I put my arm around Claire. Was this the beginning of a new life neither of us wanted—one in which our daughter was only a thought, a memory, a love revived from within us?

Jack's voice broke my train of thought.

"Let's assume the killer used the same gun for each of the four murders," he said. He must have sensed that we needed a distraction, that we needed to drag our minds out of a forlorn future and into the present.

"Why would they use the same weapon?" said Claire. "Travelling around with a gun would be risky."

"True," said Jack. "But we know a Glock was used in the Anaheim murders and in Miami. And let's assume, for argument's sake, that the bullets in Kyle Chambers' ashes came from a Glock.

If the killer didn't use the same gun, he'd have to source a gun on the black market in three different locations. Why go to all that extra trouble when you're confident you've already got an untraceable weapon?"

"Okay," I said. "But if that's the case, he would have crossed the border into Mexico with a gun. Obviously, that's not unheard of, but like Claire says, it's a big risk."

"A risk that can be minimized," said Jack. "It's easy to conceal a weapon in a car's body work, inside a door panel. He only had to hope customs would give the vehicle a light once over instead of pulling him aside for a thorough search."

"And if he's driving, or being driven in, a late-model Lincoln, wouldn't customs be more inclined to wave him through?"

"You'd have to say yes. Unless they took him for a drug lord."

"But are we talking about searching border customs data for a car we don't have the license number for?" I said. "If we are, then we're nowhere. All we have is the fact that the guy drives a black Lincoln. That hardly narrows it down."

"And who's to say he even took the Lincoln over the border? He could well have been in a rental car."

"Exactly."

"What if he didn't drive?" said Claire.

"Well, if he flew, we'd have to discount him using the same weapon," I said. "No one's going to be able to jump on a plane strapped with a sidearm."

"Not unless you're law enforcement who's done their flying armed training course," said Jack. "Transport Safety Administration regulations. And we have no reason to believe this guy is a cop."

"He could pack a weapon case into his carry-on but then he'd have to declare it to the airline, which again would leave an unwanted trail."

"What if he didn't need to?" said Claire.

"What?"

"What if he flew himself? What if he could somehow bypass the normal security protocols?"

Jack and I looked at each other. Claire was onto something.

"Right," Jack said. "But if we're talking a single-engine Cessna, he's still going to have to deal with customs and immigration, just like everyone else."

"What if he doesn't?" I said. I was suddenly springing with fresh energy. It was a lead. A thin one, but still a lead. "Jack, what are the dates of the murders in both Florida and Mexico?"

Jack took half a minute before replying. "Aaron Rybka killed in Miami, September 6, 2016. Kyle Chambers killed in Puerto Escondido, August 13, 2016."

"Charlie," I said, but I didn't need to ask her to drop what she was doing.

"I'm on it," she said. "I'll scan all the registered flights in and out of those two destinations around those two dates."

"How long do you think—" I began.

"I'll know within two minutes," she said.

No one spoke a word as the seconds ticked by. I went over to Charlie to watch her work. She flicked rapidly from one program to the next, one window of dense code supplanted by another. Every few seconds she brought up another small black window into which she quickly typed lines of code. She only paused when her computer's memory spun its wheels trying to keep up with her commands. In less than two minutes, she was done.

"A plane with the registration number N651MM flew LA to Miami a day before Aaron Rybka was killed and left the following night. Then, on the morning before Kyle Chambers' death, the same plane flew LA to Puerto Escondido and left four hours later."

Charlie had the details up on her screen. Jack leaned in to read them.

"Hell, this guy's got some cash. That's a Bombardier 45XR. A Learjet. Thirteen mill' brand new."

"So the guy's minted," I said. "Who's it registered to?"

Charlie knew that question was coming. She already had the registration details up.

"The Halo Council," she said.

"The Halo Council? What's that?" said Claire.

To everyone else in the room, the Halo Council meant nothing. But the name shot me back years to another country, to what now seemed like another life. And now that life was coming flooding back—and this time it wasn't a bad dream, a PTSD episode I'd have to ride out and recover from, it was real life. It was a wide-awake nightmare, because suddenly I knew Bella's abduction had nothing to do with her Instagram account or Claire's attitude towards her social media profile—it was all to do with me and what I'd done in Afghanistan.

"It's an NGO," I said, trying to keep my mouth moving as my mind raced through the memories of a time and place I wanted to keep far behind me. "A non-government organization. The Halo Council was running a few development projects in Afghanistan when I was there."

My body had gone cold. I was weak with nausea.

"Brad, what is it?" Claire said.

"My unit was involved in an incident in Nangarhar Province. Our patrol came under attack in a crowded marketplace and we

277

engaged. About twenty civilians were killed in the crossfire. There were women and children. One of the casualties was a female foreigner who worked for the Halo Council. Her boss gave us hell afterward. Blamed us for every death, demanded courts martial, dismissed the military investigation as a cover-up. Slandered us in the press."

"Who?"

The face was coming back to me. I recalled how he'd confronted me once outside the Bagram Air Base, where we'd been stationed after the incident. A tall man, intense nature. He'd raved at me like a preacher. He had drills for eyes and a spear for a tongue, and my Marines and I were the target of his ferocious outrage.

"Victor Lund," said Charlie, as I sounded the name in my head. "He's the founder and owner of the Halo Group, formerly the Halo Council. Here he is."

She had brought up a photo. We all crowded around her laptop to see the image of a man staring back at us—bald head, hollowed cheeks, deep-set intense eyes.

This was not the man I remembered. Back then Victor Lund was overweight and double-chinned. The difference in appearance was striking. But there was no doubt whatsoever: the skull-faced individual staring back at me from the computer screen was the man who'd kidnapped my daughter.

CHAPTER 32

"Where's the plane now?" I asked Charlie.

"The last record I can find says it returned to LAX from New York five days ago," she said.

"It'll still be there," said Jack. "No plane's going to move without the flight data being recorded."

I called Cassinelli and told him to forget about Alvarez. I needed him to get to LAX pronto to stake out the area where Lund kept his plane.

There was no reason to think Lund was heading for the airport. My gut feeling was that he was buying time to get to a location that he felt was secure, and from there he'd contact us again. With some difficulty, I reasoned that if he'd merely wanted to kill Bella, she'd already be dead. He wanted something, and Bella's life was his bargaining chip. Still, if there was any movement around his plane, I wanted to know about it. We were only a twenty-minute drive away, and I had to trust that Cassinelli would stay sharp and sober on his watch.

Charlie pulled up all the freely accessible information that she could find on Lund and the Halo Group. It turned out Lund had been born into serious money. He was the only son of Jens and Mette Lund. His father had headed up Nordec, a pharmaceutical giant founded by Lund's grandfather. After his father had taken the reins of the corporation, he'd relocated its headquarters to New York City and turned it into one of the world's biggest conglomerates. Victor, a devout Christian, had used his inheritance to found the Halo Council ten years ago. He said in one interview that he wanted to invest his wealth in helping people who were less fortunate. But more specifically, he said he wanted to repair some of the damage wrought by America's various military interventions in the developing world. To that end, the Halo Council established aid programs in Iraq, Afghanistan, Yemen and Uganda. Halo's programs in Afghanistan were aimed at turning farmers away from growing opium and helping them grow alternative crops. The combined cost of these efforts had amounted to a tiny fraction of his fortune, but he'd been happy to run them all at a loss.

Francine Holmes had been part of the Halo Council from its inception. She was based in Kabul for five years as development director while I was there, but I couldn't recall ever meeting her. That didn't surprise me. Most foreign aid workers in Kabul never left the city. They just moved about in their bulletproof four-wheel-drives, going from the guarded razor-wired compounds where they slept to the guarded razor-wired offices where they worked. They filed reports on projects being carried out in rural villages they'd never dare visit. Then after work, they'd be escorted in their bulletproof cars to guarded razor-wired bars. After a few months, they'd return home to the States feeling heroic, having earned their "worked in a war zone" badge of honor.

Charlie continued reading out her findings. The Halo Council had withdrawn from Afghanistan five years ago, she said, and that coincided with a promotions company started up by Lund called UpliftInc. As Francine had told me all those months ago, the newly formed Halo Group company ran an operation designed to advance the careers of a select group of YouTubers. The Halo Group donated money to their channels and managed their public performances. Most of the YouTubers in their stable openly declared themselves as Christians, but that didn't seem to be an absolute requirement. Cicily Pines was just one of many members whose subscriber bases had exploded with Halo's help.

"Good old wholesome entertainment," said Charlie. "Nothing wrong with that. God knows, the internet is swimming in trash."

"That may well be true," I said. "But according to Cassinelli, Victor Lund is not out to just promote the Good Word, so to speak. He wants to send the competition to hell."

"What do you mean?" said Charlie.

"I mean, the theory is that he's cleaning house, ridding YouTube of its most offensive members. But not just any old online brat— he's got his sights on the big influencers whose subscriber numbers rank in the multi-millions."

"Give me the names again," said Charlie.

Jack was back to his laptop and called them out.

"Luke Jameson, Toby Connors, Aaron Rybka and Kyle Chambers."

While Charlie worked away, Jack and I discussed tactics. I asked him to start property searches. If Lund was not taking Bella to LAX, he must have somewhere else to go. Somewhere that wasn't obvious.

"This is interesting," said Charlie. "Three of the victims were once backed by the Halo Group."

I went over to her.

"See here. They are listed among the live creator appearances at three UpliftInc events two years ago. Jameson, Rybka and Chambers. Not Connors, though."

"So maybe one of their crimes was disloyalty," I said. "I've seen how Francine responds to what she perceives as treachery."

"Looks like it went way beyond that," said Charlie. "All three began to make names for themselves for all sorts of horrible behavior—trolling, making offensive remarks about disadvantaged people, fat people. Chambers alone was known for being outrageously misogynistic."

"I thought you got kicked off YouTube if you breached community guidelines," Claire said.

"That's true," said Charlie. "But these guys saved their worst material for other platforms. They kept their YouTube channels relatively clean while indulging in vile behavior on Twitch or 4chan."

"Twitch? 4chan? I've never heard of them," said Claire.

"Practically no one under thirty has heard of them," said Charlie. "But they've become the favorite platforms for young guys to behave deplorably towards other people. As someone who's been a target of unrestrained misogyny, I can kind of see the point of this Lund guy's crusade."

Claire turned to me.

"But why in God's name has he taken Bella? This makes no sense to me whatsoever. She's done nothing hurtful. She hasn't got millions of followers. What the hell has she done to upset this maniac?!"

She looked at me like I should have an answer. I did of sorts, or at least I had an educated guess. But it was too painful to share it unless I absolutely had to.

My phone sounded a message alert. Everyone heard it. As I took the phone out of my pocket, I looked at Claire, expecting hers to buzz too. But it didn't.

A message from an unknown number was displayed on my phone. I opened it to find someone had sent me an audio file.

I pressed play.

"Mr. Madison," a woman's voice began with a whisper. "This is Francine Holmes." She sounded emotional and rushed. Out of breath. "I'm so sorry about your daughter, but I have to tell you something. Victor Lund intends to kill her. You must believe this was not what I had agreed to, but I'm telling you now in the hope that you can stop him. But you must hurry. We're in Reseda. Seven-three-four-one Enfield Avenue. Victor has locked her in ..."

The message ended. I played it again. The way Francine kept her voice low and hurried, it seemed like she'd made the call secretly and then suddenly feared she was about to be discovered.

"What's the cell number?" asked Charlie.

I read it out to her. Charlie tapped away for a few seconds and then waited. Moments later, she spoke again. "It checks out. Her phone location is the same address. In the back yard to be precise."

"Come on, Jack."

We headed to the door, Jack keying the address into his maps app as he walked.

"Brad, what if this is a hoax?" said Claire. "What if she's just drawing you into a trap?"

"What choice do I have? I have to go."

CHAPTER 33

Before we'd reached my car, Jack's phone had calculated the estimated travel time.

"It's going to take us about an hour twenty to get there," he said. "The freeway's jammed in a couple of places."

When every second counted, eighty minutes seemed like an eternity. A fat slab of time we just didn't have to waste. I sidelined my agitation and kept my focus on the road. There was only one way to access the San Fernando Valley: the heavily trafficked San Diego Freeway. Once we'd reached the 405, I took every chance I could to get ahead, flicking the Mustang from lane to lane like a getaway driver.

I kept replaying Francine's message in my head, particularly the part where she had said Lund intended to kill Bella. But Claire's question nagged at me—was this a set-up?

"Do you think she was being genuine?" I asked Jack.

"Francine? Seemed so to me. I don't think it's a con. She seemed truly frightened."

As we drove, Jack found the Reseda house on a real estate website and gave me a rundown of the property.

"Not much to it. Three bedrooms. Single story. Short driveway on the left and a kidney shaped pool out back."

"Inside?"

"Inside it looks like the sort of place where ambition goes to die. It's as ordinary as it comes. Why would a guy who owns a thirteen-million-dollar Learjet buy a dump like this?"

"Beats me. But it is strange. Who knows, maybe there's some family connection to the property. What's the layout?"

Jack walked me through the floorplan. We then planned how we would move in on it.

As we talked, Jack reached into his jacket and released his sidearm from its shoulder holster. It was a .40 caliber Smith & Wesson semi-automatic pistol. He dropped the magazine out, checked it, and then rammed it back home with the heel of his palm.

"I didn't know you were packing," I said.

"I guess I had a feeling we were going to need backup. And I even thought of you."

Jack bent forward and lifted his bag into his lap. He dug his hand in and pulled out a nine-millimeter Springfield.

"Say hello to my little friend," he said as he repeated the ammo check. "Never say I don't do anything for you."

He put the weapon briefly up to his face and sighted it. "Sorry, I can't say this is the most accurate piece, but if you're close enough, it's good enough."

"Thanks Jack. I'll be sure to wait until I see the whites of his eyes."

Jack put the Springfield back in the bag just as I swerved to change lanes again. His head banged hard against the window.

285

"Jesus, dude. You trying to take me out of play?"

"Not on your life, my friend. I want you there every step of the way."

"Well, quit doing the Mario Andretti tango. I'm no good to you unconscious."

"You should have brought a helmet," I said stomping on the throttle to seize another gap and then shooting sideways. This time Jack had taken a firm grip on the passenger handle.

My phone started ringing. I took it out and saw it was Charlie. I put the phone on speaker and placed it in the hands-free cradle.

"Charlie, what's up?"

"I'm just looking at the property records," she said. "Lund just bought the place recently."

"When exactly?"

"January nineteen."

"The day of Demarco Torrell's verdict," I said.

"Why would that have any significance?" asked Charlie.

I couldn't say. But I had a growing feeling that this was more about me than anyone else, and this new evidence made me think it could be more related to the trial than Afghanistan.

"I don't know. But Lund would have been following the trial. If for nothing else than to take satisfaction in the fact that his plan had worked out perfectly. That an innocent man was being convicted of two murders that he, or one of his helpers, committed."

"There's something else about the property you should know about."

"What's that?"

"It's got a fallout shelter in the back yard."

A fallout shelter? Maybe that's what Francine had been about to divulge before she'd cut her message short. My thoughts swung to an image of Bella, my darling child, enduring the terror of a makeshift prison, her life in the hands of a serial killer who I now realized didn't really need a motive. He enjoyed killing. He got off on playing judge, jury and executioner.

God, please let her still be alive.

"They were all the rage in the 1950s, apparently," Charlie said. "People built them in their back yards to hide in if the Russians nuked LA. They were designed for survivors to stay inside for a few weeks until the radiation danger eased off."

"What, then walk out and resume life in a nuclear wasteland?" laughed Jack.

"Yeah, that's why a lot of people didn't build them. That was not the kind of world they wanted to live in."

"Do you have any images you can send through?"

"I'll send you both the link. It only has photos of the shelter's interior. It doesn't say where it is actually located." Charlie was perceptive—she knew we'd need to plan how we were going to storm the shelter without getting Bella killed.

"Thanks Charlie. Good work. Talk later."

Fallout shelter. Nuclear apocalypse. What an awful fear to have for your family. But I'd take that over some psycho having his hands on my child.

***

I pulled the Mustang up fifty yards short of the address. Jack handed me the Springfield, and as I stepped out of the car, I tucked it into my pants at the small of my back. We jogged up the sidewalk to the house next door and took cover behind a parked car. I sneaked a look around to the target house. No cars in the driveway. More specifically, no Lincoln. We scanned up and down the street, but there was still no Lincoln to be seen. We knew the lot had no back entrance—the house backed onto another residential property. So either someone had taken the car out for a spell, or they'd all moved on. That, or we'd been led on a wild goose chase. I hoped like hell it wasn't the latter. I wanted my daughter back. And I wanted to make Lund pay royally for his actions. I hadn't decided yet whether I'd take him alive or dead. I preferred dead, but revenge was secondary. I just longed to hold Bella again—that was all that mattered.

The curtains were drawn across the home's two front windows. I turned to Jack.

"Let's go."

We dashed to the front left of the house and crouched. I snuck a peek into the front room through a small gap between the blind and window sill. There was nothing in the room at all: no furniture and no people, just white walls and floor boards. I darted across the front of the house to the other side. That was the plan. Jack would scan one side, I'd scan the other, and we'd regroup at the rear.

I waited for a while, listening. There was no noise. A cool, gentle breeze was blowing, and it carried the sweet scent of cypress from the hedge behind me. There were three windows on my side of the house. I'd memorized the floor plan. The first window was the family room, the second the bathroom, and the third the laundry. Through a slit in the curtains, the first room also looked empty. And there was neither sound nor movement coming from the other two. I soon reached the back of the house where the pool was. A small rectangular lawn extended from the pool's fence and paving stones to the lot's back boundary. A shed sat in the corner on Jack's side.

When Jack appeared, he shook his head. With that, I leapt silently over the pool fence and landed in a crouch. In one fluid motion, I aimed and swept my weapon across the kitchen and dining area through the home's rear floor-to-ceiling windows. Again, the space was totally bare. I motioned to Jack that I was going in and quietly slid the glass door open. Jack was right behind me. We cleared the entire house room by room but found nothing. The place was deserted.

I rushed out the back door and around the pool, cleared the fence, and then approached the shed. I could hear nothing but a few birds and a dog barking from a few houses down.

The shed was wooden with old paint tins stacked up against the window, completely blocking the view inside. I put my back to the shed as I readied to enter. I scanned the rest of the lawn area, but there was no sign of anything but grass. The entrance to the fallout shelter had to be inside the shed.

I turned the handle slowly and silently but was betrayed by badly squeaking hinges. I stopped and then pushed the door open fast and hard. It worked—I'd gotten it ajar without further noise. Jack covered me as I entered. The room was only dimly lit by sunlight. A few rusted tools were stacked in one corner alongside a lawn mower that looked like it hadn't been used for decades. But there, set into the floor, was a round, rusty trap door with a lever handle.

I stepped quietly towards it and took hold of the handle. My heart was pounding. Opening the door could trigger many outcomes I didn't want to imagine.

Lund could be poised underneath, waiting to pick me off.

I could find the body of my daughter.

Or I could find nothing at all.

I slowly opened the hatch. The shelter was lit with fluorescent light. A ladder descended to a floor lined with cheap black carpet. Still, I heard only silence. I fell to my stomach and motioned for Jack to hold my legs. I then positioned myself over the hole, brought my weapon up and quickly swung my upper body down through the hatch. As I hung there, scanning the room upside down, all I could hear was my breathing. There was no one there. No one alive, that is.

I saw two bodies: a man and a woman.

"Bella!" I shouted. My voice disappeared into the walls, and I got nothing in reply. I swung myself up and climbed down.

It was like the shelter had remained untouched since the people who built it had moved on. It had been preserved like a museum exhibit. The small room was fitted with two bunk beds, one against each side wall. Some shelves at the far end were stocked with tinned food and a stove, and a sink was bolted to the opposite wall.

The dead man was lying face down on the carpet. The dead woman was face up on one of the bunk beds. I didn't have to get closer to see who it was. Francine Holmes had died with her eyes open in an expression of mild surprise.

Jack followed me down. He bent over the man's body.

"Who do you think this is?" he said.

"Don't know. Could be Lund's driver. Perhaps Lund had no more use for him. Or maybe, like Francine here, he made the mistake of being disloyal. Check his pockets for ID."

While Jack searched, I turned my attention back to Francine.

Her left hand rested on her abdomen, the fingers drenched in blood. Her right hand lay straight beside her body. Then something caught my eye. I bent down for a closer look to find Francine's hand clutching a wad of bank notes.

I took the money from her hand. A message was scrawled onto the top note:

"Madison. Cash for your daughter's life. Sound fair?"

I felt violently ill. I forced back the urge to vomit.

I counted the money, but I already knew what it would add up to.

Five thousand dollars.

Jack stood beside me and read the note.

"What's that about?" he said.

"That's what we paid the Afghan families for each civilian my unit killed in Bati Kot. Five grand. And then we moved on."

I looked down at Francine's face.

"So this has nothing to do with social media," Jack said. "And he's not going to be asking for a ransom."

"No. This about one thing and one thing only—vengeance."

Just then, my phone buzzed. I took it out and opened the message.

"YOU'LL SEE YOUR DAUGHTER SOON. PROMISE. BUT FORGET ABOUT SAVING HER."

It was punctuated by a string of the same emoji—tears of laughter.

But maybe Lund shouldn't have been too sure he'd have the last laugh, because he'd just screwed up big time.

Charlie's trap had worked.

There, on my screen, was Victor Lund's number.

At last we knew exactly where this son-of-a-bitch was.

CHAPTER 34

As I hurried back to the car, I sent Charlie the number. I called as I got behind the wheel, put the phone in its cradle, and hit the ignition button. I pulled out with no plan besides putting Reseda behind me. Charlie soon had the phone's radio signal traced.

"Got it," she said. Then she paused. "That's weird."

"What's weird?"

"Hang on, just double checking. Yep. He's in Nevada."

"Nevada? Are you sure?"

"Yes. He's just outside a place called Ely, near the Utah border."

Where the hell is he going? I did a quick mental calculation to account for the time that had elapsed since I'd received Francine's tip-off. It had only been two hours. How could he be anywhere near Utah already?

"He couldn't have driven that far that fast," I said.

"He's not on a road," said Charlie.

"Jesus Christ!" I checked my mirrors and pulled over hard.

"What's going on?" asked Jack.

"Transmission's gone," said Charlie. "He's just turned his phone off—it's no longer transmitting."

"He's not in a car," I said. "He's flying. He's got Bella in his goddamn plane!"

My anger had returned in full force, and it quickly found a new target.

"What the hell is Cassinelli doing?! Why haven't we heard from him? Charlie, I'm hanging up to call him."

Cassinelli answered first ring.

"What's up, Madison?"

"Jesus Christ, Cassinelli, what have you been doing? Lund is in the air!"

"He can't be. I've been watching the terminal. I've got eyes on the hanger he keeps his plane in, and there's been no movement whatsoever."

"Are you sure?"

"If you're about to ask if I'm sober, don't. I've been watching that hanger till my eyes went dry. No one's been in there—no ground crew, no flight crew, no coffee and cake trolley—nothing. If he's in a plane, it did not leave from here, I'm telling you."

Suddenly it dawned on me.

"Van Nuys," I said. "He must have flown out of Van Nuys!"

Van Nuys Airport was just minutes away. I hung up on Cassinelli, swung the car around, and hammered the accelerator with all the delicacy of an enraged blacksmith.

I tapped redial on Charlie's number.

"Charlie! How did we miss the fact that Lund's plane was at Van Nuys Airport and not LAX?"

"Van Nuys? Never heard of it."

"It's in the San Fernando Valley, where we are right now. Lund had his plane ten minutes from his Reseda house all along."

"I'm checking it now. When I looked earlier, its last stop was LAX, I'm certain. But yes, it moved to Van Nuys."

"When?"

"About two hours ago, which was after I'd checked."

"He must have had it delivered there," I said. "It had already left by the time Cassinelli arrived."

Where the hell is that prick taking my daughter?!

My grip on the wheel could have choked out a lion.

"Charlie, can you find out where he's headed?"

"Checking the logs now. Here it is. Gallatin Field BZN, wherever that is."

"Bozeman," I said. "He's heading to the Bozeman Yellowstone Airport in Montana. Charlie, I need you to find what ties Lund has to Montana."

"I'm on it."

She hung up and we raced to Van Nuys.

"What's the plan when we get to the airport?" asked Jack.

I hadn't really thought that far ahead. But there was only one answer.

"We need to get our hands on a jet."

Jack pulled out his phone.

"I think I know someone who can help."

"You're kidding me. Who?"

"A Fortune 500 friend I did a big favor for. The one who was going to lend me that chopper before you rudely interrupted my Napa Valley date."

"Has he got a plane at Van Nuys?"

"No. At LAX. And it's a she."

"A rich lady you did a favor for?"

"Yeah. Carla Pearson. I exposed her cheating husband and saved her a mint on the divorce settlement. She was very grateful."

"Grateful enough to lend us her private jet?"

"You bet. And I'm sure she'd throw in the pilot too. We just have to hope he's available, and sober."

Jack tapped a call and put the phone to his ear.

"Carla," he said, making sure his million-watt smile shone through in his voice. "How are you doing this fine afternoon?"

After a minute or so Jack thanked her and hung up.

"She said her plane's out."

"How come? I thought you said—"

"Steady on, dude. Let me finish. Carla said that if time is of the essence, we shouldn't wait for her plane anyway. She's going to book us a charter jet. She said we can take it wherever we want for however long we want."

A shot of warm gratitude hit my wretched heart.

"That's very kind of her."

"We'll be in the air within the hour," Jack said. "She's going to secure a mid-sized jet. It'll have us in Bozeman in two hours ten minutes."

I thanked Jack. It would be getting dark soon after we arrived. I tried to send a thought to Bella, not that I believed in telepathy—or that I disbelieved it either. I just hoped that some part of her was holding onto the hope that her daddy was going to come get her, that he would cross the planet on broken glass to put an end to her ordeal and see her smile once more. After the Anaheim shooting, I promised Bella I'd always be there for her. And, God help me, I was going to deliver on that promise.

I did the time sums in my head again. The result wasn't what you'd call a relief.

"He's got about a three-hour start on us."

"Yeah, that's true," said Jack. "But we do have one thing going for us."

"Yeah? What's that?"

"He doesn't know we're coming."

✳✳✳

The Gulfstream 100 sped us north at point eight of the speed of sound—about six-hundred-and-forty-five miles an hour in land-speed terms. It was of significant consolation to me that even though we didn't know where Bella was, we were chasing her at about the fastest speed humanly possible.

At Van Nuys, I'd told the charter company we didn't need a flight attendant, just the pilot, Captain Hank Seger. Having someone waiting on us at a time like this seemed frivolous. Similarly, while it was hard not to be impressed by the plane's plush interior and massive leather seats, I couldn't lapse into anything remotely close to comfort. The plane had wi-fi, so I waited keenly for whatever Charlie could pull up in terms of Bozeman property and business data.

But it wasn't Charlie I heard from next. It was Lund.

A new message appeared on my phone.

"HAPPY VIEWING," it said.

There was a link below the text and some login details. I tapped on the link and it took me through to a YouTube channel. The frame was black. With a sickening feeling, I keyed in the username and password Lund had provided. Once I hit "enter" a still of the video appeared.

I felt like someone had punched me in the solar plexus. It was Bella. Gagged and bound. Lying down on her side.

Jack was at my shoulder.

"It's a private video," he said. "Only you can see it."

I hit play and immediately wished I hadn't. I could hear Bella breathing hard through her nose. She was whimpering quietly. And after a few seconds I realized she was trembling. I looked closer.

"She's shivering," I said as tears stung my eyes. The anger welled up again, and I had to control the violent urge to smash my phone to smithereens.

"There's a comment," Jack said. "Added five minutes ago."

I flipped the video up to bring the comment into center frame.

"See, Madison? I told you you would see your daughter again," it read. "As you can see, she is in a very cold place with not much to shield her from the elements. She will probably be dead in about three hours."

Even at the speed we were flying, we didn't have enough time. Beyond Bozeman, we had no idea where to go next.

I had to try and engage Lund. I had to find a way to change his mind, change the course of my daughter's fate.

"Is this about Bati Kot?" I wrote.

"You know damn well it is," came the reply. "Your unit destroyed dozens of lives and just walked away blameless."

"It was a firefight."

297

"Liar! I knew many of the local people. They told me what happened. Your patrol took a suicide hit and then pulled out shooting everyone in sight."

"That's not what happened. We took fire. Many of those civilians were killed by AK-47 rounds. There was a full investigation, and my unit was exonerated."

"Right, an investigation by the US military into civilian casualties inflicted by the US military. It was a total sham."

"I was there. I saw what happened."

"Then you saw at least one of your men maintain fire as your patrol withdrew, killing men, women and children as he went."

It was true. While I'd denied it for as long as possible, Lund was telling the truth. It was the darkest day of my military career. As we pulled out following the attack, a brief skirmish ensued before I ordered the men to hold fire. But Private Alan Halloway was caught in a fearful mental lock and kept his turret-mounted .50 caliber M2 firing as his Hummer sped away. The M2 was a heavy machine gun with devastating power. Any victims that weren't killed by Halloway's weapon lost either their arms or legs. Weeks later, I'd been part of the team that went to visit the villages where the victims and victims' families lived. To the wounded we gave three thousand dollars in green backs. For each of the dead, their families received five thousand. The investigation confirmed we were engaged in a firefight, but it buried the undisciplined actions of Halloway, whose bullets caused half the human carnage. It had come away ruling that while a deeply regrettable number of Afghans had been killed and injured by bullets from both sides, the conduct of my unit had fallen well within US military combat guidelines. In other words, the civilian casualties were deemed to be within the justifiable bounds of warfare.

I had no reason to defend Private Halloway now despite my innate allegiance to the Corps. Speaking against a fellow Marine was not an easy thing to do—standing by each other to the hilt was sacrosanct.

"That is true, I admit," I finally wrote. "I wish I could have gotten closer to our shooter to stop him, but in the heat of battle, he was beyond reach."

"The heat of battle? Can you hear yourself? You're an apologist for mass murder."

There was an incoming call. It was Charlie.

"What's up?" I said.

"Victor Lund has a property in Montana. It's a few acres located in the mountains near Big Sky."

That's why Bella was shivering. She must be in the mountains somewhere. Mid-winter at God only knows what altitude. This time of day, this time of year, the temperatures would have to be well below freezing. My whole body ached at the thought of her pain.

Charlie sent an address through.

"We're going to need a car," I said.

"Claire's onto it," Charlie said. I could hear Claire talking in the background. "Claire says it's done. She's booked you a Ford Expedition. You just have to do the forms at the Hertz counter."

I thanked them both and hung up.

We were due to land in thirty minutes. Both Jack and I keyed in the address Charlie gave us for Lund's property plus a link from a real estate site. It was a sixty-acre lot on Latigo Road, nestled in the foothills of Wilson Peak on the side of the valley opposite Big Sky's iconic Lone Peak.

Just like we had for Reseda, we studied the layout of Lund's house. It was a huge, six-bedroom lodge spread over three floors. We checked the snow depth and found Montana was having a very good ski season. Big Sky was reporting five feet of snow at the base. That's what we could expect at Lund's property. From the maps app, it was hard to get a read on the landscape and how close to the house we might be able to get undetected. We'd just have to see when we got there.

The thought occurred to me that we were taking a huge punt in assuming that this was where Lund had taken Bella. There was no certainty that we were right. And if we were wrong, Bella was dead.

I looked out the window. Everywhere I could see was white, divided here and there by a road or a fence. On the mountain faces, dark cliff bands were left exposed where it was too steep for the snow to hold. For all I knew, we were flying directly over her.

Hurry up, I urged the pilot inside my head.

Out the window the cold blanket of white rolled past.

Where are you, my little angel? Just hold tight. Hold tight, my darling. I'm coming.

A new comment appeared beneath Bella's video.

"Still there, Madison?"

"Yes," I wrote. "Where have you taken her? If she dies, I will skin you alive and feed you to the wolves."

I had to encourage him to believe we had no idea where he was.

"Funny you should say that. Because you won't be seeing your daughter ever again. There will be nothing of her to bury. The wolves and bears will see to that."

I buckled over and screamed out loud.

"Is everything okay back there?" asked Captain Seger over the intercom.

I looked up the aisle. The cockpit door swung open and Hank was there leaning over and looking our way.

"Yes. All good, Hank," I shouted and waved. "How long?"

"Dropping the wheels now, Mr. Madison. We'll be touching down in no time. I'm going to need you to buckle up, if you wouldn't mind."

I waved at him, sat back, and clipped my belt. I kept my eyes glued to the window. My legs were jiggling. My hands clutched the arm rests. I was prepared to sprint through the terminal to get to the car rental desk.

"We're going to get her, Brad," said Jack.

And while I appreciated his attempt to reassure me, I couldn't escape the string of horrific thoughts that sat in the back of my mind like toxic waste.

What if we don't get there in time?

What if Lund decides not to wait for Bella to freeze to death?

What if he hasn't taken Bella to his Wilson Peak property at all?

The Gulfstream landed and Hank taxied the plane over to the terminal. As soon as it stopped, Jack and I were up front, ready to exit.

Hank emerged from the cockpit.

"Mr. Madison, I took the liberty of making some very discreet inquiries to see if there's been any movement out of Gallatin Field."

"Yes?" I said warily.

"It seems Mr. Lund keeps a chopper there. Flies it himself. And twenty minutes after his plane landed, his chopper took off. He has not returned."

I shot a quizzical look at Jack. He smiled.

"I told Hank we were on Lund's tail, hoping he might get some info out of the control tower staff at Gallatin. Turns out he could."

I turned to Hank.

"Thanks Hank. Do they know where Lund went?"

"They said he headed south. And given the elapsed time they don't expect him back. They're sure he's landed somewhere."

As Hank spoke, Jack zoomed in again on Lund's property on his phone.

"Here," he said, showing me the screen. The Google Maps image revealed the property in summer. There was no helipad, but there was a tennis court. "That's where the bastard is. For sure."

We stepped out of the Gulfstream into the brisk Montana air and bolted for the terminal.

CHAPTER 35

While Jack handled the paperwork at the car rental counter, I called Charlie. I wanted her to dig around and see if there was anything she could find about Victor Lund on the Bati Kot incident. In short, why would he bear such a personal grudge against me? I was fully aware of his efforts to brand my unit as a bunch of callous murderers, but I wondered if that was the full story behind his lasting wrath.

I suggested to Charlie that some of his correspondence with the US military might be in the Afghan War Diary, the trove of classified documents released by WikiLeaks.

"Jeez. WikiLeaks. Sounds so dated. That's kind of the Middle Ages in the history of hacking. I mean, props to Assange and all, but the world's moved on."

"Can you just check it, please?"

"Of course. But I haven't been laying idle, you know."

"That doesn't surprise me. Do you have something?"

"I dug into Victor Lund's medical history," she said.

"You mean ..."

"Yeah, I hacked his records. Piece of cake, really. Most medical clinics are. And the Camden in Beverly Hills is no different. They charge their patients double what you'd pay elsewhere, but their database is easier to crack than a freshly laid egg."

"Well done. What did you find?"

"Victor Lund is a bulimic. Has been for years."

Bulimic? A man in his sixties? I thought only young people had that, young girls in particular.

"That accounts for his emaciated features," I said.

"Exactly," said Charlie. "Other tell-tale signs include a raspy voice and coughing."

"Go on," I urged.

"As far as I could tell from the doctor's notes, his bulimia was triggered by a traumatic episode. Lund did not go into detail with his doctor, but he did say it began after he returned from Afghanistan and entered divorce proceedings initiated by his wife."

"Right. Anything else."

"Yep, the doctor noted Lund seemed to harbor a burning anger but rebuffed his attempt to steer him towards therapy."

"Why address it when you can take it out on the world?"

"You and I both know that's what men prefer to do," said Charlie, reminding me of her nasty experience at the hands of online trolls. "But Lund was hurting in other ways too."

"Like what?"

"He was suffering chronic pancreatitis early last year. Typically, that's caused by alcoholism, but in Lund's case it was bulimia. To make matters worse, the pain intensifies when he eats something. So he's been prescribed enough Fentanyl and Oxycodone to drop a herd of cattle."

"He might be drugging Bella with that stuff," I said.

"Maybe, but he's also being prescribed Restoril to help him sleep."

"Restoril?"

"It's a sleeping pill. Also goes by the name of temazepam. It's more likely he's keeping her sedated with that. He probably has a stash on hand because his quack has strongly advised him to use it sparingly—it can put you in a coma if you use too much in conjunction with opioids like Fentanyl."

"Right, thanks for that, Charlie. Keep digging, please," I said the words quietly. The wave of dread had come back in force. I felt depleted, exhausted once more.

Jack slapped me on the back. It was enough for me to snap out it.

"Let's go," he said. "I'm driving. You can keep an eye on Bella as we go. And play navigator."

"No worries."

It was about an hour to Big Sky heading south along US101. Snow covered everything in sight. The township gave way to a rural landscape of flat paddocks sheeted in white. The roofs of ranch houses were capped with up to three feet of snow, and a still mist hung over the Gallatin River, which ran alongside the road. Light was fading from the overcast sky. In an hour it would be dark. That had its positives and negatives—good because it meant we could approach the lodge unseen, bad for Bella because the temperature would soon drop rapidly. The readings I had from Big Sky were that it was presently thirteen degrees, and it would fall to eight by seven o'clock.

I didn't want to watch the video stream, but I had to. I could see Bella was still breathing from the movement of her chest, but her eyes had closed. Whether that was from pure exhaustion, drugs or the beginnings of hypothermia, I didn't know.

"Stay with us, my darling," I said to the phone as if Bella could actually hear me. "Please, stay with us. Daddy's coming."

We were approaching the turnoff to Big Sky when Charlie called again.

"Brad, does the name Bianca Vanek mean anything to you?"

The name drew a blank initially, but after a few seconds the penny dropped.

"Yes, she was the Czech aid worker killed at Bati Kot."

"Well, Victor sent several emails to the officers investigating the Bati Kot massacre. He was urging them to come clean about what happened. He said the US military was responsible for Vanek's death even though her autopsy reported two bullets fired from an AK-47 had killed her."

"That's right."

"Vanek's family and the Czech government accepted the findings but Lund refused to. But there was something the military knew but only revealed to Vanek's family."

"What was that?"

"She was pregnant."

"And the father? Did they say who the father was?"

"No. But about five minutes ago I managed to contact one of Vanek's Facebook friends. From photos on Vanek's account, they appeared to be very close. So I reached out to her on Messenger and she got back to me right away."

"What did she say?"

"She said Vanek was two months pregnant. And she knew the sex. It was a girl."

My blood was stone cold.

"My God. And the father?"

"The friend told me she didn't know who he was, but Vanek told her he was a married man, an American. He was going to leave his wife and they would bring their daughter into the world together."

"She just told you this?"

"I can be very persuasive. I told her it was urgent, that it could not be more critical. I told her a young girl's life was at stake."

"Thank you, Charlie."

It was now perfectly clear what was driving Lund's madness. This was an eye for an eye. He believed I'd robbed him of his daughter. Now he was determined to take mine.

CHAPTER 36

As we began the climb up the winding, icy Latigo Road, Jack killed the headlights. The vehicle crept upwards between six-foot walls of snow that almost glowed in the dying light. It was like driving through a glacier.

We were confident Lund had no clue we were onto him. His tone in our comment exchange on YouTube was sickly smug. He was certain he was treating me to the hell of seeing my daughter die without being able to do a single thing about it.

"Stop here," I said.

We were two hundred yards short of the entrance. Jack pulled out his gun. I retrieved mine from the glove box. In unison, we both dropped, checked, and reloaded the magazines.

"Let's go get your daughter," said Jack.

The walls of snow provided cover as we trod our way up the road. Ahead I could see a break—the driveway into Lund's lodge. I motioned for Jack to stop and raised my head above the snow. The slope fell back from the road, providing a clear side view of the lodge, save for a few small pines. Several lights in the house were on. But, almost obscured by the house about fifty yards beyond, I could just make out the tail of a helicopter. My heart skipped a beat—Bella was here, somewhere.

I ducked back down and informed Jack. He had to take a look at the chopper himself.

"Brand new Bell 407," he said, "Not bad."

"Lights are on, but he could be out and about, so we have to watch our backs too."

"Sure, let's keep it our surprise."

From the top of the driveway, fresh tire tracks led into one of the garage doors. A car had been used here recently. There were only a few back windows overlooking the driveway, so we dashed quickly down to the lodge.

Darkness had just about closed in now. The clouds had cleared to reveal an obsidian sky littered with crisp pins of light and a fingernail moon. I was on edge in a good way—hyper alert, armed and utterly present in the moment. For a fraction of a second, I savored the heightened sense of being. It was the same kick that combat provided, the kick plenty of soldiers miss when they get back home.

Three feet of untouched snow was going to make moving around the house difficult. We'd sink deep with every step and our tracks would be obvious. But we had no time to lose. In Reseda, we'd split up. This time, we stuck together for cover. We headed down the side of the garage for the back.

My legs sank up to my lower thighs with each step into the soft powder, and it was an effort to haul them out. But we reached the back undetected and came to a door. I looked in through the glass. It appeared to be the ski room. I turned the handle, thankful it was not locked. I opened the door slowly, giving myself just enough room to move inside. But even that movement was enough to let a ski pole that must have been placed against the door slip onto the slate floor. At the sound of the clattering, I heard footsteps coming from the far side of the house. I stuck my head into the passageway, looking left toward the main living area. As soon as I did, a gunshot sounded, and a bullet flew past me six inches from my face and buried itself in the wood-paneled wall.

I pulled back and listened for Lund to stir. Nothing.

I was about to tell Jack to cover me when I heard what sounded like a very powerful motocross bike kick to life. Half a second later, its engine screamed under the throttle and the volume dampened quickly.

Snow mobile. Lund's making a run for it.

I launched down the passageway in pursuit. At the far end of the house a door led into a large shed that opened out onto the snow. We got there just in time to see the tail light of Lund's sled race into the pine forest and climb further up the mountain.

"He's going to kill her," I shouted.

There was another snow mobile in the shed. A Polaris RMK—a beast of a machine. Growing up in Idaho, I'd done many a snow mobile trip into the back country with my buddies to ski untracked powder. I jumped on, but the ignition was missing its keys.

Damn it!

I quickly hopped off the machine, lifted its plastic hood, yanked the ignition plug out, and dropped the hood back into place. I then hopped back on, pulled the choke switch out and ripped away at the pull cord. The Polaris snarled to life. I gave it some throttle and turned to Jake.

"Hop on," I said.

But he shook his head.

"I've got a better idea," he shouted and ran out the door into the snow. Straight for the chopper.

I wrenched the throttle and the Polaris leapt out of the shed like Secretariat. I flicked the lights on and pointed the sled into Lund's tracks. It was a hell of a machine, and it drove the belt with ferocious power. As I opened it up, it bucked forward and spat out rooster tails of powder.

Lund's tracks weaved upwards and across. I could see he was following a trail that had been used several times. I wondered how Lund knew it was me, opening fire like that and running. I guessed I was on the short list of people who'd be sneaking into his house in the remote Montana woods.

The track flattened as it crossed a wide snowfield then turned upward again into a steep climb and through another section of trees. Just as I reached the woods, I heard the sound of a chopper coming up loud and low behind me. It passed overhead and continued climbing, skimming over the trees.

I came to another clearing. We must have climbed fifteen-hundred feet at least. Up ahead against the ridge line I saw the chopper bank around.

Three shots rang out. It was Lund firing at Jack.

Suddenly the chopper lit up with red smoke. Initially, I thought the bullets had found their mark, but then I saw a red light leave the chopper and fall down onto the mountain. It was a flare. Jack was telling me where Lund was. I hit the throttle hard again and rode the machine as fast as I could. Above the noise of the sled I heard more gunfire. Jack wasn't just playing sitting duck; he was shooting back.

Just as I was thinking Jack should pull back, the chopper made a sudden turn. The tone of its engine changed, and I saw smoke pouring out of the rear as the machine dipped awkwardly down. This time it wasn't a flare. Two seconds later, the craft dropped rapidly behind the far side of the ridge. I didn't have to be an expert on piloting to know Jack was struggling to control her.

A few seconds later, I heard a sickening thud. Then came a powerful blast and a flash of light before smoke erupted high above the ridge line.

I was stunned momentarily. The idea that Jack was now dead was not something I could quickly dispel from my mind. But he'd risked his life to guide me towards Lund, and possibly Bella. I had to get there as fast as I could. I'd go and look for Jack as soon as I was sure Bella was safe and sound and I'd broken every bone in Lund's body.

The mountain up ahead was dark. There was no sign of Lund's taillight now. I was about two-hundred yards from where Jack dropped the flare when I saw a muzzle flash and heard a bullet tear through the air about three feet away. I let go of the throttle and rolled into the snow. Lund fired a few more shots at me, but his aim was stray. Away from the sled's lights, Lund could not see me. I moved into a copse of trees to my right that extended almost all the way to where Lund was. The trees were thin, and I realized we were almost at the tree line, the altitude at which trees stop growing. That meant we were about nine-thousand feet up. The snow was fresh and deep here too, and walking even a short distance was physically taxing. But I forged on, hunched over, and got to the refuge of the trees as quickly as I could.

I kept my eyes fixed on Lund's position as I darted from tree to tree, pistol at the ready. Lund was not going to be taking any more pot shots at me without getting some heat in return. But as I climbed higher, I was not fired upon. And that made me worry and want to run to Bella as fast as I could, cover be damned.

For a second, I wondered whether Lund would get back on his sled and race off. Perhaps Bella's location was much further ahead. It was almost a habit now—no matter how close I thought I was getting to my daughter, there was a nagging feeling that she was only pulling further away. The feeling told me I was utterly useless to her, and that the idea I could protect her, save her, had always been an idiotic delusion serving nothing but my ego.

I was breathing heavily. Once or twice I became extremely light-headed and short of breath. It was the altitude. Thankfully, the dizzy spells were short lived, and I was able to resume moving steadily. Soon my eyes began to make out the shape of a small cabin up ahead.

"Bella!" I said to myself and trudged on as silently as I could. As I neared the cabin, it became obvious that Lund was not standing guard or waiting to pick me off. He had either escaped, or he was inside.

The thought of him hurting Bella right now was so horrifying that I almost broke cover and made a final headlong dash. But I kept control and reached the cabin unchallenged. My greatest risk was that my heavy breathing would give me away. I got it under control as I moved carefully toward the front of the structure. When I reached the corner, I heard Lund's voice for the first time.

"Come in, Captain Madison. Let me assure you, there is no way you can shoot me without me seeing you first. I have a gun to your daughter's head. And I will pull the trigger unless you signal your immediate cooperation."

Lund's voice was hoarse, and he coughed twice as he got the words out. I remembered what Charlie had told me about bulimia affecting the voice. Well, I'd be only too happy to see him choke on his words.

I peered around the corner to check out the entrance. The windows on either side of the central door were bordered up. The only way to see in was by going through the door.

"Madison! I know you're there!"

"Alright, alright. I'm coming in."

I stepped square into the door frame with the gun in my right hand hanging next to my thigh.

"Drop it," said Lund.

There was Bella, crouched on the ground with her head resting back against the cabin wall. She looked beyond terrified, shaking with cold and fear. And there was Lund, seated on a chair beside her with his gun pressed to my daughter's temple. I considered

313

whether I could draw quickly and put a bullet in Lund's brain, backing my speed and accuracy against his reflexes. If I was holding my service weapon, I may not have thought about it too much. But this Springfield was unfamiliar. I hadn't fired it once, and I couldn't take the risk of missing.

I let my gun fall to the floor, thinking desperately that there still had to be some way out of this. There had to be some way to appeal to Lund's humanity. But I knew I was kidding myself. Maybe if I got close enough I could ... I took a step toward Lund.

"Stay where you are," he said with a clip. The force of his speech prompted yet another cough.

My eyes shifted to an old Louis Vuitton trunk sitting on the floor to my left.

Lund laughed.

"Your daughter travels in style, Madison. Limousines, Learjets and Louis Vuitton. It's a family heirloom handed down from my grandfather. Nothing but the best for your little Instagram star. She was carry-on not check-in, of course."

My breathing grew rapid and my chest heaved. The outrage of him shoving her in that trunk. I wanted to leap across and lock my hands around his neck. I blocked out the thought of Bella crammed inside the trunk, frightened to death and fighting for air. It took all my restraint to address Lund in a calm, rational manner. The imperative was to engage him in a conversation, one that could hopefully become a negotiation.

"I don't understand what's going on here, Victor."

"Oh, yes you do."

"I'm not talking about Afghanistan, because if you wanted to hurt me, why wait till now? You've had years to get your vengeance."

"The mission to make you pay is a recent one. The product of fate. I was busy with my other projects, and you just happened to walk into my web, so to speak. It was all quite serendipitous, really."

"So I distracted you from your killing spree?"

"Well, first you appeared, then your little slut caught my attention, and it seemed that the planets had just aligned. Imagine my surprise when I found out you are not only a murderer, but you are also quite happy to prostitute your daughter on social media."

"I always warned my wife there would be hideous creeps following our daughter—turns out I was right."

Diplomacy be damned.

"Who's the creep here, Madison? I have used my money and influence to promote YouTube creators who enrich America's youth, both spiritually and creatively. And I have removed a few whose only mission in life was to degrade the minds and morals of this country's children."

I was reminded of when Lund accosted me outside Bagram Air Base all those years ago. Back then he was merely a zealot. Now it seemed, he'd drifted into madness.

"I didn't think God bestowed the right on anyone to act as judge and jury in His name."

"With a reprobate like Luke Jameson peddling a life of strippers and lies, I don't need permission to dispense divine justice. He didn't just turn away from God, he mocked Him."

"So he committed the crime of apostasy? That's why you killed him? That's straight out of the Taliban's playbook. I'm surprised you didn't stone him to death."

"Very funny, Madison. But your attitude doesn't surprise me in the least. You are also a problematic heathen who is completely ignorant of the moral havoc you have wreaked as a soldier, a father and a lawyer."

315

"What, defending an innocent young man who is now sitting on death row for the murder you committed?"

"Unfortunately, delivering on my calling obliged me to take a few casualties. Cracking eggs to make omelets, as they say. But my understanding is that Demarco Torrell has made peace with God and himself. So I guess I did him a favor. His life would have remained meaningless had it not been for Francine's intervention."

"Was that under your instruction?"

"Why yes. I needed a believer if my plan was to work. And it did, beautifully."

"He's a seventeen-year-old boy locked up in San Quentin."

"Yes, and he'll die with a heart devoted to God. A true martyr."

I had to refrain from flat-out abusing him. I wanted to call him every name under the sun, but it was clear I was confronting a man who was thoroughly consumed by a belief of his own making. God and religion were simply an excuse, a package in which he boxed his toxic view of humanity and his role within it.

"What about Toby Connors? What was his moral crime?"

Lund scoffed as though I'd complained about there being one cloud in an otherwise clear sky.

"I told you there had to be sacrifices."

"You're doing God's work? Really? You harangued us for civilian casualties in Afghanistan yet you're totally okay with it when it suits you."

He shrugged. "Call it a necessary cost in the war against evil. That is the only war that is acceptable. Not the bloody invasion and occupation of a weak country, which is what you were part of. That is just plain bullying. But we have a problem in this country and you're so caught up in your own affairs that you don't even realize your dereliction of parenting has been a huge contributing factor. Don't kid yourself, your daughter is doing what so many other

316

seven-year-old girls are doing—she is a vehicle for her mother's avarice and her father's moral sloth."

"So we just happened to cross paths over the Torrell case?"

"Fate brought us together. Or, as I see it, God did."

"Not to mention Bianca Vanek."

Lund started, and went to speak, but paused. It was silent long enough for me to know that even the mention of her name was a stab to his heart.

"Yes," he said, lowering his eyes briefly before directing a hateful glare back at me. "Bianca. She was just another civilian casualty to you and the military. She was just a—"

"She was pregnant."

Again, there was that slight twitch in his expression—another blow he did not see coming.

"With your child."

"Yes. That's right. A girl. She would have been ten years old if she were alive today." Lund sighed deeply. "You see, Madison? Do you see what you have done?"

"Victor, I did not kill your girlfriend."

"Oh yes, you did. And she wasn't just my girlfriend, she was the love of my life."

"How can you dispute the fact that Bianca was killed by the Taliban? Her own family accepted that that was the truth. There was no cover up about her death."

"Bullshit. The US military closed ranks around your unit and lied to Bianca's family, to the Afghan people and to me. Bati Kot wasn't a firefight—it was a civilian massacre plain and simple."

I hadn't meant to get a rise out of Lund but I'd managed to. His blood was boiling. Part of me was glad, just to see him hurting. I couldn't have hated a man any more than I did him, the sad fucking hypocrite.

"Victor, Bianca Vanek died from two bullets shot from an AK-47. She was killed by an enemy fighter. An enemy of the United States who fired on my unit. Yet you choose to put the blame entirely on us."

"What do you want me to say, Madison? Thank you for your service?"

Lund shifted in his seat, shrugged his shoulders, and straightened his back. "Now, enough talk. It's time to prosecute this mission once and for all. Now that I can watch you feel the pain that I felt, we're all set."

"Victor, no. This is not the way."

"This is the way, Madison. It's my way. It's God's way. You have brought this upon yourself."

I shook my head.

"No. This hell is all your own making. You have infected the world with your own demented actions, not cleansed it. She is an innocent little girl!"

"Okay," Lund said, shaking his head, making it clear my words were not reaching him. "Enough of your cheap words, Madison. It's time for you and your daughter to die. But I will leave the choice up to you. Who should I shoot first—you or her?"

Given such a horrific choice, I froze mentally. What was worse—watching my own child die, or forcing her to see me die?

Lund looked at his watch.

"You have ten seconds. Starting now."

"Me!" I cried. "Let her go, for God's sake, Victor." I hoped that my words could stop him from pointing the gun at Bella and get her out of the firing line, if only for a few seconds. Lund pulled the gun from Bella's head and turned it on me.

"As you wish. You first. But your daughter will be joining you presently, I can assure you of that."

I had to make a move. I had to charge him. But at four yards, I presented a big target. He couldn't miss. I was sure to take a bullet, maybe two, but if I crouched, changed angle and sprinted, I might just get my hands on him. If I died, at least I died trying.

"Lund, can you at least let me hold my daughter one last time? I'm begging you."

I took a half step towards him.

"Stay where you are!" he shouted fiercely and pointed the gun between my eyes. "No, Madison. This is it. No last requests. No deals. No talking your way out. Bianca never had that luxury. You get no say in how you die. That pleasure belongs to me."

His arm straightened. He took aim at my heart.

I was still just four yards away. It seemed like a mile.

"Daddy!" Bella cried, beyond distraught.

"Bella. Close your eyes," I said. "Please, close your eyes."

She shut them tight and tucked her head against the wall. Without betraying any movement to Lund, I visualized my attack. *Crouch, step and sprint like hell.*

"Bella, my darling. I love you with all my heart. And I am so proud of you. I will always be with you, my precious. Always. Please don't ever forget that."

Lund was smiling. He tilted his head. His lips went taut. Then his eyes hardened with intent. I had to go.

Now!

The instant I moved, a deafening shot rang out with concussive force. But I felt no pain. It must take a second to come on, I thought, confused.

319

Poised to launch at Lund, I froze. A dark spot had appeared on his forehead. Then a drop of blood began to form there. Another shot exploded. Lund's jacket compressed—right over his heart—and he collapsed forward to the ground.

I turned around to see Jack standing in the doorway wondering if he should put a few more bullets into Lund's body for good measure.

I swooped on Bella and put my arms around her.

"Bella. My darling. It's okay. I've got you now."

She lifted her face to me and then immediately buried it in my chest and cried. Her body felt so cold. I sat on the chair Lund had occupied, lifting Bella up onto my lap and holding her tight. I unzipped my jacket and wrapped it around her.

"It's okay," I kept saying over and over again with my lips pressed against the top of her head.

I heard Jack's feet shuffle around the small cabin. He was inspecting the camera that Lund had set up and various other items in the room.

"I'll be outside. I'll give you a moment," he said before turning for the door.

"Hang on," I said. "Where the hell did you come from? I thought you were dead. Last I saw, you were inside a stricken helicopter."

"Normally, you're supposed to go down with the ship, so to speak. They train you to stay on the joystick, doing your best to control the descent. But I had nowhere to land. It was all cliff. Except for a wide chute full of snow. So I did my best to make a steady pass over the chute, got as close to it as I could, and jumped."

"You jumped? How far?"

"About sixty feet."

"What?!"

"Yep. Straight into the loving arms of deep Montana powder. It was like landing in a feather bed. But before it crashed, the chopper spun back towards me, real close. Almost gave me a haircut. So I guess it didn't all quite go to plan."

"So what took you so long?"

"Climbing out of that chute was a real bitch."

He went outside.

Soon afterwards I could feel Bella's body was calm and relatively warm. It was time to move.

"Come on, darling. Let's get you off this mountain. We need to call your mom."

Her weak arms tightened around my neck.

"I'm here, sweetheart," I whispered. "I'm here."

"I knew you'd come, Daddy," she said quietly. "Just like you promised."

CHAPTER 37

A white van made its way towards the open gates of San Quentin prison. A few yards beyond the exit it stopped, and the passenger door bearing a large California Department of Corrections badge opened. A guard stepped out. He took two steps and then turned back to face the van. Another guard took the handle of the sliding door and threw it open. Demarco Torrell emerged holding a small white plastic bag containing the sum of his belongings. The first guard stated Demarco's name and gave him his release papers and a handshake. Demarco then turned to me and crossed the yellow line separating the free from the incarcerated. He managed a half-smile as he took my hand and we bumped shoulders.

"Welcome back, Demarco," I said.

"Thanks, man."

"Let's go see your mom."

It had not taken long to secure Demarco's release. On the return drive from Big Sky to Bozeman, there were a couple of things to do. The first was to get Bella—who was safe, warm and comfortable but still quiet and subdued—some FaceTime with Claire. Next, I'd sent Jessica Pope the link to Lund's private YouTube stream, along with the login details. She didn't need me to tell her a grave miscarriage of justice had been carried out by the state of California. She was not the type to take it personally or impede any effort to free my client. She acted with haste.

I also told Jessica I'd be handing over a large folder of supporting documents that would not have existed had it not been for the hard work, instinct and tenacity of Dino Cassinelli.

"Dino Cassinelli? I thought he was a spent force."

"Far from it. He's a terrific cop, Jessica. You need him. The city needs him. You can't let his talents go to waste."

"I'll see what I can do. I can be persuasive."

"I know you can."

After delivering Bella into Claire's arms, I'd gone straight back to LAX to fly to San Francisco. But I didn't need a ticket for this flight. Once Jack had filled Carla Pearson in on Demarco's story, she'd told him to keep the Gulfstream's meter running and get the boy back home as quickly as possible.

This time, for Demarco's benefit, I'd accepted the offer of an air stewardess.

Once we hit cruising speed on our return to Los Angeles, Stacey approached us with a bottle of French champagne.

"Ms. Pearson thought you might like to celebrate," she said.

Demarco smiled and nodded, accepting the glass once Stacey had finished pouring.

"Have you given any thought to what you're going to do, Demarco?" I said.

"Yes, I have. And I still want to join the Marines."

"Are you sure that's really what you want to do, Demarco?"

"I know the cost of war more than just about anyone, Mr. Madison. But I want to defend my country and stand up for my people just like my dad did. I feel like it's my family duty."

I had the most powerful sense of deja vu. I could have sworn Tank had once uttered those exact same words.

"Here's to your father, Demarco. He'll always be my hero. And believe me when I say you remind me so much of him. Cheers."

"Cheers," he said, and we clinked glasses. "That's good to know, sir."

THE END

NOTE FROM J.J.

Thanks so much for reading *Divine Justice*. I hope you enjoyed the ride. Please consider leaving a review on Amazon. The number of reviews a book receives daily has a direct impact on how it sells and how high it ranks. So just leaving a review, no matter how small, helps me to keep writing.

All the best

J.J.

GAME

OF

JUSTICE

(Brad Madison Legal Thriller, Book 3)

J.J. MILLER

CHAPTER 1

As the two men hauled the woman toward the cliff, the storm's first drops of rain doused her face and blended with her blood. The drug they'd given her had turned her body rag-doll limp and rendered her all but speechless but it didn't dull the horror she felt at the sound of the pounding waves coming closer. It was as though the sea was ravenous for her, somehow knowing that the men were set to toss her into its jaws.

Just moments earlier, in the parked car, the woman realized they were going to kill her. Whatever they had put into her drink had taken effect.

They must have drugged her at the younger man's apartment, she thought. That's where the mood had gotten weird; just after she made that stupid joke about what she thought the two of them were up to.

The joke was meant to feel them out, to pave the way for her to ask them some more serious questions. But it didn't just fall flat, it crashed with a chilling thud. The younger man was visibly jolted. The older man, whom she hardly knew, gave her a wry grin. But she didn't have to be psychic to see that his amusement was forced.

She then decided to try and extract candor from the uneasy mood and pushed forward with a bold accusation about the men. She tried to sound like she knew exactly what their game was and that there was no point in them denying it.

Their stone-cold silence unnerved her even more.

She then quickly tried to backpedal, saying her friend Erin dared her to raise the subject with them.

She waited for the men to respond, thinking they still might confess to an unwelcome truth. But they offered no affirmation whatsoever. They just stared at her. She thought she saw hatred in the older man's eyes.

She felt compelled to speak next.

"Don't worry. It's not like I've pitched it to my editor. You're not going to be front-page news." She was flailing, trying desperately to dispel the tension, but only making things worse.

Abruptly, the men sought to make light of it.

"You are so wide of the mark, it's not funny," the younger man said. "It's complete and utter nonsense."

"Who's this friend of yours Erin?" asked the older man, looking at her like she'd lost her mind. "And where the hell does she get this kind of crap from? I never thought reporters would be so desperate for a story."

"Forget it," she said with a laugh and excused herself to go to the bathroom.

She thought she heard them arguing in hushed tones.

When she returned, the older man apologized for reacting so awkwardly.

"Look, you really caught us off-guard with that stuff. I didn't think you could be serious. But, hey, listen: it's cool. Everything's cool. No offence taken, okay?"

She nodded, somewhat relieved.

"You've sure got some balls on you, though," the older man said, shaking his head and smiling. "For a second there, I thought I was sitting with Barbara frickin' Walters."

She warmed at the complement. They hugged and laughed. The good mood was reinstated but not fully—an undertone of tension remained. Where did she stand with these two? Should she ask more of what she wanted to know? Or should she just drop it?

Then the older man seemed to read her mind.

"Listen, you want a story? I'll tell you a story. And, I swear, it'll make your toes curl. Might set you on the path to breaking something big."

She asked him, practically begged him, to elaborate.

"Later," he said. "But I promise I'll fill you in tonight, okay. Now are we here to party or what?"

He then pulled out a small Ziploc bag of cocaine and racked up two lines each. He told her it was the best gear in LA and that he had a bottomless supply. He said anytime she wanted some to just give him a call.

With the coke and a few more drinks, her disquiet gave way to excitement. She was wired.

What was the older man going to share with her?

Could it be the story that would make everyone in the *LA Times* newsroom take her seriously as a journalist?

She was stuck in the Lifestyle section, churning out breezy articles on anything from Lady Gaga's cosmetics line to the top ten vegan dips. She could write that kind of piffle in her sleep but had long ago lost the buzz of seeing her byline attached to it.

No one else in the newsroom saw her as being stuck. To them she was perfectly positioned. What more could that quiet, pretty blonde girl from Tennessee aspire to?

Plenty, but her confidence was so underdone she could barely tell her closest friends that she wanted to be an investigative reporter, and even that took some convincing.

Could the older man's information be the game changer? She was twenty-six now. It was time, once and for all, to forge a new career path, one that she felt was her true calling. She couldn't wait to hear what he had to say.

After more lines, the older man pulled another small bag out of his pocket and slid it across the coffee table to her.

"Here. Take this. I've got more than I know what to do with," he said. Her eyes lit up. That quiet, pretty blonde girl from Tennessee did love her cocaine.

The older man went to the kitchen to fix some margaritas.

She stepped out to the balcony with the younger man. The night sky over the Pacific was lit up now and then by distant lightning.

"Let's go watch the storm," said the older man, joining them on the balcony with the drinks. "The lightning show over the ocean will be incredible."

She said she didn't want to, that she was happy to stay put, do more lines and drink more margaritas. She walked back inside with her phone in hand to change the music on Spotify.

She didn't see what was coming.

The older man stepped up behind her, swung her around by the shoulder and punched her in the face with all his force, his right fist cracking into her cheek. She fell backward and brought her hands up to her face. When she took them away, she saw they were covered in blood. She started screaming at him, but he leaned in and punched her again. And again.

She collapsed onto the tiles then tried to get to her feet but couldn't.

"Come on," said the older man. "Let's get her into the car."

"What about the blood?" said the younger man.

"Get some paper from the john. Wipe her down. Make sure there's none on the floor."

From that point on, it was like she was just a spectator of her ordeal.

The older man drove. The younger man sat in the back with her, occasionally wiping her face with Kleenex.

It was a huge effort for her to speak.

"What's going on?" she moaned. "Where are we going?"

The younger man spoke to her softly.

"Don't worry. Just keep quiet. I'll take care of you."

And, for some reason, she believed him. But why did he stand by and say nothing of the attack?

What have I done to deserve this?! What?!

She had no answer. All she knew was that she was now in grave danger and that she was utterly powerless to save herself.

After thirty minutes the car pulled over and the older man got out from behind the wheel.

"Where are we?" she asked hazily, hoping her worst fears were only that.

Her door flung open and she was yanked out roughly into the night. She tried to scream, but it only came out as a whimper.

They grabbed her painfully on each side and escorted her toward the sea.

A flash of lightning exposed the location to her.

It was a place she recognized.

A year ago, she'd come here in despair, when she thought her world had collapsed beyond hope and she'd wanted to end it all, to end her pain with one final act of resolve. But she'd called him to say goodbye and he'd come and taken her home and gotten her help.

Now, though, she did not welcome death; she desperately wanted to live. She summoned every ounce of strength to fight, but her limbs could not rise to her will. In contrast to her limp body, her mind was as turbulent as the sea, cresting in bursts of panic, fear, disbelief and desperation.

What have they given me?

Why do they want to kill me?

How could he do this to me?

"Car!" the older man hissed and the three of them fell forward. She hit the ground face first. The older man fell on top of her.

"Keep your mouth shut!"

When she opened her mouth to breathe, it filled with dirt and grass.

They lifted her up. She started coughing after inhaling dirt down her throat.

Then she felt the rain on her face and the shudder of the crashing surf through her feet.

They hauled her over a wall and kept marching.

When they reached the edge of the bluff, they stopped.

Maybe they're having second thoughts.

Maybe this is just a warning after all.

"Grab her legs," said the older man.

She looked out over the ocean as they swung her over the brink and back.

Now came the horrible certainty that this was it.

As though reaching out for help where there was none, she thought of her mother and father, who both loved her dearly. And

334

she wanted to hug them so tightly and never let go until she'd woken from this nightmare.

But this was not the work of imagination.

Suddenly, her insides were swept hollow by the rushing descent. The terror of falling was all-consuming; her muted scream lost amid the clamor of the wild surf.

CHAPTER 2

I shouldn't hate on Jim Rafferty but I will. Take it as me cashing in some frequent flier miles on a friendship spanning twenty-odd years.

I don't know what was worse: the way he pointed his little finger as he popped an aioli-laden french fry into his mouth or the smug rapture that came over that fairway-tanned, entitled face of his as he chewed. Leaning back and taking in the view of Los Angeles from the patio of the prestigious California Club, Jim looked like a man so comfortable in his element you might as well have called it a birthright.

And maybe he was always destined to be here, despite this being the very thing our younger selves swore we'd never become: a fully franked member of the Establishment, someone who perpetuated rather than addressed inequality, someone who devoted his whole working life to serving the rich and in return getting the gold-plated version of the American dream: the mansion, the prestige cars, the private schools, the uber-exclusive club memberships.

That was how we saw it back then when we were cramming for exams at Stanford with Audrey Hollander—without doubt the smartest of us three—and listing the countries we wanted to help via the Peace Corps and then later with USAID or even the UN. We knew graduates not much older than us who were advising government ministers in Africa and Central Asia. They were building new legal justice systems for broken countries on the mend. How's that for serving the world, making an impact?

But that was a long time ago, a time when our idealism ran down to the marrow. Look at fat cat Rafferty now. He has it all and I'm sure he'd tell you he deserves it. You know, all those fourteen-hour days he puts in. Like no one else works fourteen-hour days and for a fraction of what he banks. Like no one has earned it more than him.

I'm no socialist, but this whole swanky lunch scenario was putting a bad taste in my mouth that the grilled sea bass and unoaked chardonnay couldn't wash off. But then I'd arrived with a bad taste in my mouth. The truth was that I, too, was the subject of my own contempt. This little get-together was actually my idea.

I'd come not to bury Jim but to butter him up. A couple of lean years, a new landlord who'd almost doubled my office rent in eighteen months and a belly full of nefarious clients had me looking out for other options. And so Jim came to mind.

On the face of it, I came armed with a couple of ideas on how we might collaborate. But that's the spin: the truth is I wanted to hitch my wagon to the corporate gravy train while I still could. I'd come prepared to offer myself to Jim's firm—Cooper, Densmore and Krieger—a collection of uber-rich lawyers who advised the people who owned Los Angeles, and I hated myself for it.

"How's the fish?" Jim asked as he leaned forward to cut into his filet mignon.

"Very good," I said distractedly. It was time to ask what I'd come to ask. "Jim, remember a year ago you approached me about a job at CDK?"

"Yup, and you should have taken it. I wish you'd listened to me. We've got some real interesting stuff coming on deck that we could have been working on together."

337

"Well, that's what I wanted to talk about."

"I can't tell you shit. Only that we are going all-out on what's going to be a massive case. You'll be reading about it, that's for sure."

I took a slug of wine.

"No, I understand you can't divulge details of your case. What I meant was I've been thinking and I've reconsidered."

Jim stopped chewing momentarily before dabbing his mouth with his napkin and reaching for his glass.

"Reconsidered what?"

"The job offer. I've decided I want in. That is if the offer's still open."

Jim leaned back in his chair.

"You're talking about the offer you threw back in my face a year ago, right?"

"Well, now—"

"You mean the offer that I put to you on behalf of our managing partner who was so keen to hire you it was like he thought you were the fucking Don Draper of the law?"

"Jim," I said. But Jim wasn't going to be interrupted.

"You mean that day when you had the gall to crap all over my career choices, my firm and told me there was no way in hell you were going to sell out like I did?"

"I'm not sure I put it like that."

"Believe me; you put it like that. I had to drag my ass back to the office and tell Harold Krieger that, basically, I was full of shit. He had his sights set on you like Captain Ahab and I assured him that I could get him his fucking white whale. Sliced and diced. Served up to him like sashimi. I was stupid enough to tell him that I was sure my old Stanford buddy could be persuaded into becoming a

338

senior partner at CDK. With your high-profile cases and connections, there was even a suggestion that that tight-ass bastard would even waive the half-mill joining fee. And I was stupid enough to believe you were a chance. You'd proven yourself as a crack trial lawyer, you'd made the papers with some brilliant wins. Every firm in the city would have given their left nut to have you, but I'd promised Krieger that if anyone could haul you in it was me."

"Jim, I'm sorry."

"You're sorry? That's the first I've heard it. Exactly when did you start to feel sorry about what went down?"

"Jim, I felt bad about—"

"You didn't feel bad about anything, you arrogant son of a bitch. I never heard from you until a few weeks ago. You know you almost cost me *my* senior partnership?"

Jim's face was burning with resentment. I'd hurt him more than I could have imagined, and I'd never cared to ask.

"No. I wasn't aware that my decision had any impact on you at all. I'm sorry, Jim. What can I say? I was caught up in my own world. I didn't feel I needed anyone."

"That's right. You were about to sign Tremaine Drake, one of the biggest drug dealers in California."

I may have grown somewhat tired of defending crooks, but I never tired of reminding people we're all entitled to a fair trial. It's chiseled into the Constitution. Worse was hearing other lawyers trying to make themselves sound virtuous by maligning defense attorneys. I tried to keep it nice.

"Everybody's got a right to a sturdy defense, Jim. You know, the Sixth Amendment and all?"

"Keep telling yourself that, like it's the noblest of truths."

339

"Well, it just about is as far as the law's concerned: making sure innocent people don't get punished for crimes they didn't commit."

"Right. You get Tremaine Drake off conspiracy to distribute twenty keys of heroin, among other charges; he hands you a check, walks away and next thing three of his lieutenants are executed on the mere suspicion of betrayal. Case closed. Society can't thank you enough, Brad."

I didn't want this to become an argument. I had to bring it back to the personal. Him and me.

"I'm not trying to tell you things have changed, buddy. I've changed."

"What do you mean?"

"I've had a change of heart."

"About what exactly?"

"If Harold is still out to land his white whale, well, you can deliver it to him."

"You want in?"

"I want in."

"Really?"

"Really."

Jim picked up his napkin and wiped his mouth.

"Well, that's too bad, Brad."

"Too bad? If this is about the half-million buy-in—"

"Five hundred grand won't get you an equity partnership at CDK now, Brad. Nothing will."

"What are you talking about? Last year—"

"Last year was last year. This year, Harold Krieger has a dartboard with your fucking face on it. At least he did for a while.

But I can tell you he's not interested in you whatsoever. You know why?"

"No. Why?"

"First is your love-in with Tremaine Drake."

"A love-in?" I could accept Jim unloading on me for letting him down last year but only up to a point. But I bit my tongue.

"Yeah, a love-in. Like it or not, Brad, your brand changes with every high-profile client you choose. And you chose the lowest of the fucking low. What, you were thinking you could dangle the billings from a drug lord as a carrot for us to let you in?"

I had to admit I was kind of thinking that.

"Well, you're out of your mind," Jim continued. "You want to sleep well at night being the courtroom Zorro for that scumbag, go right ahead. But don't expect Krieger to be impressed. You tainted yourself with the Drake case, and you know it."

"It's called justice, Jim. It's not my fault the state of California failed to meet the burden of proof."

"Cast yourself as the white knight any way you choose, Brad. A blind man can see through that bullshit."

"You're claiming the moral high ground? Really?" I could hold my tongue no longer; job scrounging be damned. "Are you seriously saying there's a moral chasm between who I defend and who you protect? The fucking corporate vampires of this world who defraud investors, who screw dying policyholders, who use public funds to fuel their political ambitions. What was that case you closed a month or so ago? Oh, that's right. Paul Spears, CEO of Calbright Properties. Paid off City Hall to get a zoning exemption for a fifty-million-dollar development in West Hollywood, and you pulled the legal strings that allowed him to get away with it."

"That's different? It was—"

"I bet you wrote that revised land-use ordinance. Didn't you?"

"Look—"

"For Paul Spears, no less. One of the most corrupt developers in the city. And he's so much better than Tremaine Drake? How?"

Jim held up his hands for a truce. For a moment, I wondered if there was a scrap of honor in anything either of us did. Both of us took a few deep breaths then we ate in silence for a minute or so.

"We're a long way from Stanford, Brad."

That reminded me of the other proposal I had for him.

"It doesn't have to be like that, Jim."

"What do you mean?"

"We can still deliver on that promise we made to each other all those years ago."

He scoffed, took a sip. "Yeah? How exactly?"

"Start our own firm." Jim's face went blank. I pressed on. "One that takes on class-action cases. I'm sure we could convince Audrey to come on board. Last time I checked she was lecturing at Stanford. We could—"

"I'm going to stop you there," Jim said, putting both elbows on the table and leaning in. "Jesus, Brad. Listen to yourself. Do you actually believe this three-amigo bullshit? Let me be clear: I'm fine with where I'm at. You may not like it that I'm happy at CDK, but I don't care. Harold Krieger has got a few more years and I'm gunning for his managing partner spot. And after a few years there, I'll be running for office." Jim's future was a series of Tetris blocks that he would spin to fit exactly where he wanted them to go. "So, you understand that I'm perfectly okay where I am. But clearly you're not? What's going on?"

What's going on? Good question. And the truth mostly came down to money. The new landlord that had taken over my floor eighteen months ago had raised the rent twice already. Last week he was at it again. I couldn't keep justifying staying there. And that train of thought had me wondering if I could justify other things I was doing with my life, making money defending the likes of Tremaine Drake for one. But I had big financial commitments. There was no alimony for my ex-wife—Claire was doing very well for herself as a designer—but I'd insisted on covering our daughter Bella's education, which was currently at thirty grand a year for fifth grade at the Crossroads School. I also had a mortgage and my escape-LA-once-and-for-all plan to fund. Then there was Megan, my brilliant secretary who I could never do without, whose engagement to her high school beau had fallen through and who now, single and unsure about her future, feared every financial hurdle that came my way spelled the end of her job.

But it was about more than money. I guess I was in the midst of a mid-life crisis without actually realizing it.

"Nothing," I said to Jim. "Just think I need a change."

"Well, if it's just a case of you looking for where the grass is greener, then I don't think you've scoped our firm properly. And that tells me you don't really have your heart set on joining us. So I wouldn't be recommending you even if that offer was still on the table, which it isn't."

"You said there were a couple of reasons it no longer stands. The first was Drake. What was the other?"

Jim sat back.

"We're all hands on deck with this big new case and there's a freeze on hires. It's a closed shop until further notice."

"What's the case?"

"You know I can't say."

"Yeah, yeah. But what can you say?"

Jim leaned in.

"A massive property development down in Costa Rica has failed. There's going to be some heavy damage to investors here and our client needs to circle the wagons."

Costa Rica... Property development... There was a bell ringing in my head, and I didn't like the sound of it.

"Your client. Who is it?" I was sitting up straight now.

"Brad, you know I can't tell you that."

I leaned forward.

"Jim, I need you to tell me. Okay, not the client. Just the name of the development. That's all."

Jim paused a moment or two before answering in a low voice, almost just mouthing the words.

"Playa Dorada."

My stomach dropped.

I shot straight to my feet.

"I've gotta go," I said.

Alarmed by my reaction, Jim grabbed my arm as I passed and held me.

"Brad, you can't say anything to anyone! I swear, if you do..."

I pulled my arm away.

"Thanks for lunch."

CHAPTER 3

A cold sweat was coming over me as I made for the elevator. I pressed the button. I couldn't wait and took the stairs. Out on the street, I tapped a speed dial.

"Bradley," my mother answered. "How nice to hear from you." Her voice was happy and warm and buoyant as usual.

"Mom, that investment you bought into in Costa Rica."

There was a slight pause before she answered.

"Yes?"

"What's it called again?"

She brightened as though my question was a pleasant surprise compared to what she'd expected.

"Playa Dorada. It's Spanish for Golden Sands."

My shoulders sank as I exhaled deeply.

"Have you heard anything about it recently?" I asked.

Another pause. Then her voice resumed with apprehension. "How did you know?"

"Know what, Mom?"

Her voice began quivering.

"It's gone. It's all gone."

My worst fear was realized.

"How much did you lose?"

"A lot, dear. Almost a million. I have to sit down. I can't bear thinking about it."

"Mom, does Dad know about this?"

"No, dear. Of course not."

It was a stupid question but I'd asked it on reflex. I still wasn't used to Dad being ignored about anything when it came to my parents' lives. But the Alzheimer's had come on quickly. So much so that you'd no more seek his opinion on an investment than you would a toddler's. Mom had good reason to go it alone on what she did with their money. But I was sure she hadn't gone it alone. There was no way she'd drop a million on something so risky all by herself.

My blood was boiling.

My parents had just lost a huge chunk of their retirement savings. And that put me in a hole: there was no way I was going to stand by and watch them be reduced to food stamps. I'd beg, borrow or steal whatever it took to keep them living in the comfort they'd always wanted for themselves.

So much for thinking I had five hundred grand to buy my way into a firm.

All of a sudden, I realized that I was going to struggle just to keep my own practice running.

I felt sick.

From out of nowhere, I was in the middle of a financial catastrophe I never saw coming.

Mom wasn't keen to feed me any details about how this debacle came about, but she didn't have to. I knew exactly who was to blame: a smooth-talking, self-absorbed weasel who, in pursuit of easy money, was ever happy to run his morality gauge down to zero.

My brother.

CHAPTER 4

I knew he wouldn't answer my calls so I didn't bother trying. That didn't matter—I knew where to find him. At two o'clock on a race-day Thursday, there was only one place he'd be: the track. Santa Anita Park, to be exact.

I cursed his name a thousand times on the twenty-minute drive out to Arcadia and my fury hadn't abated as I entered the famous racetrack. I made my way up the escalators to the top bar where the balconies overlooked the finish line. I knew this was where he would be—he'd taken to calling it his "lucky spot" years ago. And when I crossed the bar and caught sight of him, that's exactly where he was headed.

There he was in a figure-hugging long-sleeved shirt, jeans, new Vans sneakers and one of those idiotic trilby hats on his head. He clutched a Corona in one hand and the form guide in the other; one of those fools who thinks throwing good money after doped-up animals is what you call "sport".

It had been six years since I'd last seen him and a couple since we'd last talked, but he was still up to his old crap and hurting the one person who couldn't help but love him. Our mother.

The air hummed with the drone of the caller's voice. A race was in progress and Mitch and two pals necked beers as the field rounded the bend and hit the straight. I stepped out onto the balcony and stood at Mitch's shoulder.

"Got money to burn, have you?" I said. Mitch's head swung around quickly. Although the shock of seeing me was evident, he played it cool.

"What are you doing here? If you want to see me, call. Don't come here."

I grabbed him by the shirt with both hands and slammed him up against the glass window.

"You and I are going to talk right now or I'll take all your fucking tickets and flush them down the john."

Mitch's two buddies stepped closer. One of them raised a hand to touch me. I released my grip on my brother and smacked the guy's hand away, stepping forward.

"You better think very carefully and real quick about your next move. I've got some business to take care of with my brother. And if you don't like that, then you and I can sort things out first." The guy, shocked by my intensity, raised his hands.

"Is this true, Mitch? Is he your brother?"

Mitch nodded.

"Yeah. Drop it, Josh. It's cool. Actually, can you guys give us a minute?"

The other two obliged and slid past us on their way to the bar.

"What's with the hostility, Bro?" said Mitch. "What the hell are you doing here?"

That lying face of his hadn't aged much these past six years. That was always one of his gifts. And how the chicks dug that tanned skin, generous smile, and easy wit of his, not to mention the long, light brown hair he liked to pull back into a ponytail. Nowadays the hair was shorter but it was slicked back and tied beneath that stupid hat of his. He was a charming piece of work was my younger brother, I'll give him that. He had everything going for him. Even money. What he lacked was the sense to keep it.

While I was at college, he got into real estate. He made plenty of money but knew of only two things to do with it: spend and gamble. The only thing he knew how to do better was to spend and gamble with other people's money. And on the subject of marriage, Mitch only had two problems: gambling and monogamy. Two women had loved him enough to walk down the aisle with him and both ended up walking out to the same divorce lawyer's office.

"I told you to keep Mom out of your schemes. I remember the conversation clearly because I was happy for it to be the last thing I ever said to you. You called me up out of the blue and pitched me some dodgy property investment."

"Brad, that's not right. I didn't pitch you anything dodgy."

"I told you to shove that deal because I was done with your conniving schemes."

"You think I'm going to stand here and take shit from you?"

"I told you not to get Mom involved!" I shouted.

A Hispanic man in a white tie and dark waistcoat appeared at the doorway.

"Is everything okay, Mitch?"

"It's alright, Carlos. My brother's a little upset is all."

Carlos backed away inside.

"I told you to keep that shit away from Mom and what did you do?"

"I don't know, Brad. What did I do?"

Mitch didn't know what I knew, so he wasn't keen to admit to anything.

"You talked her into that Costa Rican development that's gone belly up. Playa Dorada."

His face dropped.

"Brad, I didn't push it on Mom at all. If you think that's what happened, you're wrong!"

"Her money's gone. Mom and Dad are practically broke. Don't try to make out like you didn't persuade her. What did you talk her into?"

"Brad, it was a sure thing. Never been surer of anything in my life. I still don't know what went wrong, or how. I know you don't believe that, but I've been in the property game a long time and I did my due diligence and it all checked out. That's why I felt confident about approaching Mom. I thought I was doing her a favor. And look, the dust hasn't settled on this thing. She may well get her money back."

"That's not what I've heard."

From my conversation with Jim I knew the money was shot.

"What have you heard?"

"It doesn't matter."

"Look, Mom made it clear she could afford half a mill for one of those properties."

"Half a mill? What are you talking about?"

Mitch realized his mistake immediately.

"She told me she'd lost a mill. So that means she lent you money to buy one for you."

I was struggling not to hit him. He raised his palms.

"Brad. Brad! Look, I can make this right."

"No, you can't. You've just screwed up Mom and Dad's life. And I'm going to have to bail them out. So, you haven't just stuffed up their lives, you've stuffed up mine. And I swore to God that would never happen again. That's why I've wanted nothing to do with you."

"I'm going to make this good, Brad. I swear."

"How are you going to do that? Have you got a million tucked away that you can hand over? Because that's the only thing that will fix this mess. Have you got that money?"

Mitch looked ashamed, which surprised me because I always thought that feeling had somehow been surgically removed.

"No, not exactly."

"You mean 'no'."

"No."

For a second I was lost for words. Mitch sensed this moment was an opportunity to deliver his pitch.

"Brad, I work for the guy who put together the whole Playa Dorada deal. What's happened is not right. No one saw it coming, but if there's any way to salvage this mess he'll find it."

"You really expect me to believe that? Who is this guy anyway?"

"His name's Rubin Ashby. Real smart guy. Like genius smart. If we've been burnt badly by this deal, he has too. I know he put a lot of his own money into this thing. The Costa Ricans must have screwed him over."

"You sound like a naive little girl. You want to help? Then get Mom's money out of this Ashby guy's pocket. Can you do that, Mitch? Can you?"

Mitch shook his head.

"Didn't think so. Whose money are you gambling with today?"

"Mine."

"Show me."

He pulled out a thick bankroll. I snatched it out of his hand.

"Hey? What the fuck, Brad?"

"Consider it a down-payment on your debt to Mom."

I counted the money. It was almost three grand.

"Only nine hundred and ninety-seven thousand to go," I said as I pocketed the cash.

"Jesus, Brad. That's my winnings. How am I supposed to—?"

"Ask someone who cares."

I left him there and walked back into the bar area.

I was ten minutes from the office when my phone rang. It was Megan, my secretary.

"Where are you?" she asked. "I've been calling you for an hour."

"I left my phone in the car. I'm on my way back to the office now. What's up?"

"There's someone here to see you."

"But I don't have any appointments."

"No, I know. He didn't make one. He just arrived."

A walk-in. Is it too much to ask people to pick up the phone and make an appointment?

Megan's voice lowered. I could hear her walk away from her desk and into my office for privacy.

"I told him I didn't know when you'd be back and he said he'd wait as long as it took."

I didn't like the sound of this. It's happened too many times. I know the kind of guy who strolls into a defense attorney's office unannounced and on a mission—unstable, hyped-up, drug-fucked, twitchy and paranoid. I wasn't far away, but I didn't like Megan being alone with a potential lunatic.

"Did he now? Who is he? Is he behaving himself?"

353

"Yes, he's fine. I'm fine, Mr. Madison, I assure you."

"Did he give you a name?"

"Yes. He said his name was Rubin Ashby."

END OF PREVIEW

Printed in Great Britain
by Amazon

84901515R00205